ABOUT THE AUTHOR

Melissa Hemmings was born and raised in Surrey. Having put a pin in a map in her twenties, she ended up in the Bristol Chann~~ Not enamoured with the prospect of living on a s~~ ~~he decided to cheat and moved the pin dow~~ ~~lt, she upped sticks to live by the se~~ ~~ereupon she awoke one day and~~ an organic delicatessen. This ~~ has blighted Melissa's life and w~~ ~~tedly, afforded her a very rich an~~ ~~hings, she now finds herself in nee~~

Hence the advent ~~ ~~g. She has always written. All ma~~ ~~m stern letters of complaint to p~~ ~~ving the pleasure of ghost-writing ou~~ s.

She is also an artist and w~~ ~~he's not writing, she's creating pictures. All artwork promoting her books are hers and more can be found hung on people's walls, in books and magazines.

This is Melissa's first novel.

OTHER BOOKS BY MELISSA HEMMINGS:

Meanderings Of A Cuckoo

Fortitude Amongst The Flip-Flops

OBSERVATIONS FROM THE PRECIPICE

By

Melissa Hemmings

Published by Happy Mayhem Media Ltd

20 – 22 Wenlock Road, London N1 7GU

This is a work of fiction. Names, characters, businesses, places, events and incidents are either the products of the author's imagination or used in a fictitious manner. Any resemblance to actual persons, living or dead, or actual events is purely coincidental.

The rights of the author of this work has been asserted to her in accordance with the Copyright, Designs and Patents Act 1988. No part of this book may be reproduced in any form, by photocopying or by any electronic or mechanical means, including information storage or retrieval systems, without permission in writing from both the copyright owner and the publisher of this book.

ISBN: 978-0-9927277-8-9 (Paperback)

First published 2013 by Shameless Miming Ltd
Published 2022 by Happy Mayhem Media Ltd

Text Copyright © Melissa Hemmings 2013

All Rights Reserved

Cover Illustration Copyright © Melissa Hemmings 2022

A CIP catalogue record for this book is available from the British Library

Printed in the UK by
Biddles Books Ltd, King's Lynn, Norfolk

For Jack

It was only a sunny smile, and little it cost in the giving, but like morning light it scattered the night and made the day worth living.

F Scott Fitzgerald

Prologue

The front door opened and Lewis Wakeley threw his coat over the lounge chair, shifting uncomfortably from foot to foot, he watched his wife crawling around on the floor; face on the carpet with an arm outstretched, scrabbling around under the settee.

'Eli, I have some news.' Lewis announced from behind her spread-eagled frame as she retrieved a half-eaten rusk with a look of triumph on her face.

'No Tom, you can't eat it. It's been under there for heaven knows how long. We would have to introduce a three-month rule to allow you to put that near your mouth.' admonished Eliza as she scooped her toddler up under one arm and went towards the kitchen to throw the food away.

'Hello love. Good day? Ooh, news?! I like news.' Eliza called over her shoulder as she wandered through the dining room.

'I saw Mrs Mitchell today,' Eliza continued, 'and she said you can borrow the dodgy lawnmower after work tomorrow. The blades aren't too exposed so it'll do for our little patch as long as Tom is indoors and you don't wear shorts, otherwise all the stuff flicking up will lacerate your shins.'

'Eli, can you stop walking and talking. Please!' Lewis appealed. His urgent tone caught Eliza by surprise and she stopped where she was and spun round to face her husband of five years, mouldy rusk in one hand and Tom in the other.

'Eli. I'm leaving you.'

In shock, Eliza dropped the rusk into the bin and along with it her dreams of a happy marriage.

Status: *"One thing you can rely on about your father: He can't be relied on."*

The Main Characters

Eliza Wakeley:

This is Eliza's journey. This book is her mental ramblings and view on the world as she adapts to her new life. She talks to herself, a lot, and often in the third person. Don't worry, you'll get used to it. You should like her, she's quite funny and you'll want her to do well. Whether she succeeds in her mission to keep a grip on life is another matter.

Lewis Wakeley:

He's the catalyst for the happenings in this story. You'll not take to him much. That's a bit unfortunate as he does have quite a nice face but, nevertheless, your dislike of him will be quite just. Truth be known, he is somewhat dull. He reads instructions and is a stickler for straight lines. Eliza learnt to live with this but she's rebelled since he left and insists on everything in her house hanging squiffy. There's a lot of that sort of defiance going on. She'll not wash the cups before bed now, just because she knows it would irritate him if he knew.

He's not a very good father and, as you just read, a pretty bad husband too.

He left Eliza for Geraldine. You'll definitely not like her.

Geraldine Copeland:

As I just mentioned, she's the old hussy Lewis left Eliza for.

Tom Wakeley:

The lifeline of sanity for Eliza. Her beautiful, funny and endearing little boy. He'll probably make you want children. Sorry about that, because the bad bits of having a child have been left out. Well, that wouldn't make the best reading, would it?

If you have a child as a result of reading this book, please don't write to me and complain if it turns out to be the spawn of Satan.

Michael and Christine Turner – Eliza's parents:

Eliza's name is because of an "in" joke between her parents. Her father is the Managing Director of Turner and Holsten, the country's top publishing house and in Eliza's formative years worked long hours to make the business a success. He'd met her mother whilst doing the weekly shop as she had worked on the tills in his local supermarket.

She hailed originally from Stratford in London and spoke with a broad East End accent, whilst his was the finest Oxbridge. He sought her out whenever he could see she was working and their union blossomed and they married within a year. They have been happily married ever since. Eliza's name had been dreamt up in the womb and during her upbringing there was lots of 'by Jove, I think she's got it!' exclaimed.

You'll learn more about her parents as the book goes along. They have a lot to answer for.

Lydia Perkins:

Lydia is Eliza's best friend. I shall fill you in on her back story. Lydia left her husband, Roy, as he was abusive and it became worse after their daughter, Freya, was born. Having made the decision that she couldn't take being used as a punch bag with a child to support, her parents helped her by putting up enough money to put the deposit down on a rented house for her and Freya.

Outwardly, Lydia is brash, confident and appears to have it all going on. A few close people know the truth, Eliza being one of them. Lydia truly loved Roy and was desolate when the realisation dawned that he wouldn't change.

Lydia was one of the true friends who sat with Eliza through her manic ramblings of loss after Lewis left and was a constant support.

Be warned though, Lydia is a bit near the knuckle and not to put too fine a point on it, her morals are somewhat, erm... flexible. If you see a lot of yourself in Lydia, you might want to rethink your lifestyle a bit.

Roy Perkins:

See above. A bit of a shit.

Charmaine Wilson:

The bit of a shit's new girlfriend.

Brian and Clive:

Eliza has known Brian for nine years. He was a pre-Lewis friend and he's firmly in her camp. He is married to Clive. They are utterly devoted to each other and live in a pristine semi-detached house ten miles away from Eliza on the edge of town and run a restaurant together called Manners. It is THE place in town and Eliza absolutely adores them both.

She'd gone to Manners to celebrate her birthday one year and Brian had sat down during the second course to share a birthday drink with her. They'd started chatting and that was that. They have been firm friends ever since.

Dave:

Owner and general dogsbody of the Merrythought Café. Eliza and Lydia's usual greasy spoon. Dave is smitten with Eliza and has a strong dislike for Lydia. You'll feel a bit sorry for him. Some people in life induce that reaction. It can't be helped.

Philip Hargreaves:

Divorcee and Eliza's eccentric new neighbour. Barmy as a badger. You'll hear a lot about him during this book.

Ellington:

Ellington is a three-year-old border collie who, along with his penchant for eating Tom's toys is generally in a world of his own. Hyper one minute and desperately emotional the next. Whilst he is a welcome addition to Eliza's household, he is proving to be a handful. She'd been asked to have him some months ago by her brother, James, when he upped sticks to travel the world. His dog had been named after Duke Ellington. James' love of jazz music being the main cause for this convoluted name. When Eliza had questioned why he hadn't just called him Duke, James had replied 'He's not a Great Dane.' As if that was explanation enough.

Norris:

Eliza and Tom's grey Persian. He's a cat and whilst I went into a pre-ambulated explanation into Ellington's arrival into their household, Norris' arrival is less noteworthy. He was a present from Eliza's aunt. The loony one, the one in the family they affectionately call the 'Mad Cat Lady'.

Others:

There's plenty of them; you will be introduced as the book proceeds.

You're now fully armed with the characters. Plump up a cushion and grab yourself a drink. I hope you enjoy.

Chapter One

Affirmation for the day: *I welcome new people into my life.*

Eliza slammed the transit van's backdoors shut and unclipped Tom from his car seat in the front.

Holding Tom under one arm and a potted plant under the other, she went up her new garden path.

From the front door of the adjoining cottage shot out a very red-faced, middle-aged man who was wearing an apron emblazoned with the outline of a woman wearing a yellow and white polka-dot bikini. Eliza noted he was holding a bloodied meat cleaver.

Cleaver wielding man: "Hello, allow me to introduce myself, dear lady. I am Philip Hargreaves. You may call me Philip."

He extended his non-cleavered hand.

Eliza: "Philip, nice to meet you. Sorry, I need to put either a child or a plant down."

She sized up the situation and felt that under the circumstances shaking his hand by way of greeting wasn't an option so nudged Tom and he held out his hand to Philip.

Philip: "Oh yes, there's a child! Hello little person! What's your name?"

Eliza: "He's called Tom."

Philip: "And your partner, slash, husband, slash, boyfriend, isn't helping a pretty little lady such as yourself?"

Eliza: "No, my slash husband is with a new partner, slash, another woman."

Philip: "Oh, my dear girl. Give me the plant. I'll help you."

Philip practically yanked the Peace Lily out of Eliza's hand and strode into the kitchen ahead of her.

Philip: "Your name, my dear lady?"

Eliza: "Eliza."

Philip: "As in Elizabeth?"

Eliza: "No, as in Dolittle."

Philip looked at her, momentarily stupefied.

Philip: "Oh. Yes, of course. Anyway, let us be friends Eliza. If you need anything at all, day or night, you only have to ask. I am at your service and I am delighted you and your little offspring have come to live next door to me."

He was almost spitting he was so effusive with his pleasure at making their acquaintance. She noticed when he spoke white spittle formed in the corners of his mouth. She felt compelled wipe it with a tissue for him.

She spoke to the settled spittle, resting in the left corner of his mouth.

Eliza: "Thank you. I'll bear that in mind, Philip."

The spittle replied and flew out of his mouth as a result and Eliza instinctively stepped back to miss it.

Philip: "Dinner. You'll need to eat! I shall make you dinner as a "welcome to your new home" treat. Just you and me. How about that, dear lady Eliza?"

Eliza: "Erm, thank you but I have Tom."

Philip: "Oh dear, I'm not used to children. Can you leave him here?"

Of course, I'll leave him boiling the kettle and running a bath, shall I?

Eliza: "No. I don't think that's legal, Philip."

Philip: "Typical. That's this bloody government for you. You can't even leave your children unattended now for fear of retribution."

Okaaay.

Eliza: "Er, quite. Right, I must be getting on, I've parked the van badly and I want to get the rest of the stuff unloaded before it gets dark. Lovely to meet you, Philip."

Philip: "Yes, dear girl. I'm just chopping up a cow. Toodle pip and many joys of the day to you."

He turned heel and waved his cleaver by way of departure and went back into his house.

Marvellous, a barmy neighbour. Welcome to Pilkington on the Moors; the village where the mentally imbalanced converge.

I should fit right in.

Status: *"Toto. I've got a feeling we're not in Kansas anymore."*

Chapter Two

Affirmation for the day: *I can cope and stay alive.*

Eliza shook the cereal packet into her mouth and put it on the work surface and stared at it with a look of disgust.

What has happened to my eating habits since Lewis left me? I'll be drinking milk from the carton next.

She had given up using cutlery wherever possible and had dispensed with mealtimes. Tom was fine. She regimented him ok. She was an automaton mother regarding his welfare but she ate the most peculiar combinations by way of sustenance. Take today's "lunch" for example. A lump of cheese, literally bitten off out of the packet and a gingerbread man which had been festering in the tin since last week's baking session with Tom.

No wonder I look wane. Bloody Lewis. I used to eat a decent roast before he went off with that posh bint. I bet she eats roast beef every Sunday. Beef eating cow!

So here she finds herself, in a rented cottage, in a new village with her beautiful little boy. A constant reminder of her soon to be ex-husband. Tom has Lewis' stubbornness, a trait that tests a fragile Eliza frequently, but he also has Lewis' beautiful blue, expressive, kind eyes. The eyes that made her heart melt and her soul break when he left her. Whenever she looks in them, she feels a squeeze of sorrow in her heart. A regret that she couldn't be what he wanted even though she gave him the ultimate gift of a son.

Lewis had cried that he wasn't ready for the responsibility.

Selfish bastard. It was a joint decision to have a baby mister but off you go. Just because it's not the walk in the park you'd thought it'd be.

Run along into the arms of Miss Perfect Pants. Her of the ever-present G-string and black bra under a white shirt.

Eliza had seen Geraldine at Lewis' work parties. She was evidently paid enough to shop in Karen Millen and could afford enough styling products to have her hair ironed within an inch of its life.

God forbid it might have a wave, nay, any movement, in it. That is obviously the work of the frizz devil.

Geraldine in Eliza's eyes was the antithesis of everything she was which was the most humiliating kick in the teeth Lewis could ever have provided. Eliza had borne him a child and not only had he dismissed her, but he had also set upon his new path almost to the exclusion of Tom, which Eliza could not ever forgive or comprehend.

In the weeks after he packed his bags, he announced they needed to sell their home as he wanted to move in with Geraldine. Her mother had consoled her by assuring her most men were immature and shirkers of responsibility if a new proposition came along. Lydia, Eliza's oldest female friend and single mother in arms, had consoled her by assuring her all men were weak minded bastards who only thought with their cocks. Fair comment by both parties Eliza, acknowledged.

It was that rebuff from him, the seemingly considered and easy elimination of Tom from his life, that proved to be both the breaking and pivotal point for Eliza. His actions had allowed her to switch from loving him with all her heart to dislike. The anger his separation caused had made her want to show him she could cope. The survival instinct kicked in and she gathered what emotional and physical possessions she had left and let him go.

She had been too worn out to put up a fight.

As a result, she dealt with each day on a "suck it and see" basis. She never quite knew how she would be when she woke up. On the good days, she made the most of them and made sure she got out and enjoyed the simple pleasures in life.

****

Eliza sat down at her computer and flicked open the internet shortcut and went to her bookmarked pages. She had started writing a blog; "The Adventures of an Incompetent Mother". It was her electronic doodle pad of idle meanderings. She didn't know how many people stumbled across it or even comprehended it, but that was irrelevant. She found it a release and that, in itself, was reason enough in her eyes.

She started to type.

"Is it me?" A question I find myself asking on a daily occasion.

After nearly thirty-five years on the planet, I'm starting to think it probably is.

Then again, the world may be filled with people thinking "Is it me?" and that goes a long way to explaining why we are in the state we are.

I find myself an ill prepared single mother to a toddler, who has more about him than I do of a morning. I rely on him to co-ordinate my outfits and decide the evening menu.   He also informs me when a trip to the supermarket is required. I'm teaching him how to use the vacuum cleaner and his natural toddler inclination to line everything up is a blessing.

I liken my life to gold panning men like the olden days. I think I'm the chosen one and whilst sifting through the pan of my life, think I've struck gold. I run up and down the riverbed hollering to all and sundry I've found it! My life will change irrevocably! No more mundanity! I can do whatever I want, I'm rich!! Only to be told by some wiser stalwart within the whole panning business that my wonderful find is in fact a lump of old gravel after all.

You get the picture. Your life too? You see, it's not only me.

To my credit I have abounding optimism which I would figure is god's way of helping me deal with the blows life seems hell bent in lining up for me. He must be a Libra.

The phone rang. It was her mother.

Eliza's mother down the line: "Hello Sparrow, how are you doing? Any chance of coming over to see your old mum on Tuesday? I've got the day off."

Eliza had been given the nickname Sparrow by her mother as a child. One spring day, when she was six, she had been sitting outside in the garden making little mud pie nests out of twigs and grass. Asked what she was doing, Eliza had replied she was a little birdie making her nest. As a result, the nickname to follow her through the rest of her life was born, or hatched, if you prefer.

Eliza could hear the end of a TV theme tune in the background.

Ah, we're in between soaps. I'm in the advert slot.

Eliza: "I'm not sure mum, I've scheduled my mental breakdown in for then. I'll let you know, if that's ok?"

Eliza wasn't in the mood for either a close inspection or interrogation from her mother at this particular time. Eliza had lost weight and had massive eye bags from lack of sleep. There was no need to worry her mother so had decided it prudent to keep away until her life had been metamorphosed into something akin to normality.

Eliza's mother: "Ok dear."

Her mother sounded more hurried

Eliza's mother: "As long as you're alright."

The theme tune to another programme started up

Eliza's mother: "You know where I am. Big hug to Tommy."

And she was gone. On to her next fix of make believe which had become her reality.

I just said I was going to have a breakdown, mum.

Eliza sighed and replaced the handset and decided a sugar rush was the curer of all ills. She got herself a fork and opened the wrapping on a lemon drizzle cake. She delved into the middle of it.

Shame to make a knife dirty. A quarter will do... Oh ok, I'll neaten the edges up. Seems a shame to leave it uneven... Oh, half a cake. That's more than enough... Oh dear, I feel a bit queasy now.

Status: *"Frankly my dear, I don't give a damn."*

Chapter Three

Affirmation for the day: *I can handle people with ease.*

Eliza stood looking out of her kitchen window. She watched her unnervingly ebullient neighbour, Philip, wrestle with a lawn mower and then proceed to hit it with a spade when it wouldn't start.

Yes, that'll teach it.

He was well meaning enough but his joy at her marital status was palpable.

He'd told her he had lived on his own for a number of years after his wife left him for gutting fish on the dining room table.

Their gardens were separated by the lowest fence known to man and, as such, it was rendered somewhat pointless. A mere marking of territory. Philip just stepped over it whenever he wanted to speak to her which, as it transpired, was quite a lot. He had taken to standing out in his back garden at eight in the morning, in his saggy boxer shorts, hollering on the phone. Eliza never understood what possessed him to find the need or to whom he was rebuking. On his birthday, she'd bought him a dressing gown in the vain hope he'd wear it and save her the need to look. She wished she had the ability to divert her gaze but she subscribed to the other camp and just stared at him with a mixture of delight and horror. Delight that he didn't have a care in the world and horror at the actual physical specimen.

She, absentmindedly, watched him whacking his lawnmower whilst she drank her tea and made a mental check on her emotional chart.

How do I feel today?

The sun's out. How lovely.

Do feel I can leave the house without shaking?

I do.

I could even make eye contact with strangers.

Steady on Eli, don't want to overdo it now do we?

Hallelujah! Today is a coping day.

Right. Make the most of this and get the crew together and do something positive.

She decided to take Ellington and Tom to the local park.

When they got there, Eliza took in her surroundings. The village had a lovely large park with a pond in the middle and flowing down the far end was a river. She took in the boat hire shop, which was situated on the right-hand side, near the pavilion. Since she'd moved there, she'd seen many visitors and locals rowing a boat for half an hour and travel up and down the river. She watched a young couple wobble off a boat and head off for a steadying beer at The Anchor, the village pub, which was positioned alongside the river.

Eliza threw a tennis ball.

Eliza, hollering: "Fetch!!"

She paused and watched as her toddler set off to retrieve the ball thrown for the bemused dog, who proceeded to circle the park aimlessly, sniffing at unknown scents in the grass.

Eliza: "Not you, Tom. Get it you dopey dog!!"

Ellington looked up with disinterest then continued his circuitous quest for sniffs.

Eliza: "Right, I'll do it then shall I? Ok Tom, go on then. Save mummy's legs."

Tom ambled off at a wobbly pace, stopping at every tuft of grass along the way.

Hmm, we could be here a while. If a job needs doing...

Off Eliza strode, scooping Tom up on the way and hoiked him under one arm as he giggled joyously. Seeing movement, Ellington bounded back and fell into step looking very pleased with himself.

Eliza, playfully scolding: "I don't know what you're so jolly about dog. You're useless."

She bent down, retrieved the ball and wedged it in her jeans pocket.

Eliza: "Right then crew, a cup of tea is in order. What's that Ellington? Cake too? A good plan. Back to the bat cave we must go."

Eliza hoofed Tom onto her shoulders and he grabbed lumps of her already tousled blonde hair.

Eliza: "Easy lad! I can pull out my own hair thank you! Release your grip child! Not the throat either! Argh! Mummy can't breathe. Gimme your hands. Right, thank you. Ears. That's your handlebars."

Eliza adjusted herself and made her way across the park with Tom, intermittently, grabbing and thwacking her ears.

When they arrived at the entrance to the car park, Eliza swung Tom off her shoulders and set him down as she fumbled around in her pockets trying to locate where she'd stashed the dog lead. Ellington, meanwhile, continued strolling off across the car park.

Eliza, authoritatively: "SIT!"

Tom obediently dropped like a stone and started foraging around at the kerb.

Eliza: "Not you, Tom... Ah yes, nice stone. Oh ok, we shall take it home then. I'll put it in my pocket."

She looked up.

Eliza: "Ellington!! Stop! Come here!"

Nothing. The disobedient dog continued across the car park.

Eliza: "HALT!!"

Ellington stopped in his tracks in the path of an incoming car and mooched back.

An elderly lady joined them at the kerb.

Elderly lady: "You want that dog on a lead, deary."

She was accompanied by a Yorkshire terrier with a tartan lead and matching coat. The Yorkshire terrier didn't seem very amused by his attire and looked up with pleading, bulbous brown eyes.

Eliza, somewhat piqued: "Yes, thank you. That was my intention."

She roughly moved Ellington's collar, tethered him up and gave him a stern look. Tom, meanwhile, was placing stones in the hem of her trouser turn ups.

Tartan Dog woman: "Disobedient dogs are down to the owners, you know."

Oh, shut your face.

Tartan dog woman continued, obviously glad to have a passer-by to berate.

Tartan dog woman: "Be a shame for him to get run over now, wouldn't it?"

Eliza: "Indeed. A run over dog would certainly muck up my day."

Go away now please. Can't you sense I'm demented and could swear at you at any given moment?

Eliza gave the interfering woman her best will-you-go-away-now-please stare. It worked on Dave at the Merrythought Café but it appeared this lady was immune.

Years of butting into situations that have nothing to do with her has made her oblivious to boundaries.

I wonder if her husband has chosen to live in the shed.

Meddling Tartan dog woman: "My Percy, here, is a very well-behaved little boy."

The old woman warmed to her theme and smiled down fondly at her dog who looked up, balefully.

Meddling Tartan dog woman: "I rescued him, you know."

Well, that's debatable.

Eliza: "Lovely. Nice plaid, Kennedy Tartan, is it? If you'll excuse me, I've got hem-loads of stones to remove and a kettle waiting."

With that Eliza gave Ellington's lead a yank and pulled up Tom.

Eliza, commandingly: "MARCH!"

She strutted off, purposefully, back towards her cottage.

When they'd got out of the car park, Eliza got her mobile phone out.

She pulled up her social media account: "Do any of my friends know of a good dog obedience class near me? My dog only responds to military commands. DM me xx"

When they got back, Eliza set Tom down with his crayons and paper and lobbed a chewy bone at Ellington. She pulled up a chair, sat down and armed with her cup of tea and a slice of chocolate cake, she opened her blog.

I need to earn some money and fast - am in dire need as a growing boy is an expensive one - but my brain is no longer functioning on an "any use whatsoever" level. I am really annoyed with myself for not coming up with anything or finding anything I can do. The money my deserting husband gave me from the sale of the house is dwindling. I've put aside what I thought was enough for my child's – I shall refer to him as LP going forward as in "little person" - future and the rest to secure the cottage but the remainder is rapidly depleting.

Now, we live in what they class as an "affluent" area - i.e., they ride horses, all wear gilets and patterned wellies round here. My friend, we'll call her "L", moved here a couple of years ago when she split up from her husband. She loves it, so it seemed a natural place to move to in the absence of anywhere else to plonk my roots. We're starting a trend. It's where the divorced mums go. They should write it on the bottom of the "Welcome to" sign, twinned with "Errant Husbands".

My parents asked if I wanted to move nearer to them but I think twenty miles away is close enough. Don't get me wrong, they're lovely but they are my parents. ☺

I'm settling into the village and I think it's helped that LP is so young. He doesn't know or register any changes. He won't have any memories of his dad living with us. I'm the constant in his life and I am attempting to keep a grip due to the responsibility of such a task.

LP has been poorly the past couple of days, I think it's his teeth. He is normally quite stoic about the whole gnashers coming through thing but this has knocked him and he's very grumpy. He's even gone off his food which means things must be bad. He keeps flicking his ears so he must have earache with it. He's currently telling Cheddar Chicken all about it. (Named by LP as it's Chicken's favourite food, apparently). They have a lot of in-depth chats about life, the universe and chocolate buttons.

Thank you for your continued support and comments.

Virtually promise to stop moaning soon. x

She posted the blog and turned off the computer.

Status: *"I'll get you, my pretty, and your little dog too!"*

Chapter Four

Sub-affirmation for the day: *Every thought I have is positive.*

Eliza had decided to take up meditation. She had taken to doing it on the advice of her mother. Her mother had always veered towards the more bohemian aspects of life and had learned all manner of weird and wonderful techniques in her quest for understanding the meaning of life. Eliza had grown up around the new age vibe her mother reverberated. With the advent of the internet the whole 'understanding our purpose' quest had ramped up a gear.

Her father had taken to leaving the room whenever her mother had found a new course or "Eureka" technique that had been discovered and touted on the internet. These new techniques could usually be taught remotely, via a manual and for fifty pound a pop. He left her mother to it. It made her happy and that was his mission in life, to protect and care for her. The corporate world had jaded his views slightly and he knew life wasn't the skip in the meadow his wife chose to believe it was. He loved her completely and allowed her the illusion by funding her never ending merry-go-round of life enhancing courses.

Eliza had asked her father his views on it and he'd replied that it was more preferable than her taking up knitting or crochet. Eliza had nodded sagely.

When Eliza was pregnant, her mother had thrown herself into knitting and had set herself the grandiose task of producing a cardigan and booties. After the birth of Tom, Eliza had been presented with a scarf. A very long scarf. One that would mummify the poor mite. This was because Eliza's mother had realised, she couldn't turn corners. Eliza agreed with her father, the thought of everyone receiving scarves for Christmas every year was an unwelcome one.

Crochet was also a definite no-no as no-one under the age of ninety has the requirement for antimacassars.

Eliza had to concur that whilst crystals were undoubtedly very pretty, she had to seriously question whether they were the cure for stomach ache, cancer and just about every malady in between. When she had period pains, she did not wish to have a garnet strapped to her nether regions. She wanted a hot water bottle, pills and chocolate.

Perhaps that's where I'm going wrong. I'm not at one with the earth.

In the twilight period after Lewis left her, her mother had gone into full self-help mode and furnished her with a library full of positive thought books. Eliza had ascertained that it was her mother's belief that Eliza had brought on her own problems and that it was her negative mind-set that had made the whole house of cards collapse.

Marvellous. It's my fault Lewis has run off with a floozy and deserted his child. It's because my mind is wayward. I was inadvertently giving off husband leaving vibes.

Eliza's first bit of bedside reading had been a self-help book about anxiety and basically how to get a grip on life. The overall recommendation was encouragement to be at one with nature. That and to generally have very little expectation in life. Willing to give anything a bash, Eliza had grasped this new age nettle and had to concede maybe some of her earlier thoughts had been the work of the naughty fairy and that karma had well and truly bitten her when Lewis left.

Meditation allowed her mind to wander and it often resulted in what Lydia termed "contemplate your navel poems".

Today was one such day.

She opened her Blog:

Poem for the day

Purpose

I look at my back
But I see no wings
I am a mere mortal
A peasant among Kings
A lonely individual
Looking for my path
Staring at the flames
I am cinders in the hearth
An onlooker on life's meaning
A quest I have yet to find

My searching, it continues
A fight between heart and mind
I hope one day I will find
The truth I have been looking for
And the loneliness will cease
I will find peace for evermore.

Eliza Wakeley

Eliza sighed a despondent sigh.

Bloody Lewis.

Eliza saw her computer as a link with the rest of society. In her bleak moments, she perceived herself as a frail little sun-starved waif, hugging her knees, looking out of the window at a world that continued oblivious to her and her personal struggle. She sometimes looked at the sun and wondered how it could still shine when she felt so disassociated with the world. People were laughing and able to get up and function on a continuous basis. How come the ability for her to cope rationally only came in fits and starts? She wondered if this feeling of functioning under water would ever pass.

She continued with her blog:

I have entered a twilight world where some days I wish to shun society completely. It took all my strength and mental capacity to be able to get LP and my bones to the supermarket on Tuesday. I would have quite cheerfully starved if I didn't have the responsibility of other mouths to feed.

I never knew I could feel so completely unable to cope and not see joy in life on occasion. L says I'm depressed and I think she actually may have a point. I literally sat in the corner sobbing after I put LP down for his afternoon nap yesterday. Some days I just want to curl up in bed and close myself off from the world. What has happened to me?? I look in the mirror and hate everything about myself.

Today I could quite cheerfully walk in front of a bus if it weren't for the fact LP would be effectively an orphan, what with my ex-husband being the ultimate absentee father at the moment.

I realise today is not a good day but if it carries on perhaps I should go to the Doctors.

She posted her blog and got up from the computer to survey the scene in her lounge around her.

Ellington had a yellow crayon in his ear and was desperately shaking his head, Tom was dribbling juice onto his recent masterpiece and wiping it in with his sleeve and Norris was scratching the arm of the leather settee.

Norris had taken severe umbrage when Ellington turned up on the scene. He'd been the only pet up until that point and was used to a free reign in the house. The situation was not helped by the fact Ellington took immediately to sleeping in Norris' cat basket. He'd fold himself in and hang his lolling, sleeping head out over the side. Norris tried to put pay to this by biting his ear and hissing at him. When he realised his endeavours wouldn't remove a comatose collie from his bed, he'd just decided to clamber on top of Ellington and sleep two storey.

They had fights often and Norris always won. A whimpering Ellington would snitch on Norris to Eliza but she had enough on her plate without bickering animals so left them to sort out their pecking order.

Eliza, shouting: "Oi, Norris! Pack it in!"

Eliza leapt and grabbed the scarpering cat and lobbed him out the back door and went to assist Ellington with his crayon removal.

Eliza: "Ellington, stand easy. There you go. As you were."

Ellington gave her a look of gratitude and flumped down on the floor, a safe distance from Tom.

Tom, meanwhile, had dispensed with the paper entirely and was doodling on the oak table that Lewis and she had spent months saving up for.

Ah well. Easy come, easy go. You need to get a grip girl. You have a beautiful son, ok so he's just inserted a crayon in the dog's ear but it is all going ok. You're keeping it together. He's alive, in fact you all are. Result.

Status: *"We all go a little mad sometimes... Haven't you?"*

Chapter Five

Affirmation for the day: *My friendships are filled with happiness and joy.*

There was a knock at Eliza's front door. Ellington leapt up in shocked reaction and barked a deep involuntary woof. He then flopped back down with one eye following Eliza as she went towards the door.

Yeah, no worries pooch, I'll go and attend to the axe wielding murderer at the door who's here under the pretence of selling me new windows.

Eliza checked herself briefly in the mirror by the door and shook her head in dismay.

Oh dear. I must wash my hair tomorrow and I really should start wearing make-up again.

She opened the door.

Eliza: "Hello, Brian! What a lovely surprise! Come in!"

Eliza was genuinely delighted to see her friend.

When Lewis left her, Eliza had been shocked at how quickly she had been dropped by people she'd thought of as true friends. Lydia said it was because she had instantly become a man-eating threat to all husbands and it was more down to the wives being crap in bed and scared of keeping their bored husbands, than any threat Eliza actually presented. Eliza had been appalled. When she'd needed support from people whom she'd thought of as real confidants, they'd ignored her calls.

Too trusting, that's my problem. A lesson learned.

Brian: "Hello, poppet. I've come to check on the mentally infirm. How are you?"

Brian looked her thin bedraggled state up and down.

Brian: "Oh dear! Looks like I came by just in time!"

He walked into the cottage with one hand holding something behind his back, he bent down, tickled Ellington's ear with his spare hand and went and ruffled Tom's hair.

Brian: "What's that you're watching, Tom?"

Tom looked up and uttered "White Gardin," before returning his gaze back to the television, transfixed.

Brian: "What did he say? Translate, poppet."

He hadn't trained his ear to the burblings of a toddler and always needed subtitles.

Eliza: "In the Night Garden."

Brian: "Is that where the bear thing stacks stones and cleans everything with the same sponge?"

Eliza: "Yes."

Brian: "Very educational, I'm sure. Set him up for life that will. Stone stacking. What have you eaten today?"

Congealed peach porridge.

Eliza: "Erm…"

Brian: "Hmm, as I suspected. Still eating left over baby slop as a main course. I've brought you something. Tadarr!"

He presented from behind his back a foil covered tray full of canapés, wraps and nibbles.

Brian: "I know cutlery is an alien concept for you these days, so I've brought finger food. Shove it in your chops or next time you have a bath, you'll slip down the plug hole."

Eliza: "Yay! Thank you, Brian. I love you!"

Eliza threw her arms around him.

Brian: "I love you too."

Brian hugged her; tray outstretched in one hand.

Tom scrambled up and grabbed both Brian and Eliza's legs.

Tom, demanding: "Cuddle mummy."

Eliza scooped him up and proffered him a mini spring roll.

He put it in his mouth and promptly went "Pleugh!" and spat it into Brian's hand.

Tom: "Gistustin!"

Brian, drawling: "Lovely child."

Brian inspected his palm and strode off to the kitchen to put down the tray and wash his hands.

Brian: "I'll make us a cuppa. Where's the sugar?"

Eliza, hollering after him: "Cupboard above the kettle."

Eliza joined him in the kitchen.

Brian opened the kitchen cupboard and a tin of beans fell out, narrowly missing his face.

Brian: "Fuck me! I need to straighten your tins. Look at the state of this! How can you find anything?"

He looked at the haphazard arrangement of the cupboard.

Eliza: "Language! There's young ears present."

Brian: "Oh shit, sorry!"

Twenty minutes later they were slumped on the settee drinking tea, eating hors d'oeuvres and her cupboard was lined up with military precision with all the labels the correct way and easy to decipher. She realised she had five tins of spaghetti hoops and no tinned tuna.

I shall make a shopping list in future and consult the cupboard before entering the supermarket.

After Brian had left and Tom had gone down for his afternoon nap she sat at her computer and let her mind wander.

Blog: *Poem for the day*

Confidence

So, to all those who question
What is their plight
All one's desires
Is well within your sight
Ask and you will be shown
The path you are to take
All life's decisions
With confidence you will make
Enjoy all that you see
As this enriches the soul
If you know your purpose
You will reach your goal.

Eliza Wakeley

She reread her poem.

Ooh, I'm feeling a bit better. Thank canapés for that!

Status: "*Leave the gun. Take the cannoli.*"

Chapter Six

Affirmation for the day: *I accept new challenges with zeal.*

Eliza sat down at her computer and updated her blog:

Thank you for putting up with my mental ramblings the other day. I was having a massive down day and felt utterly useless. I look at other mothers and they seem to have it all going on. Baby under one arm and career under the other. Doting husbands and helpful family. I'm trying not to wallow but I just feel so alone sometimes. I've got a grip for the moment so today is a lucid day ☺

Thank you for your replies and I know what you mean about setting goals – little steps - but I find it very hard to remain motivated with a crazy little person demanding my attention most of the time. I'll think about going to the Doctors then, seeing as a lot of your responses were quite so insistent.

I have a confession... I haven't made it to playgroup this week as LP and I had a conversation and the library won. I reasoned with him that there were many different ways of depressing mummy without adding stuck up rude mothers to the list. He was remarkably agreeable and no lasting damage was done to either of our nerves. I asked L if she'd taken her daughter – to be known as F - to these playgroups and she said "not on your Nelly" so I had sympathy in that corner as well.

In the olden days they didn't have playgroups and we didn't all grow up emotionally stunted so I will make it a few times a month occurrence instead of a weekly one.

I have written you all a poem.

"Wordsworth Had No Friends"

I wandered lonely as a cloud
O'er hill and dale
When all a sudden I trod on

A host of golden daffodils
Bugger, I thought, where'd they come from?
As I trampled on their finery.

I wandered lonely as a cloud
O'er hill and dale
When I fell over a passing cow
Whilst dodging a host of daffodils
Bugger, I thought, where'd she come from?
As she trampled on my finery.

I wandered lonely as a cloud
O'er hill and dale
When I fell off a precipice
Whilst running from a cow
When dodging a host of daffodils
Bugger, I thought, where'd that come from?
As I landed on a rambler's finery.

I wandered lonely as a pissed off cloud
O'er hill and dale
And thought sod this for a lark
I'm off to have a drink
Where I dodged a host of imaginary daffodils
Bugger, I thought, how many have I had?
As I landed on the pub's carpet finery

I gave up wandering lonely as a cloud
As I never did like Wordsworth.

I thank you ☺

As Eliza switched off her computer there was a knock at the door.

Ellington woofed a solitary woof and Eliza scrambled to the door quickly to make sure Tom wasn't awoken from his afternoon nap. She opened the door to Lydia who breezed in.

Lydia: "Mwah. Hello. How are you feeling? Ooh, you're only looking half as ghastly as usual."

Eliza: "That's nice. Hello."

Lydia: "I've been thinking. We need to talk."

Oh dear. I may need caffeine flowing through my veins for this.

Eliza: "Oh ok, I'll go and put the kettle on."

Lydia followed her and sat down at the kitchen table. She rubbed her hand up and down it.

Lydia: "This table, how much did you pay for it?"

Eliza: "Twenty pounds, I think. Why?"

Lydia: "And how much did you spend sanding it down, repainting and making it look worn out again?"

Eliza: "I don't know, probably about another twenty. Why are you asking?"

Lydia: "I've got an idea. I must get off Jobseekers. I can't take it anymore, Eli."

Lydia had been on the dole for a year. When she finally left Roy, she'd ended up reliant on benefits. It was acceptable in her eyes for her not to work as she had a young child and only had to go into the Job Centre once every six months. During that time, she'd thrown herself into bringing Freya up the best she could.

However, when Freya turned five and went to school, she had been forced to go on Jobseekers Allowance which changed the whole situation radically. She'd tried to find a job but she lacked experience. She'd married Roy at eighteen and he held the archaic view that wives should stay at home and look after their men. Lydia had accepted this lifestyle and preferred it to working as it meant she could have her hair and nails done during the salon quiet times. She relished the fact she could go shopping any day she liked and before Freya came along, she used to take daytime college classes. One was a life art class, she realised during this how much she enjoyed art and it transpired she was a talented artist. After this, she'd practiced and had started to do the odd nude (not odd nudes, they wouldn't be very saleable, no - hers were very lifelike) and put them up for sale in a nearby gallery.

On her fortnightly trips to the Job Centre, Lydia had seen enough despondency to sap even the strongest of spirits. She used to dress in her best outfit every two weeks as a show of defiance and tell anyone that asked, she was off to a meeting with her business advisor. Which, in effect, was true. Eliza knew it broke her heart to be in the position she was.

The most demoralising moment for Lydia was when she saw a man she recognised as the former Marketing Manager from Roy's work. She recalled him as such a proud man and so dominant. She confessed on occasion to Eliza to having a crush on him purely on the merit of his authority and glint of cheekiness in his eyes. To see him being spoken down to by the hardened souls who were employed within the Job Centre had been a sobering sight for Lydia. He had recognised her, she knew he did, but he'd sat the other side of the waiting room and not made eye contact again. To see such a man in this position made her realise that no one was immune from falling through the drain cover of society.

Eliza: "What's your idea then?"

Lydia: "You are good at doing up furniture, just look around your cottage. We could do it together. We could make a business out of it. We could have a little shop in the village. I was given the idea when I drove past Hicks Bakery and noticed it's up for let. I spoke to my neighbour about it as he knows all the goss. Apparently, it's quite a reasonable rent. We could go all green and upcycle old crap. Green's the new black. We'd be very 'now'."

Eliza: "Ah, that's a shame about the bakers. What's happened to Mr Hicks?"

Lydia: "I don't think the business quite recovered after that time Mrs Reynolds found half a dead mouse in her bloomer. He's decided to take early retirement."

Eliza: "It's a lovely shop but not a lot of room out the back with the kitchens in there. We'd have to have majority of the furniture in our houses whilst we did them up."

Lydia: "That's doable though. It would be so exciting, Eli; a new venture for us both. What do you think?"

Eliza: "I'm thinking it might be a bit costly, but it does sound appealing. It might be what I need to get back some adventure and focus in life."

Lydia: "I'm as poor as a church mouse but you've got some money left, haven't you? Couldn't you invest a teensy bit into setting it all up?"

Hmmmm.

Eliza: "Let me think about it, ok? So, you're thinking furniture. Is that it? There's quite a lot of money in this village. Shall we include gifts? Continue along the green route? Fairtrade is very big. We could do all that sort of thing. It'll help my karma recover; helping the underprivileged."

Lydia: "Yes! Let's go the whole hog! Oh Eli, it's so thrilling. We'll be earning a living with our own business and you'll get good karma back. You might even meet a man and have sex again!"

For the first time in months Eliza started to feel a flutter of excitement.

Oh, thank the Lord, I am still capable of some form of feeling.

Think seriously about this, Eli. This might really help you.

Eliza: "It does sound very intriguing. Let's have a think and we'll arrange to see Mr Hicks, ok? See what the deal is with the premises."

Lydia: "Yay! Thank you, Eli. You won't regret it."

Eliza: "I haven't said yes, yet. It would mean the last of my savings. We'd have to start making money quite quickly for us to be able to both survive on it."

Lydia: "I believe in you, Eli. We can do it."

The lure of good karma is swinging it for me.

I'm turning into a hippy. I blame mum.

I'll stop shaving under my arms next.

No. Never stop doing that, Eli. You'll never get a decent man like that.

Don't ever turn into something from the Planet of the Apes and neglect your bits and bobs.

Think of the shock on a man's face if he got down there to be faced with non-attended to nether regions.

Lady gardens get a lot of attention these days.

Eliza: "Would you ever have a vajazzle?"

Lydia: "Eh? Random. Lord no! There's enough perils for a man to contend with as it is in that vicinity, without the poor bugger ending up in A&E due to choking on a lump of diamante. The only use I could think of for them is if they were in the shape of an arrow, by way of a guide. I just opt for minimalist. Anyway, I must go. I'm having my roots done."

They finished their tea and Lydia flitted off to the hairdressers to get her low lights done.

Status: *"Hold your breath. Make a wish. Count to three."*

Chapter Seven

Affirmation for the year: *If it all goes tits up at least you had a bash.*

Sub Affirmation for the year: *You are marvellous so everything you put your mind to will be a massive success.*

Yes, the sub affirmation was better. Stick with muttering that one.

Eliza sat down at her blog

Inventiveness and Confidence

We make our own limitations and listen to what others say far too much. Our inner voice is all but forgotten. Our confidence is dictated by others.

Question - Have you ever thought "That could work" or "that's a brilliant idea" then share it with someone and they are not very positive? That's the idea done with and your confidence dented. Only a few pursue the thought.

Remember - everything around us has been created from the same matter. Someone had the vision to carry their thought out. Look around the room, everything in it has been sourced from the planet and created.

By someone. Someone no better or different than you.

Have confidence in your abilities and ideas.

Poem:

When you look in the mirror
What is it you see?
A woman with flaws
Or a spirit that lives eternally?

Look beyond the façade
Don't judge by what you think may be
There is a light that burns beneath
For now and eternity.

Eliza Wakeley.

This self-help lark was, perhaps, starting to pay off. It could be that or just the passing of time. Whichever, Eliza had to concede she was starting to feel the cloud lift. She still experienced bad days but she was learning to accept them and knew that they would pass. Just having that knowledge allowed her to cope more. She had also made the decision to take charge of her life and feel less of a victim. She was going to move on and try and experience life again in the hope that it would alleviate the numbness she felt. She used to feel excitement and joy at simple pleasures and she was starting to remember how she used to feel. She had been writing less and less in her blog and she took this to be a good thing as it meant she was actually experiencing rather than reaching out through a computer for solace.

It was a gentle thawing out of her mind, body and soul; a dissipation from the emotional stupor the loss of Lewis had rendered her immobile with.

It had been a year now since Lewis had walked away and the time elapsed had helped her come to terms with not only the hurt he'd caused but her whole life as she knew it.

Over the months she had, in an automatous fashion, got on with her new life and she had created a self-imposed regime for her and Tom. She had booked him into the local nursery three days a week to allow him to mingle with other children and it afforded her more time to set up the business.

After continued coercion from Lydia, she had invested her remaining savings into setting up a business for them both "Illusions of Grandeur Crafts" in the old baker's premises. Mr Hicks had rented them the shop on an annual basis and on a good rent on the proviso he could continue to live upstairs and bake bread in the kitchens when he felt the need.

He cut a lonely figure; Mrs Hicks had upped sticks five years ago after she met a twenty-year-old Portuguese waiter on holiday and moved abroad to live with him. Never to be seen again. The only clue Mr Hicks had that she was still alive was the arrival of the divorce papers some months later. The result of these actions had led to the slow demise of Hicks Bakery and the added extra of a rodent in the bloomer.

Lydia had told Eliza that if the "shit hit the fan" then at least she would know she'd tried it. She was reliably informed you only regret what you don't do in this life, not what you do and was adamant their venture was going to be a success.

Eliza was a hard worker and was keen to prove herself and having agreed to invest what savings she had left into the business; they had drawn up an agreement that she'd take her capital out as and when funds allowed.

****

There was a knock at the door. Eliza put down the paintbrush and opened it.

Lydia swept in with an air kiss.

Lydia: "Hello angel. Mwah."

Eliza: "Oh, hello. I'm painting that table we bought last week. Go and put the kettle on, I'll just move my brush so Ellington and Norris don't get covered."

Eliza picked up the paintbrush and wrapped it in a plastic bag. She put the bag on the kitchen unit and leant on the doorframe, watching her friend breezing around her kitchen.

Lydia filled the kettle, turned and looked at her friend intently. Hands on hips.

Lydia: "What in god's name are you wearing? Tracksuits are so not you, darling. You must buck up. Are you still having off days? You either need to go to the Doctors or have a shag. Which one?"

Oh god. She means business.

Eliza, flatly: "I'm painting. I can wear what I want."

Today was not a good day. The determination she had felt a few days before had not lasted and she felt morose again and unworthy.

Lydia: "Pills are tricky to wean yourself off. Nooky is what Nurse Lydia prescribes. You wouldn't get me wearing a tracksuit even under sedation. What if the man of your dreams knocked at the door?"

Lydia busied herself plonking the tea bags in the cups.

Eliza: "He did, remember? Then he left me for a G-string-wearing-husband-taker. But you're right, you are the only woman I know who renovates a dresser wearing a maxi dress and wedges."

Eliza bent down and picked up Norris and he instantly started purring.

Lydia: "Oh Eli. Won't you please consider going on that dating site I'm on?"

She's pleading and using her best 'come on darling' face. Oh, I'm so not in the mood for this.

Eliza: "What, that millions of manky men website? No thank you. I'd rather go quietly out of my mind. I'll just line myself up for more heartache. Who is going to want me?"

Eliza cradled Norris like a baby and tickled his tummy as he purred loudly. She leant over and nuzzled his tummy with her nose. He grabbed round her head with his front paws and started kicking at her with his back ones.

Arrgh! Not a good move. Mental cat!

Eliza: "Arrgh, gerroff cat! You've got claws and you're kicking my face."

She extracted herself from his grasp and dropped him on the floor. She stood and attempted to tame her unruly hair out a bit. A lost cause. It was long, curly and with a mind of its own.

I wonder if I should invest in hair straighteners. Then I'll just be like oh-so-perfect Geraldine. Straight hair obviously lures husbands. Do I want someone else's husband, though? No. I'd just wanted my own.

Oh, I thought in the past tense. Wanted my husband. Not want. Hmmm.

Lydia: "You're nuts! You're beautiful, funny, clever and a brilliant mother! Any man would give his right arm to be with you. And a few other body parts I should imagine. Please do it for me; it'll take your mind off things. Let's have some fun. We could double date."

Oh, she's still talking. Concentrate Eli.

Lydia rubbed her hands together with excitement.

Lydia had been on several dates with guys she'd met on multitudeofmates.com and whilst a couple had been five years older and ten stone fatter than their photos, a few of the others, Eliza had to concede, did appear outwardly, relatively normal. They didn't wield machetes and their car boots lacked rolled up carpets and shot gun created air holes.

Always a bonus.

Lydia: "I'm worried about you, Eli."

Here we go...

Lydia: "You need to start coming out of this. Lewis is a fool and he'll regret it soon enough but move on. Please."

Leave Lewis out of this. I'm not in the mood. Anyway, I just thought of him in the past tense, so shut your face.

Eliza: "Stop nagging me, I'm fine."

Eliza shot her a warning look and put Norris out of the back door.

Lydia: "You're not fine. Have you been talking to the pigeon again?"

Lydia eyed her speculatively.

Oh shit.

Eliza: "Erm..."

Eliza didn't look at her friend.

Lydia: "Eli. It's not normal to befriend a pigeon in your garden and tell it your inner most thoughts. I know you're now all at one with nature and you've got all that hippy thing going on, but you're too young for the onset of senility. Eccentric is acceptable. Quirky almost, but there's a line and having a pigeon as your best friend is it."

Lydia was shaking her head in dismay.

Eliza: "He's very tame. Winky likes pork pie."

Don't think about what you just said, Eli - you'll be designated a carer.

Lydia spat her tea out.

Lydia: "Winky?!!"

Eliza: "He winks at me when I talk to him."

Eliza giggled and got a piece of kitchen roll and mopped her friend's top.

Lydia: "Ok, that does it. Either you set up a dating profile or I'll do it for you. I'm not having a looper for a friend. You'll be having canaries next and dressing Ellington up in a smoking jacket and sunglasses."

Ellington would look quite the wolf in a smoking jacket.

Lydia pushed past Eliza to the computer.

I give up. It's the easiest option. I've got table legs to paint.

Eliza: "Ok! God woman!!"

I am powerless when she's on a roll.

Eliza held her hands up in surrender.

Eliza: "Fine. We shall do it but I won't date anyone."

Just so you know, madam.

Eliza trailed behind her.

Lydia: "Yes, yes. Whatevs. Let's strike whilst the iron's hot and I've got you in a weak moment. I can only assume you're high on paint fumes. Marvellous! Get your tea and we'll set you up. How frightfully exciting!"

Beyond words.

Lydia pulled up a chair and clicked on the internet shortcut.

Eliza: "Thrilling."

Eliza was dripping in sarcasm. Though, secretly she had actually started to feel a bit of a rush at the prospect.

Perhaps I am ready to go out and date the odd guy again. Not an odd guy. Obviously.

****

Twenty minutes later Eliza had 4 photos, a name of SHAKESPEARESISTER1 and a profile up on multitudeofmates.com:

Well, it is with either unbounded optimism or sheer stupidity I find myself on here!

I run a craft shop with my naggy friend. Naggy because it is due to her, I have relented and gone on here. She mentioned something about not ending up as some crazy old bint with thirty cats and talking to pigeons during the "get yourself on multitude of mates" conversation her and I had. I seek the quiet life and caved in!

Anyway, we scour the locality for what is technically known by special people in the trade as lumps of furniture, or if you rather "tat" and upcycle them into objects of beauty that'll hopefully grace people's homes for... oooh... another year or so at least!

I am training to be a hippy and I'm told I speak fluent new age twaddle. You need to be open to this way of life as, if I find it makes my life better, I shall seize this nettle with both hands (I'll wear gloves).

I am looking to spend what spare time I do have with a funny, normal, laid-back guy.

If you would like to get to know me then please apply within.

Please note: I cannot lol or omg. I can only talk in complete sentences. I also like the correct use of apostrophes.

Eliza and Lydia sat looking at the profile hovering over the "Save Profile" button.

Lydia: "I'm not altogether sure I like being thought of as naggy. Helpfully persuasive and wanting my dearest friend to clear off the cobwebs on her lower regions, yes. Naggy, no."

Ah, stop your whining woman.

Eliza: "It's that profile or nothing."

Eliza was sticking to her guns.

Lydia: "Do you have to be so pedantic about the text speak thing? It makes you look a boffin."

Oh yes, because being able to use the English language correctly is right up there with splitting the atom.

Lydia was not the greatest wordsmith and saw nothing wrong in "rofling".

Eliza: "I will not talk to anyone whose conversation I have to Google. I can't be doing with text speak. Forty-year-old men getting down wiv da kidz is the ultimate turn off."

Lydia: "Oh, all right. Keep your knickers on - hit save and let's see how many messages you get. Oooh I'm so giddy."

You actually are very excited. We both need to get a life. It's official.

Lydia clapped her hands excitedly. The profile saved and the screen cleared to the emails received page.

Eliza: "Giddy. Indeed. I can barely breathe."

Load of old codswallop.

Lydia: "You know what they say about sarcasm, darling. Lowest form of wit and all that."

Lydia got up and fetched the biscuit tin and upon her return, hit refresh.

Lydia: "Ooh blimey O'Reilly! You've had three messages already. I told you, you are marvellous! Didn't I say you turned heads? Didn't I?!"

It's not the medication she's on after all. I have men writing to me. That's a turn up for the books.

Eliza: "Crikey! Haha! Let's look at them then. They're probably ancient."

Eliza straightened in her chair

Lydia: "Oooh, he's lovely. Look at Mellowman70. I'll have him if you don't want him!"

Lydia was practically dribbling.

Good heavens. Stroll on woman!

Eliza: "Lydia! It's not the out of date chucking out section in the supermarket. Have some decorum!"

I must agree though, he does have a certain something about him.

Lydia: "Bollocks! Behave! This site is a man supermarket and believe me, a lot are near their sell by date!"

Lydia was laughing and scrolling through his pictures.

Eliza: "Actually, he does look quite nice. Get out of the way then and let me see what the message is."

I'm here now. I may as well enter the spirit of things.

Ahem.

Eliza pushed her friend away from the computer. She clicked on the email and with it opened a whole new world of internet dating.

Status: *"carpe diem, seize the day boys, make your lives extraordinary."*

Chapter Eight

Affirmation for the day: *I am totally loveable.*

Eliza was busy decanting own label shampoo and conditioner into posh pots when the phone rang. It was Brian inviting her to a launch do for their new menu next month. They'd employed a new chef, Carlos, and from what Brian described, he subscribed to the Heston Blumenthal School of Creative Cooking so they wanted to test out his new dishes on friends and family prior to releasing them on the public.

Brian: "Bring a date, poppet. The more victims the merrier! I want you to get back on the world. I agree with Lydia, you're too good to be festering away, plus you'll go to seed in a few years. Get yourself kitted up with a man before everything sags southwards. No man, no free food! Make sure he's not a vegetarian. Can't be stressing Carlos out that much, he's very volatile. Clive says it's his creative nature. Speak to you soon. I love you!"

Oh great. I am back in the realms of "bring a partner" or I risk being shunned from all social events for the rest of my life. I truly will have just a pigeon for a friend. Time to act and believe all that positive affirmation stuff.

Stand aside Winky; I have been set a mission.

Eliza threw her empty cheap hair product bottles in the bathroom bin and went to check on Tom. He was happily chatting to his teddies in his room and feeding them cheese strings. They were having a picnic. Cheddar Chicken was at the head of the picnic rug and master of pretend tea pouring proceedings.

Eliza: "Alright darling?"

Tom: "Yes mummy, we have pickernick. Cheddar, he love tea."

Eliza: "Naturally darling. Tea is the elixir of life. Don't depend on anyone who doesn't like tea, Tom. Be instantly suspicious of them. They're not to be trusted. That's the lesson for today."

An impromptu sermon about tea to a three-year-old. That's rather unexpected.

Tom: "What?"

Eliza: "Pardon, not what. Nothing love, carry on. I'm off to do some very important work. Call me if you need me."

Tom: "Ok mummy. Wuv you."

Aww my darling child.

Eliza, cooing: "I love you too, baby."

Eliza went downstairs, flicked on the computer and went on to multitudeofmates.com. Since she'd joined a fortnight ago, she'd been inundated with messages. She'd taken to cutting and pasting her replies. No one had particularly rocked her world. Mellowman70 turned out to be as dull as dishwater so she had rid herself of him, sharpish.

The conversation had gone like this:

SHAKESPEARESISTER1: Hello, thank you for your message. I'm very well, thank you. What have you been up to today?

MELLOWMAN70: Hi, I've been to Screwfix and bought some rawlplugs.

Can I engage any further with this person?

SHAKESPEARESISTER1: That's nice. Take care.

No, apparently not.

She found the website peculiarly compelling viewing and from an egotistical point of view, good for her morale. She'd learned she was cute, cheeky looking and had a beautiful/sexy/naughty/adorable (tick as message appropriate) smile. Eliza was quite the onlooker in all this and was strangely fascinated by it all.

Lewis never said any of those things. He only informed me when my roots needed touching up.

Some of the guys on the website were downright peculiar. MEATHEAD50 was holding a gravy boat in his profile picture. She'd flicked on to another picture of him and it was of an extreme close up of a Yorkshire pudding.

I like a Sunday roast as much as the next person but to take a picture of your dinner does take the biscuit, or pudding, as in this case. And you wonder why you're single.

Lots of other photos, she'd noticed, were of men in their bathrooms. They'd taken pictures of themselves in their bathroom mirrors on their mobile phones and invariably had their power showers and differing tastes of tiles also on display. In a virtual world of lightening decision making based on limited information, Eliza instantly took to deleting any message without even reading it if she didn't like the tiles; regardless of what the guy looked like. It became her criteria for deletion – a bad backdrop – delete.

Take, BUTCHMAN, for example. He was a spindly guy with an air of vagrant about him. He stood proudly in a kitchen where Steptoe and Son could have easily been the previous occupiers. The surfaces were literally overflowing with paperwork, open cat food tins and dirty plates.

Do they not have any presence of mind at all to look at their picture remotely objectively?!

Right then. I guess I need to find someone to take to Brian's launch do. I need someone that looks like they won't baulk at pigs' trotters served up on a bed of chocolate cake.

She'd received five messages that day. The first one was of a guy sitting on the middle of a grey Porsche bonnet, legs astride with an overconfident look on his face.

I don't know why you look so confident; you're on a dating website like the rest of us. If you had it all going on mister, you'd be shagging inside the Porsche not just showing it off.

Don't be so cynical, Eliza. It's the bitter Lewis induced side of you. Look on the upside; he is showing off he's rich. If he's rich, then he's probably eaten at decent restaurants. He is more likely to take eating bits of chocolate covered pork in his stride.

Read the message - just do it.

Eliza clicked on the message accompanying the profile picture; his username was WHITEKNIGHT1, Eliza rolled her eyes but carried on regardless.

WHITEKNIGHT1: Hi, I'm Anthony. You sound very nice. I looked at your personal ad and you look beautiful and almost sound too good to be true!

Oh, he's online. Ah well, in for a penny and all that.

Eliza started to type.

SHAKESPEARESISTER1: Hello Anthony. Thank you for the compliment and yes, I am too good to be true - I am a walking goddess.

WHITEKNIGHT1: Ah, you are there! I can be your Master and put colour in those cheeks!!

Oh, how simply marvellous. He's a perv.

SHAKESPEARESISTER1: Colour in my cheeks. Hmmm, I see what you did there.

Send.

WHITEKNIGHT1: Good morning my Mistress. Would you like me to send you some intimate pictures of me?

Really?

SHAKESPEARESISTER1: No, you're ok. I presume you're thinking of pictures of your penis. I have internet access and can search for "men's willies" should the mood ever take me.

WHITEKNIGHT1: Lol. Your so intelligent and pretty my Mistress. Being prim is quite the turn on and doesn't preclude you from having a naughty side too.

He typed lol and wrote your incorrectly. It's you're – you are. Tut.

SHAKESPEARESISTER1: You don't hear the word "preclude" used enough these days. I shall make it my mission to use it in a sentence today. In all honesty Anthony, I might not be the sort of person you're looking for. I'm more comedic than sultry but thank you for taking an interest in me.

Send.

Now bugger off and be lewd somewhere else.

Oh, he's replied.

Eliza held her breath and looked at his reply.

WHITEKNIGHT1: I like a funny woman. You must be able to laugh during the throws of passion and I like my Mistresses to be joyous of soul. Your Master will wait for you and your punishment will be meted out accordingly. You minx.

Throes not throws, you div. Saying that, maybe with you it is throws. DELETE!

I think my obsession with the correct use of words may be a hindrance in the meeting of men. I have to accept I am not right in the head with it. Is it normal to get aggravated because some random guy can't tell the difference between your and you're and their and there? I might need to relax my linguistic issues or I'll be forever alone and never invited out. Most of the world talks in initial letters. Whole conversations are conversed with "omg, c u l8r. Lol."

Be there or be square, Eliza.

Now then, who's next?

Roll up, roll up. Come and get your sexual deviants here...

She looked at another message. This guy's picture looked ok. He was sitting behind a computer screen and it was a bit of a distant shot but it was a very natural pose and there were no bathroom tiles or Sunday roasts in evidence.

He looks open enough and no 1980's power shower. Ooh, things are looking up.

She clicked on the message.

COMPUTERBOY: Hello. I read your profile and you sound very happy and funny. I expect you get hundreds of messages and wouldn't be bothered with someone like me but I felt I had to write and say thank you for brightening up my day.

That's very nice. No hint of mentalness.

She looked at his profile. Forty years old, single, no children and the owner of a software programming business. It didn't go into any other specifics. His profile looked as if he wasn't a natural on a site such as this and Eliza found that encouraging. His profile text was brief and basically said he was looking to experience something new. She liked the feeling of discomfort that emanated from his words.

I know the feeling, COMPUTERBOY. I'm hearing you.

SHAKESPEARESISTER1: Hello. Thank you for the compliments. I am happy to talk to you. You sound normal and aren't holding a severed head, which is a bonus for a start.

Send.

Eliza got up and put the kettle on.

Food. I need food. All this talk of pig's feet has made me peckish.

She opened the fridge for something to eat but couldn't find anything remotely interesting, so chain ate five digestive biscuits. Once she'd made her tea, checked on the proceedings of the tea party, let Ellington out and Norris in, she sat back down at her computer.

Oooh, he's replied.

COMPUTERBOY: Hi again, you find self-loathing attractive? You're going to love me then! Please note the correct use of apostrophes.

SHAKESPEARESISTER1: Much obliged with the apostrophe usage. You are a dying breed my friend. Were you waiting for my reply?

COMPUTERBOY: I receive them on my phone and I'm having a cup of tea at the moment and your message came through. Do you have a name? Mine is Richard.

He drinks tea. Good. He also has a normal name. Also, good. As opposed to what Eliza? Chopper? Nutjob?

SHAKESPEARESISTER1: I do have a name, yes. My parents were quite thoughtful that way. Eliza. What's a nice guy like you doing on your own?

COMPUTERBOY: Very pleased to meet you, Eliza. I could ask you the same thing. Anyway, how do you know I'm on my own? Maybe I snuck on whilst the wife was out.

SHAKESPEARESISTER1: You may well have done, indeed. I've gagged and bound my other chaps up and they're holed up under the stairs. They last quite well if I throw a crust of bread in during the day. I'm on a tea and biscuit run with the stalkers too, seems only fair seeing as they go to so much trouble to watch me putting on my dressing gown and taking my false leg off in an evening. I'm on here because my friends have given me up as a dead loss.

COMPUTERBOY: You have friends? Lucky woman! You're teasing me now, aren't you?

Bite the bullet, Eliza. You can't talk on here all day. Ask him if he wants to talk by another means.

SHAKESPEARESISTER1: Would you like to talk by some other means other than on here? Are you vegetarian?

Are you sure, Eliza? Bit forward of you. Oh, bugger it.

Send.

COMPUTERBOY: No. I'm not vegetarian. I like bacon too much. Unfortunately, I am one of those maverick law breakers who has yet to wilt to the promise of eternal happiness proffered by the constant stream of banality generated by social media sites. I have a chat app though. We can chat through our phones if you wish? I'll send you my number, if you like.

SHAKESPEARESISTER1: You mean you're not telling the world what you had for breakfast? You're not posting up pictures of every meal you cook and telling madcap stories about how you nearly ran over a cyclist who happened to not be wearing a cycle helmet? You crazy fool. It's the new black; a bit like internet dating. You'll relent eventually. Even the hardiest of souls cave in and post up their Victoria Sponges as a baking trophy. Yes, please send me your number and we can chat via our phones.

He likes bacon. Bacon means pork. He might not run at trotters. There may be light at the end of the dating tunnel.

Status: *"Seek and ye shall find."*

Chapter Nine

What's my affirmation? Oh yes. "You are an attractive, independent woman."

After consultation with Lydia, the date with COMPUTERBOY was set for Friday evening that week. A pub equidistance between their two abodes. Tom was safely ensconced at Lydia's and she could relax knowing he was safe.

Eliza was nervous but it was under control. She looked undeniably cute in skinny jeans, ankle boots, floral top and leather biker jacket. Her curly hair had been tamed slightly and it looked as though she'd made the effort but not overly so. She never subscribed to the "show them what you've got" school of dressing and always kept her limited assets under wraps. She'd lost a lot of weight with her recent dubious eating habits and, whilst on a bad day she looked gaunt and in need of a good meal, when she made the effort, she looked stunning. Today was one of those days.

She stood outside the doorway to the pub and looked through the window at the hub of activity. She straightened her limited frame, brushed down the imaginary creases in her top, breathed in deeply and exhaled quickly.

You can do this. You need a man to go to Brian's menu launch. Keep your eye on the pig.

Balls to Lewis. Life goes on.

She then strode into the pub with purpose and aimed for the bar. Then she saw him and stopped in her tracks. The sight that met her eyes looked nothing like the profile photo.

Oh fuck! I mean flip-flop!

You can swear in your head, Eliza. It's the only outlet where you can't be berated for being a bad mother.

There before her stood Richard Edwards. Possibly the most awkward, spindly, pasty-faced, socially inept man she had ever laid eyes upon. He was staring into the middle distance with a pensive expression; holding a skiing jacket under one arm with a backpack by his feet. He looked the most ill at ease person she had ever seen. Eliza stopped and assessed the impending situation.

Oh, dear Lord! He's wearing a fleece and mustard-coloured cords! He looks like he's been yomping across the fields and has strolled in to ask for directions. He has computer nerd stamped all over him. This is so not me. How could I have got it so patently wrong?! The "experience something new" bit on his profile actually meant leaving the house.

I don't know if I can face this. Shall I just turn tail and leg it now?

He adjusted his gaze and she fell into his tractor beam. His mouth dropped open slightly and he unashamedly stared at her with a mixture of fear and surprise at the pretty sight he'd managed to coerce to go out with him. His brow knotted and he went to move towards her and as he did so, swept two bar mats off the bar with his oversized jacket.

Eliza stood rooted to the spot and watched as he bent down and fumbled around on the floor picking up the mats and replacing them correctly back on the bar.

He stood, grasping all his paraphernalia clumsily and approached her with caution. Anxiety at the situation etched all over his face.

Richard: "Eliza. Hello. There's pictures of foxes and dogs all over the walls."

He swept his gaze around the pub.

Eh?

Eliza: "Is there?"

She glanced around and there were indeed a number of prints of foxes being pursued by hounds.

Eliza: "Hounds they are. On account of the pub name. The Fox and Hounds. Hello."

Richard: "Lacks a degree of imagination, don't you think?"

Eh?

Eliza: "Erm. Yes. Quite possibly."

Eliza was stumped. Of all the openers in a conversation this was a bit different.

This is all Lydia's bloody fault. I'll be having serious words with her for this.

Lydia had told Eliza to get the meeting out of the way rather than waste weeks of talking then as soon as you met them, hating them on sight. Such a waste of effort and word power. Look, text, meet. All in the space of a week.

Oh yes. Far better to go in completely ignorant and hate them quickly. Lydia will have the next ten dressers to single-handedly renovate as a result of this.

Richard: "Would you like a drink?"

A bottle of gin should do the trick.

Eliza: "Yes please, a coke."

He lumbered with his belongings back to the bar and she tentatively followed him.

Everyone's looking at us. I know they are. They're wondering why such an incongruous couple happen to be in each other's company on a Friday night.

Online dating my friends, that's why. For the record, he looked NOTHING like this in his photo. In his photo he looked as if he actually mixed with the rest of society and saw daylight.

Bucks Fizz, My Camera Never Lies? Pah, I've got news for you.

He came back with two cokes.

Richard: "I had the same. I don't normally drink coke. I don't like it."

Tut, why did you then?

Eliza: "You could have had something else. Something you do like."

Richard: "I wanted to have the same as you."

Oh dear.

Eliza: "Oh."

There was a silence. An undoubtedly awkward silence. One that Eliza knew she couldn't allow and was required to fill. If she didn't, the whole evening would be doomed from the outset.

Silence alert! This is illegal. Fill it with anything. Random words will suffice.

Eliza: "Have you booked the table?"

Oh, well saved. Food is the diversion, we can eat.

Richard: "Yes. It's for half an hour's time."

Oh no! That's a lifetime away.

Eliza: "Shall we see if it's ready now?"

Richard: "Yes, ok."

His brow knotted even more and he looked intently at her.

Take control, Eliza. You're here now. You're completely mismatched but make the most of it. You've spoken via messages, albeit briefly. He types a good conversation. It is your job to make him relax in female company and talk it as well.

Eliza assumed charge and led their way to a guy stood waiting to help allocate dining customers. Their table was ready and Richard looked visibly relieved.

Probably glad to put down his hiking gear. I wonder if he has crampons and a survival kit in that backpack. I might be requiring that survival kit before the evening is out at this rate. OR he could have a rope and an axe in there. Oh dear.

She sat down and watched as he faffed around, unloading possessions around him. Finally, he plonked himself opposite her.

Eliza: "What's in the rucksack?"

A severed head?

Richard: "Bits and bobs. You never know when you may need your tablet."

Oh. A gadget. Not a person's body part. That's perhaps worse.

Eliza: "You carry around a tablet?"

Richard: "Only a small one. Not the larger version. That would be unnecessary."

Completely unnecessary. Foolhardy almost.

Eliza: "Naturally."

Richard: "Your text earlier said today you went shopping. What did you buy?"

Uh oh, he's trying to make small talk. I bought milk, sausages and a loaf of bread.

Eliza: "Some arty bits for my next project."

That's a conversation starter. I could talk for ten minutes about painting a cupboard.

Richard: "Oh."

Or maybe not.

Eliza: "What did you do?"

Talk about yourself. Run free with the wind in your thinning hair Dicky boy. Regale tales of geekdom.

Richard: "I finished some code. I have been thinking about your business."

He grasped his chin and looked over Eliza's right shoulder as if recalling a thought process.

Why have you been thinking about my business? Don't do that. There's really no need. You'll not be seeing me again.

Eliza: "Have you? In what way?"

Feign interest. It kills time.

Richard: "You need a better angle. You have a modicum of talent, which is undeniable, but to sell, you need your own brand – your USP – unique selling point."

Modicum of talent?! Piss off!

Eliza: "Do I? What's your thoughts on that then?"

Come on, let's hear you out.

Richard: "I have been considering this."

I bet. Look me in the eyes man. Go on. See if you can. Otherwise, I'm going to end up trying to follow your gaze.

His eyes flickered briefly to hers then he looked over her shoulder again and continued talking.

Richard: "You advocate recycling yet you use paint that harms the environment. You need to practice what you preach. Your angle could be you add rubbish to the items of furniture. Truly recycle."

Flip-flop off!

Eliza: "Pardon?"

Richard: "It's an interesting concept. Attach a baked beans tin to a shelf so it can be a holder for pencils and a milk carton to hold a flower. They are examples. I haven't fully thought it out, obviously, but it is the germ of an idea. Push the envelope."

I'll push your envelope.

Eliza, tartly: "Oh yes. I can see how adding lumps of old crap to beautifully painted shelves would get me known."

He visibly blanched when she said the word crap.

Change the subject, Eliza. You're getting mardy.

Eliza: "Do you go out much? In the evening, I mean."

Richard: "No."

Shock. Not.

Eliza: "Do you often eat out?"

Richard: "No. I have particular tastes."

Eh? What particular tastes eliminates restaurants?

Live animals? He eats rabbits from the roadside. Surely not.

Oh no! I bet he eats roadkill. Badger casserole. Oh dear, poor Brock.

Eliza: "In what way?"

Richard: "I don't eat wheat, carbohydrates or dairy."

Crikey. Brock's still in with a shout though.

Eliza: "What do you eat then? What did you have today, for example?"

Richard: "I had liver for breakfast."

Oh! I wasn't expecting that. Don't laugh in his face, Eliza. It's bad form.

Eliza: "Just liver?"

Badger liver?

Richard: "Yes."

Shit. He's Hannibal Lecter reborn. He definitely has something dubious in his rucksack.

Eliza: "Did you have it with a fine Chianti?"

God, I'm funny.

Richard: "Pardon? No. Why would I have wine at breakfast? I had a glass of soya milk."

Ok, maybe not so funny. I thought I had a peculiar diet. At least mine's borne out of depression. Yours is a life choice.

You're annoying me now.

Eliza: "And this diet. Makes you feel alive and brimming full of vitality, does it?"

Eliza looked into his beady, slightly sunken eyes and at his washed-out complexion.

Richard: "I struggle with fatigue."

No shit.

Richard: "I'm hoping by eliminating all the food groups, I will find the diet that suits my metabolism."

You imbecile.

Eliza: "Do you not think actually eating a variety of foods will suit your metabolism?"

Richard: "No."

There's no reasoning with insanity.

Eliza, desperately: "Shall we order?"

Richard: "I'm not very hungry. Are you?"

I'm here now. I'm eating. I don't care if you stare blankly at the fox and hounds adorning the walls during the main course.

Eliza: "Yes ravenous. I could eat a horse."

Richard: "Have you ever eaten horse?"

Yes, every day in a bagel, you lunatic.

Eliza: "Not to my knowledge. Though, saying that it's apparently rife these days, so I may have mistakenly done so. I do like a nice pre-packed lasagne."

The server came up to take their order. Richard ordered steak and kidney pie with chips.

Please make it quick so I can eat and run.

Hang on, carbohydrates?

Eliza: "Ah, so you eat pie and chips then?"

Richard: "I won't eat the pastry or the chips."

He's a looper. It's official. I need time out.

Eliza: "Would you excuse me for a moment, I need to visit the ladies."

He got up slightly as she picked up her bag and he sat down again as she departed.

Upon entering the toilet, Eliza looked around.

What are you looking for Eliza? A window? An escape hatch back into the real world?!

Safely in the confines of a cubicle, she debated how long she could remain in there before she had to brave him again.

She got out her phone and texted Lydia.

Eliza's text: "Oh, my bloody hell. He's a dweeby liver eating murderer with an axe in his bag. If I'm not lobbed into the river or thrown myself in by my own volition, I'm going to come and get you and make you go out with him by way of punishment. Either that or I'll just kill you myself. xx"

Send.

She unlocked the cubicle and went and looked in the mirror.

Look at yourself, Eliza. What in heaven's name are you doing here? You could be at home with chocolate and a film. You'd be perfectly happy with that.

I should blame Lewis for this, not Lydia. Yes, it's all his fault, the bloody wife leaver.

She sighed heavily and looked into her reflection.

Into the breach dear friends. See it through and learn from this. All part of life's rich tapestry and all that.

Eliza fluffed up her hair and strode with purpose back to her table. Richard was picking at the quick of his nails.

He stood quickly as she returned and, due to the weight of the skiing jacket and rucksack, his chair toppled back. He swiftly turned to retrieve it and he knocked over his drink.

Eliza stood as a complete onlooker for a moment at the situation before gathering herself. She quickly picked up the glass and mopped up the spillage with their napkins.

Add clumsy to the list of unwelcome attributes.

The server came with some more napkins and Eliza shot her a look of gratitude. The server flickered her gaze to Richard and back again to Eliza and smiled.

She knows. I know she does. She knows I'm on the worst date in history. I have the sympathy vote.

Their food arrived mercifully quickly and the server imperceptibly nodded at Eliza and shot her a grin.

Eliza: "Bon appétit."

Richard: "Do you know what that is in Latin?"

Eh?

Eliza: "No."

Richard tutted and looked most disappointed.

They busied themselves with their meals and Eliza watched with fascination and bemusement as he delicately removed the lid of his steak and kidney pie and neatly placed it on the side of his plate.

He looked up and stared at her plate.

Richard, matter of factly: "You have bacon. You have bacon with chicken."

What's with the bacon obsession? I bet he grows his own pigs and eats them.

Eliza: "Er yes, it's what I ordered."

And?

Richard: "Have you ever owned a pig?"

Oh yes, I have a whole farmyard at home. The cow is currently in the lounge watching television.

Eliza: "No. Have you?"

Richard: "No. One ran full pelt at me once. I remember it vividly."

He shuddered at the memory.

Did it stamp on your head?

Eliza: "I'm sure it will remain etched on your memory forever."

He looked up from fiddling with his steak with his ever-present knotted brow.

Richard: "Ah, you were trying to be funny then, weren't you?"

Eliza: "Not really."

I've got to amuse myself somehow. I appreciate you're not used to humans. I shall try and curb it a tad.

Eliza: "You know your brain. Is it very full?"

Richard: "In what respect? Actual density or thoughts?"

Eliza: "Thunks."

Richard: "I don't believe "thunks" is a word in the context you are using it. It may be applied to the programming of computers, but yes, I do analyse a lot."

Thunks, thunks, thunks. Meh. It's a word alright.

Eliza: "Are you enjoying tonight?"

Richard: "It's a new experience. I wished to meet you and I have fulfilled that wish. You hold much interest to me which doesn't normally happen."

Oh, dear me. He's like a robotic version of Crocodile Dundee.

With that, he inhaled sharply and promptly started to choke on his mouthful.

I'm not sure I can be bothered to carry out the Heimlich manoeuvre. Why prolong the agony?

Oh, he's going very red.

He coughed violently and a lump of steak shot across the table accompanied by a mouthful of spit and gravy.

Eliza instinctively leant back on her chair and the expelled lump of meat landed on her floral top. She looked down with a mixture of disgust and amusement and promptly burst out laughing.

Hahahaha! Where's the camera? Don't laugh too much Eli, you were a bit lax with the old pelvic floor exercises after Tom. Can't add weeing yourself to the comedy of errors occurring this evening.

She picked up her napkin and picked it off her top and placed it on the table.

The people on the next table stared with unabashed joy at the unfolding situation. A suited, grey-haired man leant over and volunteered his napkin to Eliza with a wink. Eliza accepted it gratefully and commenced spit and gravy removal as best she could.

Richard had stopped coughing and having regained some composure, was staring with horror at the social faux pas he had just executed.

Richard, in utter dismay: "I spat on you!"

Perceptive in the face of impending death.

Eliza: "You did."

Richard: "I'm very sorry. I'm not used to steak."

He shook his head, forlornly.

Eliza: "Did you forget you needed to chew it?"

Eliza added the latest napkin to the ever-increasing pile that was accumulating by the condiments.

Richard: "I don't actually like it."

Eliza: "So your whole meal consists of things you don't like?"

He looked at his plate.

Richard: "Yes."

Honestly, I ask you.

Eliza: "Ah well, you could always spit the rest of it out over me and then you won't have to eat any of it."

Richard: "You're trying to be funny again, aren't you?"

Trying? How very dare you.

Eliza: "Apparently so."

I need to leave. As soon as feasible. I should just say "Piss off you peculiar, little man". Why did my parents have to bring me up with manners and social grace? I'll be having words with them about this matter.

They continued in a self-imposed silence as Eliza had lost the will to converse and Richard had stunned himself into silence with his behaviour.

He'll never go out again. Talk to him. Make him feel comfortable. The karma fairy may look on me, favourably.

Eliza looked up from her food to witness him separating and sorting the remaining pieces of steak and kidney into tidy piles.

Bollocks to that. Some people just can't be helped.

She finished her meal with haste and as she put her knife and fork together, Richard did the same with his.

Eliza, warily: "Pudding?"

Please say no.

Richard: "I don't eat sugar generally."

Eliza: "We'll give it a miss then, eh?"

Richard: "I'll watch you eat. I'm happy to do that."

Maybe he's never seen someone actually chew food before. It's a learning experience for him.

Eliza: "No, you're fine. I'll get the bill if that's ok."

Richard contemplated her with the ever-present perplexed look.

Richard: "Yes. As you wish."

Eliza looked frantically around and caught the eye of their server who materialised from behind the next table.

Eliza: "Bill! Er, please!"

She almost begged.

Server, with a massive smile: "Certainly."

She was back swiftly and plonked the plate with the bill firmly in Richard's half of the table and walked away.

Eliza: "I'll pay my half."

She started to ferret around in her handbag for her purse.

Richard: "You most certainly will not! I asked you out for a meal and I shall pay for it. Plus, the menu is hardly a la carte. Pub food is a cheap meal out."

How verbally dysfunctional.

Eliza: "Oh, thank you then."

Richard, whining: "Do I have to leave a tip? I didn't really like her much. She didn't do anything other than bring us our food."

Tightwad.

Eliza: "She was very nice. I'll leave her a tip."

Hush money.

They paid the bill and Eliza practically threw on her jacket and stood, getting her keys out of her handbag with the ignition key ready for action. She waited whilst he layered himself up and, nearly taking the diner out behind him, he put his rucksack on his back.

Eliza: "Back off up the mountain?"

Richard: "Pardon? I don't like heights."

Just give up.

Eliza: "Of course you don't."

Eliza led the way and thanked her server on the way out and the server beamed her a conspiratorial grin.

The server, calling after his retreating frame: "Thank you. See you both again soon!"

Ha de ha. You and I both know I'd need to be sedated before that would ever become a reality.

Eliza stood by her car and Richard started to move in towards her with his arms outstretched.

NOOOO!! Flipping flip-flops, no! I've had quite enough of your spit near me, thank you very much.

Eliza, hastily: "Thank you for an interesting dinner. I'll speak to you soon."

She unlocked her car and was round by the driver's side in a flash.

Richard: "Oh. Oh. Yes. Ok."

He stood in the middle of the car park, dumbfounded, arms still outstretched.

Eliza: "Bye now!"

She waved at him and, with that, she was in her car. She locked the doors and exhaled a massive sigh. Without any conscious thought, she rested her head on her steering wheel and proceeded to bang her head on it five times whilst uttering "Arrghhh!"

She looked up to find him still standing in the middle of the car park watching her with his omnipresent perplexed look on his face. She stared at him blankly from the safety of her car and watched him dithering in the car park for a few moments longer before he lumbered off to his car.

It's over. You can erase it from your memory. Start the engine and go go go!!

Status: *"I'm not sure you get wiser as you get older, Starling, but you do learn to dodge a certain amount of hell."*

Chapter Ten

Affirmation for the day: *Everyone has their place in the world.*

A week had elapsed since the liver man choking saga. Eliza picked up the phone and speed dialled Lydia's number. Lydia had met a new guy.

Eliza: "So?!"

Lydia: "We had the most brilliant time."

Eliza: "That's lovely!"

Lydia: "No it's not. It's not good for my health and I don't know when I'm going to see him again."

Oh, not quite perfect then.

Eliza: "Oh, that's bad. He didn't set up another date?"

Vagueness is not good.

Lydia: "Nope. He didn't compliment me, either. At all. And I pulled out my best smile, the one that normally gets them. Not even a flicker. I don't think he likes me. He thinks I'm an ugly pig with a crap grin."

Uh oh. Low self-esteem issues alert.

Eliza: "I need to meet him, to assess the situation. Perhaps, he just wants to be friends."

Friends? Come on Eliza, that's pants.

Eliza: "Did he kiss you?"

Lydia: "Yes, briefly good-bye."

Eliza: "Lydia! Well, that's encouraging. Why are you so despondent?"

Lydia: "I let myself down. We were talking about my art course and I said I'd like to draw him as he'd be sublime. He said he wasn't but I said to me he was. How lame am I?!"

Uncensored flattery. Not cool. Not cool at all.

Eliza: "Oh dear. Did you say anything else too flattering?"

Please say no.

Lydia: "Yes. I said he had a lovely face."

Crap.

Eliza: "Hmmm. How did he take these compliments? In the same "I'm pretending I didn't hear that" way I do when Dave ladles them out or with a thank you?"

Lydia: "He said, thank you."

Eliza: "Well, it all sounds promising. Why are you so down about it all?"

Lydia: "Because his disinterest makes me feel uneasy and I want him to want me. Plus, I've stared at his crotch. He looks very favourably attributed."

Eliza: "In what way attributed?"

Lydia: "He has a mighty sword."

Eliza: "Ohhh."

Lydia: "Men are such trouble. God. Anyway, I need to go to the shops, I'm Old Ma Hubbard. Do you want to come?"

Eliza: "Yes, ok."

Lydia: "I'll just put my face on. Pick me up in half an hour."

Yeah, right.

Eliza: "Half an hour?"

Lydia: "You're right, make it three quarters of an hour."

Eliza: "Don't worry, I'm sure he adores you! See you when your face is ready for the world."

Eliza put the phone down and promptly fell over Norris who was sitting very proudly with a gift he had deposited for her. An offering of a very wet and very deceased mouse.

Oh, that's just lovely. Lydia gets a man with a humungous willy, and I get a dead rodent. That about sums it up, quite frankly.

Status: *"I'll have what she's having."*

Chapter Eleven

Sub Affirmation for the day: *I am the perfect weight for me.*

Eliza and Lydia were trawling the aisles of the supermarket. Tom and Cheddar Chicken were securely strapped into the trolley and, as was the norm these days, Eliza had the front end of the trolley for her purchases and Lydia had the back.

Eliza caught herself picking up Lydia's normal biscuits and put them into the relevant trolley section.

We've morphed into Bert and Ernie, when did that happen?

Eliza: "I am rapidly running out of time to find a man to take to Brian's do. Help me, Lydia."

Lydia: "Blimey, you're asking me for help? Must be bad."

You're telling me.

Eliza: "Uh huh. Just one that's remotely normal and won't be afraid of all you lot."

Lydia: "That's a tall order."

At this point Tom spotted the toy aisle.

Tom: "Get out, mummy! Tom need to get out. NOW!"

Eliza "Yes ok, hold your horses. Mummy's having an important conversation."

Tom: "NOW!!"

Eliza released him and Cheddar Chicken and they tottered off to press myriad buttons on the lowest shelf of the toy aisle.

Lydia: "So how many are you talking to at the moment on multitudeofmates?"

Eliza: "About three."

Lydia: "Speed date this weekend. I'll look after Tom. Do all three. Then just pick one."

She's serious.

Eliza "Bloody hell, I don't know if I'm up for that. I don't like pig's trotters that much."

At this point, a wiry man in his fifties tapped Eliza on her shoulder.

Wiry man: "Is that child yours?"

Eliza looked to where he was pointing, to see Tom laying on his back, in the middle of the toy aisle, arms and legs out like a star. Shoppers were attempting to get round and he'd caused a trolley pile up.

Eliza: "Oh. I'd deny it but he looks too much like me. I do beg your pardon; I'll go and retrieve him."

She scuttled off and scooped up Tom.

Eliza: "What are you doing, you crazy child?"

Tom: "I Tom starfish."

Eliza: "Of course you are."

Lydia had joined them with the trolley.

Lydia: "Come on, let's get this over with and we can go for brekkie at Dave's."

Tom: "Oooh sausage. Want sausage."

Lydia: "I know the feeling, darling."

Incorrigible.

Eliza: "Good plan. Let's do a lightening dash."

Go go go!

They clicked Tom back in and whisked around the aisles hurling stuff into their trolley and joined a queue at the checkouts behind a very overweight woman. They lined up their purchases on the conveyor belt.

That's a very ill-thought-out blouse.

Tom: "Mummy! Lady, she eat cake. Cake all day... Cake all night..."

Tom was excitedly jiggling in the seat and pointing furiously to the woman in front of them.

Oh no!

Eliza widened her eyes and gritted her teeth in a "stop immediately" face.

The woman looked at the three of them with a look of utter dislike. She looked down at her line of purchases and instinctively put a bunch of bananas over a box of chocolate cream éclairs.

Thank you, Tom, she's going to have to have therapy now. When I read Chat magazine in two years' time, there she'll be posing as skinny as a rake with the headline "Random supermarket child said I ate cake 24-7." I'll go on to read how she turned to a life of drugs and cream cakes to blot out the memory until one day, half an hour from death, she had an epiphany and realised she liked carrots and apples.

Lydia: "Where's Cheddar Chicken?"

Eliza was shot back into the present.

Oh crap. The world will drop off its axis if Cheddar Chicken is lost.

Tom started to frantically look at his lap and was starting to well up.

Tom: "Cheddar!! I need Cheddar. He need me!"

He proceeded to let out a blood curdling wail.

What are you looking at cake lady? Get on with your packing. For the record, I'm only thin because my husband left me. You've got a wedding ring on so you're the one who's got it all going on, not me and my blabber-mouthed child.

Lydia: "Hang fire. I'll go and check the starfish aisle."

Eliza: "Good plan. It's alright, darling, Cheddar's doing a bit of shopping. He'll be back in a minute."

Lydia hurried off and Eliza tried to divert an inconsolable Tom.

Eliza lifted items off the conveyor belt.

Eliza: "Look Tom, washing tablets. Aren't they a lovely colour? Tell me the colour."

Tom wailed: "Bleughhhh!"

Eliza: "Blue you say? Quite correct. What a clever child you are."

People were staring.

Piss off!

Eliza: "Who's the best person in the whole wide world?"

Tom: "Mummmmmy! Whaaaaah!"

Eliza: "Ah, thank you darling."

Go back to your purchases, there's nothing to see here.

A couple of minutes later, which actually seemed like a decade, Lydia came charging down the ambient foods aisle behind them, triumphantly waving Cheddar.

Lydia: "Got 'im! He was by Thomas the Tank Engine. OH FUCK!!"

The world then suddenly switched to slow motion as Lydia skidded in her high heeled boots, lost her footing and promptly fell backwards. She put her arms out to stop herself and took several boxes of tea bags with her.

Mother of Jesus, she just said fuck really loudly. I've lost it. Hahaha!!

Eliza doubled up laughing as she witnessed Lydia flailing around on the floor trying to maintain some air of decorum but failing miserably.

Tom stopped bawling and stared open-mouthed, as were the shop staff and other shoppers within the vicinity.

Eliza ran over, grabbed hold of her friend and pulled her up.

Eliza: "Hahaha! Are you alright?"

Don't laugh too much. Remember the dodgy pelvic floor.

Lydia: "Flippin' Nora! My arse! I mean bottom. Hahaha!"

She scrambled up and brushed herself down. A prepubescent looking employee had hurried to assist and was picking up the boxes of tea bags.

Lydia: "Oh, hello little shop boy. Thank you."

He blushed furiously and beamed.

She left the pile of tea bags behind her and handed Cheddar over to a very grateful Tom.

Lydia: "Here you go, Tom. Auntie Lydia risked life and limb to retrieve Cheddar."

Eliza: "What do you say?"

Tom murmured thank you whilst wiping his nose on Cheddar Chicken by way of re-acquaintance.

At which point, the teenage server on the till, who was armed with an array of tattoos, piercings and a red streak dyed into his hair, piped up.

Till boy: "Ten out of ten for artistic impression."

Lydia: "Aren't we quite the comedian? You know what they say, where there's a skid there's a few quid. I could sue you know."

Till boy: "I think you'll be ruled out on the grounds of improper footwear for a supermarket shop."

He was eyeing up her four-inch heels with a raised eyebrow.

She leant over the card payment machine and inspected a large ear extender in his left ear.

Lydia: "Does that thing in your ear hurt?"

Till boy: "Eh? No, I'm used to it."

Lydia: "What possessed you to think it was a wise move?"

Uh oh. He dissed the boots. He's dead meat.

Till boy: "Erm. It's cool. My mate has one."

Lydia: "A friend of mine has a prosthetic limb, but I wouldn't necessarily advise emulating it unless it was a medical requirement."

She's on a roll. I need to interject.

Eliza: "Oooh look! A queue of people behind us."

Lydia shot a look up the queue of shoppers who were openly listening to the conversation.

Till boy was rubbing his left ear in contemplation.

Lydia: "Just think, you'll be having to roll your ear lobe up and put it in a little sling when you're older. Have a good day now. Come on you two. I've earned my fry up."

Eliza assumed control with the wayward trolley and wrestled it across the car park to the car.

I always get the one with the dodgy wheel.

Status: *"We're going to need considerably bigger buns."*

Chapter Twelve

Sub Sub Affirmation for the day: *Food is my friend.*

They left all their purchases in the boot and ambled into the warm, grease laden fug of the condensation riddled café that was the Merrythought.

The floor was scrubbed wood which, Eliza noted every time she went in, was in desperate need of a sand down and a new coat of varnish.

Dave was out from the kitchen door in a flash as he spotted them taking their seats. He was in his forties but life running a greasy spoon and years of inhaling cooking fat had left its mark. Mainly on his face it had to be acknowledged. He looked worn out and sallow for his age; much like an old moccasin. His brown, thinning hair was always greasy and flattened down with a neat side parting. He wore a once white chef's shirt to cover his paunch with saggy jeans. He always had a dirty J-cloth hanging out of his belt hook.

Lydia whispered loudly across the Formica table.

Lydia: "Uh oh. Stalker alert at ten o'clock."

Dave: "Oh, hello Eliza! You're looking radiant as usual."

Eliza: "Morning and thank you. You're looking knackered as usual."

Dave: "Ah, thank you."

Lydia: "I'm here too. Hello."

Lydia prodded his podgy upper arm.

Dave: "Oh yes, so you are."

He looked at her as an afterthought and turned his attention back to Eliza.

Dave: "What can I interest you in? Hmmm? I have many tasty treats for your delectation."

His eyebrows flicked skywards and he bit his lower lip.

Double entendre. Ignore.

Eliza: "Well, I've had rice crispies this morning, so probably just a five-piece fry up for me, please and sausage, hash brown and beans for Tom."

Tom: "Sausage! Tom like sausage!"

Dave: "Certainly, it's my pleasure."

He looked at Lydia.

Dave, flatly: "And you? What do want?"

Lydia: "Well, seeing as you asked so nicely, I'll have a poached egg on non-buttered granary and don't spit on it, there's a pet."

He looked at her for a moment with a stony expression then swept his gaze back to Eliza.

Dave: "I've got some marvellous new bangers in, very expensive from the cash and carry, they were. I'll cook those special for you."

Eliza: "Don't go to any trouble."

Dave fondly: "Nothing is ever too much trouble for you."

Lydia tugged his top.

Lydia: "Do I get a special banger an' all?"

Dave, tutting: "I suppose so."

Lydia: "You charmer you. I can see why you got so far in the catering trade."

Eliza: "Thank you, Dave. We'll see you with our food in a bit then."

Dave took his cue, awkwardly ruffled Tom's hair and bowed back from the table. He backed into the kitchen, nearly taking out Belinda, the waitress, who was ambitiously carrying two pots of tea and a tray of toast to a table to their right.

Eliza: "You're particularly outspoken today."

You're like a Siamese cat with piles.

Lydia: "I dropped Freya off at Roy's before going out with The Mighty Sword last night and met his new girlfriend."

Ooooh, not good.

Subjects concerning Roy are always a bit touchy. He may have used her as a punch bag, but she loved him beyond words and it broke her heart to leave him. It was something Eliza couldn't comprehend. How could you love someone who did that to you? Basically, injure you for no reason. He wielded a level of control over Lydia that Eliza found unfathomable.

Eliza: "Oh I see, what's she like?"

Beautiful and sophisticated?

Lydia: "She's called Charmaine and she looks like she's just come off a night shift at the steel yard."

Lydia screwed her nose up.

Eliza: "Don't be horrible, I feel a bit sorry for her. I wonder if he's beaten her up."

Lydia: "I should save your sympathy, darling. She looks like she could pack a punch."

Tom started bashing his cutlery.

Eliza removed his cutlery and patted him on his hand.

Eliza: "Your wonder bangers are on their way. Be patient."

Tom: "Want nangers. Want them now. Cheddar, he want nangers."

Broach the birthday party. Do it now.

Eliza: "I have something to talk to you about too, actually. It's Tom's birthday in a few weeks. I thought I'd have a party. Will you help me arrange it?"

Lydia: "Of course, we can get one of the pancetta things for them to hit with a stick."

Oh. That's a bit different.

Eliza: "A game where they hit ham with a stick?"

Lydia: "Eh? It's a horse, I think. I've not heard of hitting ham with a stick. What's the prize for that one? A sandwich?"

Dave came back to the table with their teas and a cup of milk for Tom.

Eliza: "Dave, have you heard of the party game where you get pancetta and hit it with a stick?"

Dave: "Piñata, I think you'll find it is."

Ohhhhh.

Lydia: "That's the one! You're not as stupid as you look Dave."

Dave: "I know. You are though."

And he turned on his heel back to the kitchen. Lydia poked her tongue out at his retreating frame.

Eliza: "Why do you torment him so?"

Lydia: "Because it's easy and it's a hobby of mine. Anyway, when we get back, we need to find you a man to take to Brian's ball, Cinders."

Sigh. Indeed, we do.

Eliza: "Who are you taking?"

Lydia: "If I can persuade him – The Mighty Sword. Failing that, I've got a back-up."

Back up? One would suffice me.

Eliza: "Oh, who's that then?"

Lydia: "Clarke."

Clarke? Who is this person she speaks of? Is my short-term memory loss kicking in?

Eliza sifted through the archive filing system in her brain of Lydia boyfriends past, present and future. Nope. Not there. The C file is empty.

Eliza: "Clarke? Where did you meet him?"

Lydia: "Petrol station."

Pardon?

Eliza: "Did he come free with forty pounds worth of petrol? It's a step up from the Tiger tokens they used to hand out. Think of the queues in the forecourt for that? Was he in the pump next to you? How does this sort of thing occur? I have never been chatted up whilst filling my tank."

Lydia looked down at her lap and mumbled.

Hmmm? What's that you're saying?

Eliza: "Sorry? Speak up."

Lydia: "He works there."

Hahaha!

Eliza: "Blummin' heck. You'll be going out with ear sling man off the tills next."

I feel a bit better now.

Lydia: "Shut up! He's only back up, ok."

Tom: "Shut up! Shut up!"

Sigh.

Eliza: "No, don't say that. Naughty Lydia."

Eliza gave her a look.

Lydia: "Soz Eli. Tom, you need to say, "Be quiet". Shut up is for grown-ups."

Dave came back to the table laden with plates of artery clogging food and laid them out in a grandiose fashion.

Eliza: "Thank you, Dave. It looks lovely."

Dave: "You look lovely."

Tom: "Shut up, grown-up!"

Lydia: "I echo your sentiments, Tom. Now tuck in."

Status: *"Let me tell you something my friend. Hope is a dangerous thing. Hope can drive a man mad."*

Chapter Thirteen

Sub Sub Sub Affirmation for the day: *I choose to make the best decisions for me.*

After breakfast, back at Eliza's cottage, they let various animals either in or out, plonked Tom in front of children's television and unpacked the shopping.

Tea had been made and Eliza switched the computer on and logged onto multitudeofmates.com.

First up on the menu was Chris aka HIDDENWONDER. His profession was down as retail and he had the look of a Greek Gary Barlow about him.

Lydia: "Oooh, I like this one."

Eliza, unsure: "He might like himself a bit too much."

Overconfident. Don't like cocky.

Lydia: "Nothing wrong with being good looking and knowing it."

I disagree. I don't want to fight for the mirror.

Eliza: "Really? I don't like that at all."

Lydia: "I'd go for a good looker over a Dynamic Dave any day of the week."

Valid point, well made.

Eliza: "Agreed. I'll respond to his last message."

Eliza replied to his request for meeting up for a coffee and arranged to meet him on Saturday morning that week.

Next up was Patrick, WOODMAN10, a thin man with a beard. He was a carpenter and had various examples of his work on his profile pictures.

Lydia: "It's a dating site not Etsy. Maybe, he's got confused."

Eliza: "I think he might be showing off that he's good with his hands."

Lydia: "Fair enough. Plus, I like a nice beard."

Eliza: "You do, don't you?"

Lydia: "Yeah, it tickles my thighs! Hahaha!"

Eliza: "Santa's your ideal man, isn't he? I'm going to have to watch you at Christmas. You'll be jumping the queue to sit on Santa's knee! I can imagine it now 'Eli, meet my new man. He's perfect. Jolly, has a beard, lives a long way away so won't get under my feet. Has a job for life, can give me anything I want (as long as I'm a good girl.) By the way, is having a huge sack indicative of anything else, like it is with feet?'"

Lydia, laughing: "Point me in the direction of Lapland!"

Stop digressing, Eliza.

Eliza: "So anyway, woodwork man? Yay or nay?"

Lydia: "Do it. If nothing else, he might know some good contacts for our business."

A message was sent asking if he was free for lunch this Saturday.

Last up was Neville, TAKEAPICK5050. A man. Just a man. A normal looking, walk past in the street man. Nothing extraordinary about him, but by the same token, nothing that hinted at an arsenal of weapons kept under the stairs.

Lydia: "Oh, he's a man. He's alright. Nothing wrong with a bit of bland. Probably not quite reaching the bar for you but he could be back up, like petrol pump man."

Eliza: "When am I to fit him in then?"

Lydia: "Saturday evening. Three men, done and dusted in the space of a day. You don't even need to change your outfit."

Eliza: "I'm not sure, Lydia. It's not quite my style all this."

Lydia: "What is your style, Eli? Sitting around for the rest of your life never going out? Pining after old knob chops?"

Steady.

Eliza: "I'm still smarting from Liver man but this once I will do it, to shut you up. If it all goes belly up, I'm doing it my way in future. Meet a man, get to know him, be wooed by him and feel things before jumping in."

Lydia: "That's what I love about you, you're so old fashioned. Oh bugger! I've got frozen stuff; I need to go."

With that, Lydia downed her tea and made for the door. On the way past, she picked up Tom, gave him a cuddle and kissed him on the forehead.

Lydia: "See you later, chicken."

Tom: "Bye Auntie Wydia. Wuv you."

Lydia: "Aww, don't lose that cuteness little man. Don't turn like the others."

She called back to Eliza.

Lydia: "Text you in a bit when I've refrozen my burgers."

Then she was gone, leaving Eliza sat at her computer.

About time I checked my emails. I've been very tardy of late.

There were two unopened ones from her mother. (Her mother was mastering the internet and instead of ringing her, had taken to sending emails.)

Bugger.

She read the first one, hit reply and proceeded to type.

To: Christine Turner

From: Eliza Wakeley

Subject: Re: Bird Whisperer

Hi mum,

Lovely to hear from you. I've been meaning to write back, what a wonderful bird photo. A bird on your head. How astonishing. Was it asleep? You obviously have that vibe. A feathery one or something equally ethereal. Your chakras are obviously very open to the avian world.

Things are fine here. I've got to find some random guy to take to Brian's menu launch so I'm on mega speed date this weekend. I know, it's so not me. Blame Lydia. She means well but I'm feeling a bit pushed into it. It takes my mind off things though and I have to say I do feel more hopeful for the future these days.

Will close for now. Say hi to dad for me.

Virtually sending you bird feathery vibes.

Eli xxx

She clicked on the next email from her mother which was sent the next day.

Crap.

Eliza hit reply.

To: Christine Turner

From: Eliza Wakeley

Subject: Re: Dead Bird.

Hi mum,

So sorry to hear the bird didn't fall asleep and actually died. That's a bit unfortunate, a bird actually dying on your head. Not sure that falls in the ethereal healing bracket but nonetheless, nice way to go, eh? Ensconced in something clean and fluffy.

I meant to ask; would you be able to babysit on the menu night please? Tom would love it. It's Saturday 14th.

Virtually sending the deceased bird flying into the light.

Eli xxx

Send.

That'll teach me for not reading all the emails in one go and keeping on top of my correspondence.

Status: *"To infinity and beyond."*

Chapter Fourteen

Affirmation for the day: *I am wonderful and can handle all situations with ease.*

Saturday morning arrived and Eliza dropped Tom off at Lydia's.

Eliza: "Morning, where's Freya?"

Lydia: "She's spending the weekend at Roy's. Apparently, Char - I can't talk without saying innit - Maine likes spending time with her."

Oh. Touchy subject.

Eliza: "That's nice. The more people that love her, the more enriched her life will be."

Where did that come from?

Lydia: "Did one of your hippy self-help books instil that?"

Very probably, I have them to thank for my sanctimonious words of wisdom.

Eliza: "Sorry."

Lydia: "S'ok. You look gorgeous. He'll love you."

Eliza: "Probably not as much as he loves himself, but we'll see."

Lydia: "PMA, darling."

Eh?

Eliza: "Pre-Menstrual Alert? Do you want me to pick you up some pills and chocolate on the way back?"

The least I can do after my new age nugget.

Lydia: "Positive Mental Attitude, you stupid mare."

Of course. Derr

Eliza: "I knew that."

Ahem.

Eliza: "Got to scoot. He's suggested meeting in a place I have never been to so need to use my new Sat Nav."

Lydia: "Oh dear. Allow an extra half an hour then."

Ha de ha.

Eliza: "I'm getting better with technology. Shut your face."

Lydia, dryly: "Of course you are."

Eliza: "Anyway, I must go. Tom's eaten and has brought a bag of toys to play with. I'll text you when I can."

Lydia: "Ok darling. Have fun! He'll love you. Don't worry about a thing!"

Eliza jumped into the car and set about programming the postcode into the Sat Nav.

Come on GPS. I need to get a shift on.

GPS? What does that mean? Getting person's spot. Yes, that must be it.

It's found me. Marvellous. See, I can do technology.

Eliza started up the engine and set off.

Half a mile down the road, the American woman's voice on the Sat Nav was starting to grate.

I need to get another voice. I am expecting her to ask if I want fries with every direction.

Eliza haphazardly pressed a few buttons and found a very well-spoken southern accent.

Ooh I like you, posh bird. You can tell me the way.

She continued driving, following the eloquent directions.

She's a bit slow on the old wordage. I'm nearly on the junction before she tells me where I need to go.

One needs to speed up one's verbalising, Ma'am.

Eliza approached a busy roundabout. No directions were forthcoming from the Sat Nav. She started dithering about in the lanes and a car behind her beeped his horn at her.

Hold your parping, Volvo man. I'm waiting for the Queen to tell me the way.

Eliza looked down and the Sat Nav was finding GPS.

Eliza shouted out loud at it.

Eliza: "Hurry up and get my person's spot! I need to know a lane!"

Still nothing.

Eliza, staring hard at the Sat Nav: "Oh flip-flop it, I'll choose the right-hand lane and go all the way round in the vain hope you chirp up."

Eliza went twice round the roundabout.

Eliza, hollering at the Sat Nav: "Come on then! SPEAK! Tell me a lane you languid, electronic whore!"

Nothing.

Eliza: "Fine! I'm coming off here!"

Eliza opted for a route.

Queen Sat Nav: "Make a U turn. Make a U turn."

Eliza: "Piss off!"

Eliza pulled over in a lay by and retrieved an ancient AA map from behind the passenger's seat.

Ooh retro. I'm time travelling.

She looked around and ascertained where she was and chose the route.

Not bad, only three fingernails away from date one destination. If I get a move on, I might not be too late.

Now then. What was his name? Greek Gary? No, that's not right. Chris. That's the fella!

Ten minutes later, Eliza pulled into the car park of Whitegate Floral Emporium feeling somewhat dishevelled.

At least I'm here and only a few minutes late. Phew.

He had requested they meet at a garden centre. Now, Eliza was as interested in pansies as the next person, but it wouldn't have been her chosen venue for a first date. It's something her mum and dad do on a Sunday, not the natural rendezvous destination for meeting a Greek god retail man.

She strolled into the herb section of the garden centre, whereupon she saw him, holding a potted Lemon Grass and prodding the soil. He instinctively looked up and smiled at her with a broad grin.

Blimey O'Reilly. Look at those teeth! Wow, they're white!

I mustn't stare straight at them in case they're a portal into Narnia.

Greek Gary had the whitest teeth known to man and a lot of them. A whole mouthful in fact.

And my, you're so brown. Almost luminous with it. Is that a colour melanin actually makes?

Greek Gary: "Ah, hello Eliza. What a pleasure it is."

Eliza: "Hello Gary. Lovely to meet you."

Shit. That's not right.

Greek Gary: "Chris. I am Chris. As in Christos. It means anointed one."

Anointed one? You really do love yourself, don't you?

Eliza: "Yes, of course you are. Sorry, anointed Chris."

Apologise for being late. Redeem myself with polite chit chat.

Eliza: "Sorry I'm late. I had a bit of an altercation with the Sat Nav."

Greek Gary: "It's no problem. I was looking around the herbs. I am a brilliant cook, you know. My friends are always wanting me to cook for them."

You're just marvellous, aren't you?

Eliza: "That's nice. Where did you go on holiday?"

Mykonos? Athens? The face of the sun?

Greek Gary: "Eh? When? Last year, I went to France. It was divine. The most beautiful scallops."

Oh yes, darling. Do you remember the Scallops? We go back every year to Paris to visit the Beautiful Scallops, don't you know? It's right up there with the Eiffel Tower for visitor attractions.

Eliza: "France is indeed known for The Beautiful Scallops. No, recently. Have you just got back from somewhere hot?"

Greek Gary: "No. I've been in Grimsby on a training course."

Oh.

Eliza: "You're very, erm, tanned."

Greek Gary: "I spray tan, you know. I believe one should look after oneself. You should try it."

Ooof! Cheeky bastard.

Eliza: "I have white towels."

Greek Gary: "Get maroon ones. They don't show the stains."

I'm staring. I'm staring at the gnashers. I'm transfixed.

Don't under any circumstance mention them.

Eliza: "Your teeth are very white."

My brain and mouth are not working in harmony. Anything could happen. I'm buggered.

Greek Gary: "They're simply gorg aren't they?"

Gorg? What is this word?

Eliza: "Gorg, oh yes. Are they yours?"

What the...? Shut up Eliza.

Greek Gary: "I saved up and bought veneers. Fifteen years it took."

Fifteen years to buy a set of pretend teeth?

Eliza: "Fifteen years? They must be dipped in gold leaf. Haha!"

Greek Gary: "They're porcelain. Same people what done Jordan's."

What done? What sort of grammar is that?

Hang on a little second here. Your hair is very brown for man in his forties.

Eliza: "Nice hair."

It's just tripping out of your mouth today, isn't it?

Greek Gary: "Aww, thank you, lovely Eliza. My stylist says it's the best hair he's ever seen. People try to emulate it, but they can't. I was just born with fabulous big hair."

And a fabulous big ego to boot.

Eliza: "That's nice."

Eliza realised he was still holding the Lemon Grass pot.

Eliza: "Shall we go and have a cup of tea?"

I need one.

Greek Gary: "Yes, that's a lovely idea. I must just wash my hands. I can't bear muck on them. Plus, I'm borderline diabetic. I wee a lot."

How delightful; sharing toilet habits with a virtual stranger.

Eliza looked at his immaculately manicured nails and involuntarily glanced at her own.

He's got better nails than me. Is that allowed?

They wandered off towards the tearoom and Chris excused himself to the gents whilst Eliza loitered by the tray pile in the food section.

Chris emerged a few minutes later, looking very flushed.

Eliza: "Everything alright?"

Greek Gary: "It's a three out of ten in there."

Explain.

Eliza: "I'm sorry?"

Greek Gary: "The gents. I have a points system for toilets. One is never return. Anything under a five indicates the establishment has a bad hygiene practice; I've rarely been to an eight or over. Top tip - Don't ever touch the door handles; they're covered in shit. Do you have any idea how many people don't wash their hands after abluting? Hmmm? Truly shocking."

Okaaaay.

Eliza: "I take it, that one doesn't meet expectations."

Greek Gary: "Put it this way, I won't be touching the scones."

Right you are.

Eliza: "What would you like to drink?"

Greek Gary: "Do they do a skinny vanilla latte with oat milk?"

Hang on. Let me mind meld with the ether.

Eliza put her fingertips to her temples.

Eliza, dropping her fingers: "The cosmos doesn't know. Ask the woman serving, she may have more of a clue."

Greek Gary: "Oh ok. And you lovely Eliza. You with the winsome smile. What would you like?"

Winsome? That's a new one for the smile repertoire.

Eliza: "Tea, please."

Greek Gary: "Assam, Darjeeling, Earl Grey? Oat, almond or soya milk?"

Eliza: "Normal with cow's milk."

Greek Gary: "Oh. Fair enough."

I know. I'm a disappointment, aren't I? What with my boring tea choices, pale freckly face and mouth grown teeth.

They ordered their drinks and, out of pure bloody mindedness, Eliza ordered a cheese scone.

It's not big and it's not clever, Eliza.

No, but it keeps me amused.

They sat down and Chris stared at Eliza.

What are you looking at?

Eliza: "Are you ok?"

Greek Gary, wistfully: "You have the most beautiful eyes. I like the left one."

Hahahaha!

Eliza: "Crikey, and there was me thinking they were a pair."

Greek Gary: "Oh, they are, they are. But, you know, we are made in two halves. Matched in the womb and created by the seed of love."

Oh dear. That's all quite unnecessary. I have no wish to contemplate your seed of love.

Eliza: "Seed of love, eh? Indeed."

He continued to stare at her.

Stop looking at me. I feel the compunction to go crossed eyed. The left one might not look so beautiful then.

Eliza: "I'd quite like to eat my scone but I'm rather alarmed at the level of staring that's occurring. I think I might choke."

Greek Gary: "Of course, my lovely Eliza. I shall refrain. I just find you so beguiling."

Winsome, beguiling and a nice left eye. My, my Eliza you are doing well this morning. Beat that carpenter man.

Eliza buttered her scone and bit into it.

Greek Gary: "You and I are the same, you know."

Shoot me now.

Eliza: "Really? Lucky old me."

Greek Gary: "I want to show you my world, Eliza. Be part of my life."

I'd rather not if it's all the same.

Eliza: "What is your life? Your profile said retail. Do you own your own shop?"

I'm thinking men's retail. Lots of mannequins wearing layered tops in the window display. You wafting about; red scarf in hand, bossing the staff around.

Greek Gary: "I am but a fragment of an international group of companies. We are a team and every one of us plays our part in keeping the business successful."

Did you learn all that on the training course in Grimsby?

Greek Gary, continued: "I adore that you wish to learn more about my life."

Civility, I think you call it. I learnt it on the "how to do small talk" course that I never took.

Eliza: "Quite. You're doing alright for yourself then?"

Maybe he's rich. Fake tan costs a bit, surely.

Greek Gary: "I enjoy interacting with my public, yes."

What part of retail means you have your own public?

Eliza: "Your public? Do you mean customers?"

Greek Gary: "Well, I see myself as their servant attending to their requirements."

Hmmm...

Eliza: "This shop of yours. What's it called and what do you actually do?"

Chris looked down at his skinny latte and answered quietly.

Greek Gary: "Discount Food International. I retrieve the trolleys from the far end of the car park... and sometimes the canal."

Eliza coughed on her scone and swallowed a whole unchewed mouthful and pushed it down with a swig of tea.

Oh, Mother of Jesus, I've just swallowed half a scone without chewing.

I'm so sorry stomach. You'll have to sort that out seeing as it bypassed my teeth. I'll have soup for lunch.

Eliza made her excuses and left shortly after the scone swallowing. She got back into the car and checked the time. Three quarters of an hour until Patrick.

She sent a text to Lydia.

Eliza's text: "Date one - He was a 1970s Greek porn star trolley finder with a fake tan, fake teeth and massive dyed hair. All that was missing was the moustache.

Hope Tom's being a good boy. Call me if you have any problems. Love you xx"

Eliza sighed.

NEXT!!

Status: *"I want the truth! You can't handle the truth!"*

Chapter Fifteen

Sub Affirmation for the day: *I give out love and it is returned in abundance.*

Eliza decided to dispense with the Sat Nav and opted for the old-fashioned way of navigation for her second date. This involved stopping at a petrol station and asking the way.

Eliza recited to herself on the way back to the car.

Left out of the garage. Two rights, a left up the hill, by the pub turn right again. Straight on at the lights, then it'll be on your left.

Erm...

Left out of the garage. Two rights, a left up the hill, pub er, right? Left? Whatever. One of the two. Then straight past the lights and it's on my right?

How can I forget literally in the space of eight seconds?

I thought baby brain only lasted when they were babies. That's blatant misrepresentation of the truth. They don't tell you your faculties never, ever recover. That's baby marketing that is. If they told you what really happened, procreation would stop overnight.

The conversation in bed would go like this:

Her: "No sorry, I can't have your 'seed of love' tonight. If we have a baby, I'll never be able to remember the way to the shops. I do beg your pardon, who are you again?"

Him: "I am your husband."

Her: "I do admit you do look familiar but unless it's on a post-it note stuck to the fridge, I'm afraid I'm buggered."

Having a child is akin to having your head run over by a bus.

Stop mentally rambling, Eliza, you're creating a queue by the pumps.

She glanced in her rear-view mirror. A woman in a Smart car behind her was urging her forward by waving her hands. She didn't look impressed.

Don't look at me that way, little car woman. And for the record, I can lip read. I will not "fuck off". I will drive off when I'm good and ready. So, what if I didn't get petrol? Who are you? The petrol pump police?

Eliza started her car and revved it unnecessarily, by way of defiance.

Eliza looked in her rear-view mirror and Smart car woman gave her a sarcastic "very clever" look.

I've a good mind to re-apply my make-up in the mirror just to piss you off. Anyway, at least I can fit shopping into my car. What do you do with yours? Bung it on your head like Carmen Miranda?

Anyway, don't distract me, I have instructions to remember.

Now then which way out of here? Right? Left? Right, I think he said...

****

Half an hour later, a stressed Eliza pulled into the car park of the Red Lion pub. Pulling the driver's mirror around to face her, she looked at herself.

Flipping flip-flops. I'm getting a glow on. I am never ever doing this again.

I can't even remember this one's name.

I can't even remember my child's name at this present moment.

How can travelling twelve miles across town prove to be so mentally and physically draining?

Oh no, I've got to eat again. I'm still digesting the scone.

Eliza looked at a board outside the pub.

How classy, a two for one menu.

This comes from a woman who shakes rice crispies from the packet into her chops and then has a glass of milk to follow as she can't be bothered to get a bowl out.

What do I care?

I'm not Geraldine with her cheese and wine parties. I am normal.

No, that's not right. I am not normal. Most definitely not normal.

What am I then? Mental. Ah yes, that's it. Mental.

She powdered her nose and put on a slick of lipstick.

Off we go again.

Name? Patrick.

Profession? Woodwork.

Likes and dislikes? Haven't a clue.

Age? He's an adult.

Lives? In the vicinity.

We're fully informed and ready to roll.

Eliza got out of the car and strolled into the bar.

Patrick was waiting for her and smiled when she approached.

Ooh, big beard. Lydia would be impressed. Long hair. He looks a bit like Jesus. Jesus did woodwork too, didn't he? Maybe he's the second coming.

Eliza: "Hello."

Second Coming: "Hi Eliza. Nice to meet you. Drink?"

Eliza: "A coke, please."

Second Coming: "That's full of additives, are you sure?"

Oh god. Or son of god.

Eliza: "Yes, quite sure, thank you."

It's the additives in food that keep me functioning.

Second Coming: "Fair enough."

Patrick ordered Eliza a drink.

Eliza: "What are you drinking?"

Second Coming: "Mineral water."

Why bother?

Eliza: "You pay money for water?"

Second Coming: "Yes, it's the fuel of life."

I think you'll find that's chocolate, actually.

Eliza: "Indeed. I have it from the tap at home."

Second Coming: "You shouldn't drink tap water it's full of chemicals."

I'm really doing well today. Surpassing all expectations.

Eliza: "Ah well, shall we sit down?"

Second Coming: "Good plan. You choose."

Eliza went to sit down in a booth.

Second Coming: "Can we sit by the window please; I like the natural light."

Well, don't give me a choice then if you have a preference. At least we've ascertained you're not a Gremlin.

She trailed behind him as he strode towards a table by the window. They sat down and she got the menu out.

Ok. Small talk. Here we go.

Eliza: "Bit wet out, isn't it?"

Second Coming: "Yes, it's our fault. We have only ourselves to blame."

I don't recall us doing a global rain dance.

Eliza: "Is it? What did we do? Upset the rain fairy?"

Second Coming: "Rain fairy? How quaint. No, we continue to burn fossil fuels to the detriment of the planet."

Quaint? I'm not sure that's a term of endearment. I've got a lovely left eye, I'll have you know. A man who loves himself and has the same teeth as Jordan told me so, just this morning.

Eliza: "Oh yes, we are very irresponsible. We're better off burning wood. We can always plant trees."

You see Eliza, you can hold your own.

Second Coming: "We have affected the Gulf Stream."

Surely a stream can't cause widespread flooding?

Eliza: "Where is the Gulf Stream? Oxfordshire way?"

How does burning coal clog up a stream? Maybe they dump the excess in there. That is very irresponsible indeed. Fossil fuel fly-tipping. I'm not surprised he's annoyed. The Government should step in.

Why is he looking at me like that?

He's laughing. I'm not sure if it's at me or with me.

Second Coming: "Haha! You're funny. It's off the coast of America, as you well know."

That's not a stream, it's the Atlantic Ocean you stupid man.

Change the subject. He obviously hasn't a clue.

Eliza: "Right, let's look at the menu. I'm starving."

Liar.

Second Coming: "I wonder what the vegetarian options are."

Crap. He's out of the running on the grounds that he can't go to Brian's menu launch.

Was he honestly in with a shout even if he ordered a mixed grill with extra black pudding? No, of course not.

Eliza: "I bet you like fish, though."

He's not actually Jesus, you stupid cow.

Second Coming: "I'm not a Pescatarian."

Random.

Eliza: "Me neither, I'm a Gemini."

He's laughing again. What an unusual man. At least he's happy.

Second Coming: "Haha! So, what are you having?"

Eliza: "Soup of the day, I think."

He took a note of their table number and went up to the bar to order. Meanwhile, Eliza got her phone out and sent a text to Lydia.

Eliza's text: "What month are Pescatarians born in? Is Tom alright? Love you xx"

Send.

Patrick came back to the table.

Second Coming: "So tell me about your business. I'm very interested. You upcycle products. That's very green and commendable. I make furniture from fallen trees."

Eliza: "As opposed to what other sort of trees?"

Second Coming: "I only use trees that have fallen over by natural means."

Eliza: "Instead of a chainsaw, you mean?"

Second Coming: "Yes. I don't believe we should desecrate the countryside for our own ends."

Eliza: "Do they have to fall of their own volition then?"

What do you do, will them over?

Second Coming: "Yes. I do use ones that have fallen over in the wind, though, as that's an act of god."

Naturally. What with you and him being related. It's a family business sort of set up.

Eliza's phone pinged.

Eliza: "Do excuse me. I have a message. It may relate to my son."

Second Coming: "Of course, by all means."

Eliza picked up her phone and Lydia had replied.

Lydia's text: "Pescatarians eat fish but not meat, you dozy bint. Tom's lovely, we've just made carrot cake. Hope you're having fun. Love you too xx"

Oh. That's why he was laughing. It was at me, not with me.

Eliza: "Well, I paint old furniture really. That's it. Try and give it a new lease of life. It's going ok."

Keep it brief. It's hardly rocket science.

Second Coming: "I took the liberty of reading your blog."

Ohhhhh?

Eliza: "How did you find that?"

Second Coming: "I Googled you."

Stalker warning.

Eliza: "Oh right. Ok."

I am on a heightened state of alert.

Second Coming: "I like your poems. I write poems too."

He's read my outpourings. I'm not sure I feel comfortable sitting opposite a man who knows my inner mind workings. It gives him the upper hand.

Eliza, warily: "Really, that's nice."

Second Coming: "What are you looking for on MOM?"

Oh, that's a bit left field.

Eliza: "A date that likes pork."

For goodness' sake, Eli.

Second Coming: "I can't assist you with the pork element of your request, but I have written you a poem which outlines my feelings towards you."

Poem? Feelings towards me?

I'm sorry, have I entered a parallel universe where we have met before?

Eliza: "Ok. I'm not sure what to say."

For once I am voicing my actual thoughts.

Second Coming: "Here, read it and see what you think."

He handed her a folded piece of paper from his pocket and slid it across the table. Eliza unfolded the A4 sheet and proceeded to read.

I am not your lover
I am not your friend
I am someone in between
I am your companion when you have a need.

We don't have much in common
But a physical attraction
We only meet
When we need some erotic action.

We must limit our feelings
To what we do when our clothes are off
Your eyes are the windows to your soul, and they create my lust
To meet twice monthly is certainly a must.

Be mine in the bedroom and the rest can wait
My carnal desires, you need to sate.

Eliza dropped the piece of paper on the table.

Hardly Keats, is it?

Eliza: "Erm. How long did that take you to think up?"

Ten minutes whilst you were having a wank?

Second Coming: "I was looking at your profile picture and everything just flowed."

I bet.

Eliza: "Well, it's all frightfully charming but I think I might just be looking for the pork eating element of a relationship not the regular porking."

So crude, Eliza.

It's his fault. He's set me off kilter with his 'erotic action'. I've not even eaten my lunch yet.

Second Coming: "Ah, no worries. Let's eat then instead."

Eliza: "Yes, how about we do that and forget about the carnal desires bit."

Second Coming: "You do have very sexy eyes, though. I could take you right here and now over this table."

I might have to do something about my eyes. Beer bottle bottom glasses might be an option. Or a blindfold. Might prove somewhat hazardous, perhaps.

Eliza: "But, just think, this table might have been felled by unnatural means. That would surely upset your sensibilities."

Second Coming: "Haha! You are very quaint indeed."

There's that word quaint, again. I am not quaint, you bearded pervert. Quaint to me means gingham dresses and stripy socks with a penchant for eating jam straight out of the jar.

Their lunches came and Eliza busied herself trying to not make eye contact and at the same time not slurp her soup.

They paid the bill and as Eliza put her coat on, she looked at the sheet of paper; uncertain what to do with the poem.

I need to show Lydia. Then I can rip it up into tiny little shreds and forget it ever existed.

She folded it up and put it in her coat pocket.

Second Coming: "Ah, you're keeping it. I'm very touched. Think of me every time you read it, won't you? If you change your mind, you know where I am."

Eliza: "Yes, I do indeed. You'll be the one carving up a tree your dad knocked over whilst composing filthy odes."

Patrick looked at her quizzically for a moment, with his head to one side.

Second Coming: "You're a one off, you really are. Most quaint, most quaint indeed."

Right, that's it. I'm off. Overuse of the word quaint. Get yourself a thesaurus, Jesus man.

Eliza gave him an awkward hug goodbye and headed for the car. Once inside, she sent a further text to Lydia.

Eliza's text: "Date two – He was the son of god with a yearning for no strings sex whilst saving the planet from wanton deforestation and flooding. I'm on my way back to put my head in your oven. Put the kettle on xx"

Status: *"He's not the messiah, he's a very naughty boy!"*

Chapter Sixteen

Sub Sub Affirmation for the day: *All my attitudes are positive.*

Lydia opened the door and Eliza lobbed her bag on the floor as she charged past her. She picked up a seated Tom who had been cheerfully building towers with Lydia's make-up sponges and planted kisses into his warm, podgy neck.

Tom started squirming and giggling with delight.

Eliza: "Hello, my darling. My little bit of sanity in a world full of nutters!"

Tom: "Hello mummy! I build squidgy towers. I wipe nose on them."

Lydia: "Oh, that's nice."

Eliza to Lydia: "Put the kettle on. I need my elixir of life."

Lydia: "Panic not, my little man explorer. One is on the brew. I take it they weren't a roaring success."

Eliza shot her a pained expression and plonked Tom back in optimum sponge tower construction position.

Eliza: "Build mummy a replica of the Chrysler building so she can throw herself off it, there's a pet."

Tom: "Ok, mummy."

Eliza signalled to Lydia to go into the kitchen and followed behind her.

Eliza: "Oh. My. God. Where do these men come from? They actually mingle with society Lydia."

Lydia: "I know, It's concerning, isn't it? They should be branded or something."

Eliza: "We should set up a company that administers a "Total Wanker Alert Tattoo" – TWAT for short. Think of the amount of people we'd be able to employ. We'd send our employees on training courses on how to choose the best tattoo spot. If they were bald, they could do it on their heads. We could write a manual."

Lydia: "Yes, then if we meet a man with a balaclava on, we'd know he was part of the TWAT club."

Eliza: "If I went on a date and he turned up in a balaclava I think the clues would be there to be honest."

Lydia: "See it works. You're a genius, Eli."

Eliza: "I thank you."

Eliza did a little bow and put some cake in her mouth.

Eliza: "Oooh, I must show you something. I met Jesus and he wrote me a poem."

Lydia: "Blimey, that's not a sentence I expected to hear over my carrot cake."

Eliza reached into her coat pocket and handed it to Lydia.

Lydia read it and put it on the work counter. She stared at it with disapproval.

Lydia: "Did you rip his nuts off?"

Eliza: "It was an option but instead I just said thanks, but I'll just have the soup, please."

Lydia: "You're too polite."

Eliza: "I know, the next time I go to mum and dads for Sunday dinner, I'm going to discuss this whole manners thing with them. They let me down. I'm going to learn from their mistake and teach Tom to be a rude child and have the ability to tell people to go and shove their suggestive poems up their bums."

Lydia: "Oooh, hello Tom, would you like a drink, chicken?"

Tom had pottered into the kitchen and had all the sponges wedged down his t-shirt.

Tom: "Yes please. Bums. Up their bums."

Bums indeed. Diversion tactic needed to assist in child forgetting offensive statement.

Eliza: "What have you got down your top, Tom?"

Pathetic. He'll grow up thinking you don't have the ability to spot the bleedin' obvious.

Tom: "I have bricks. Buildy bricks. I brick man. I save the world."

Lydia: "I am sponge brick man, hear me roar!"

Eliza: "Haha! Where would we be without sponge brick man to soak up the detritus of humanity? Here you are saviour of the world. Have some carrot cake and a cup of milk."

Tom: "Brick man say fank you, mummy."

Tom started to totter off back to the lounge with his bulging t-shirt, cup of milk and plate of cake and bounced off the doorframe.

Ok. Saviour of the world may require some assistance.

Eliza took the drink and plate off him and led the way back to the lounge and put it on the coffee table.

Eliza wandered back into the kitchen.

Eliza: "New coffee table? I'm sure I've not seen that before."

Lydia: "Oh yeah, I meant to say. I bought it for us to renovate but it kind of got stuck in my lounge."

Hmmmm.

Eliza: "Did you pay for it out of the business account?"

Lydia: "Err yes, I had every intention of making it our next project."

Eliza: "Have you put the money back into the business account? If you're keeping it, you need to do that."

Lydia: "Not yet, darling, I haven't had it long and I meant to mention it, but it slipped my mind."

Eliza felt a wave of discomfort wash over her.

Eliza: "You need to reimburse the company if you keep anything straight away or the books will get in a muddle. Like that wardrobe last month. Have you paid the money for that back in?"

Lydia: "Wardrobe? Oh yes, I forgot about that, but I will do. Don't worry, it'll all be sorted. Don't be so anal about such things."

Anal? How am I anal? How did my bottom come into this?

Eliza: "Ok."

Don't be a nag.

Give her a chance. She's not business orientated. Guide her. It'll be fine.

Lydia: "Anyway, less of boring old furniture. Tell me more about these loopy men."

They moved to the lounge and spent the next hour putting the world to rights which basically involved shooting all men and agreeing that the world of lesbianism held great attraction if only they could get over the fact, they like men and not women.

I have eaten an unchewed scone, soup and three quarters of a carrot cake and it's not even three o'clock in the afternoon. I have the delight of dinner as well this evening with Bland Man.

I'm so not in the mood.

I shall cancel. Yes, that's what I shall do.

Eliza: "I'm going to cancel tonight. I can't face another dire date."

Lydia: "Don't be daft. I'm having Tom, it's all cool."

Eliza: "No, I am definitely not in the mood. I'll take Tom back with me and have a film and pyjamas night. You've not got Freya, why don't you call The Mighty Sword and see if he's free?"

Lydia: "Oooh, I could, couldn't I? Does that look a bit keen?"

Eliza: "Yes, but you are keen so what does it matter? I don't understand all the dating rules thing. If he goes off you because you text him and ask him out then he's not the one for you in the first place is he?"

Lydia: "Ok, that's logic enough for me. I'll text him now."

Eliza: "Good girl."

Phew, I can message Bland Man and put him off. Say I have my child. Which is true. No lying involved so I can't have a black mark against me from the karma fairy.

Eliza: "Right then, little man and I will get out of your hair."

Lydia: "Okidokes. Oooh, he's replied and said yes. Fabulous! I'll go and sort out an outfit."

Eliza: "Ok. Let me know how you get on. Come on Brick Boy let's remove your sponges."

Tom: "Not sponges. They special guns. They shoot baddies."

Eliza: "Naturally. Let's decommission your weapons then. Come here."

Eliza removed all the sponges and put them on the coffee table.

Don't forget about the coffee table Eli, make a note to remind Lydia.

She got all Tom's paraphernalia together and left Lydia to have a clothes crisis.

You and I, my little bundle of joy are going home to flop on the settee and I am going to forget today ever happened.

Status: *"It's the wind, it's speaking to us. What's it saying? I don't know, I don't speak wind."*

Chapter Seventeen

Affirmation for the day: *Life is a joy filled with wonderful surprises.*

It was Wednesday evening and Eliza's mobile rang.

Oh, it's Lewis. What does he want? I heard from him a few days ago.

He's ascertained Tom and I are still alive which is about his limit these days.

Eliza: "Hello. What's up?"

Lewis: "Hello. Why does anything have to be up?"

Eliza: "Because you are a creature of habit and it's not your day to enquire whether your ex-wife and child are still alive."

Don't be abrasive. Actually, what do you care? As you were.

Lewis: "Haha. You are funny Eliza."

Pardon? A compliment.

Eliza: "Have you been drinking?"

Lewis: "No. I wondered if you were in."

This is not normal Lewis behaviour. Guard up. Ping! Guard is in place.

Eliza: "I am in. Perhaps you could tell me why you want to know."

Lewis: "Can I come round? Er, please?"

Politeness and a personal visit. Hmmm.

Eliza: "Do you want to collect something?"

I'm keeping the retro tea pot. End of.

Lewis: "No, of course not. I wanted to see you, have a chat. That's all."

He sounds awkward.

Eliza: "Oh."

Lewis: "Is Tom still up? Perhaps if I come over now, I'll be able to help you put him to bed?"

Whoah there laddio, that's a bit out of the blue. Over a year down the line taking up fatherly duties.

Eliza: "How about you come over after I've put him to bed, and you can tell me how you got severe concussion and forgot that this isn't your personality."

Lewis: "Haha! You and your jokes! Ok, tell me a time that's suitable for you."

I wasn't joking actually. You've had a brain transplant. I'm wrong footed. Go back to being a crap, inattentive father. I can hate you then.

Eliza: "Come over at about half past eight."

I've got time to whip round the house and make myself look in some semblance of order.

Show you I'm coping just fine and dandy thank you very much Mr Abandon Man.

Lewis: "Ok Eli. See you in a bit."

Eliza felt an involuntary stab in her chest.

The way you said "Eli". That familiar, affectionate way. I can imagine you smiling when you say it.

Bastard. Don't do that to me. Don't say my name.

Don't speak actually. Oh, and definitely don't turn nice.

Eliza: "See you in a bit."

She put her mobile down on the kitchen work surface and stared at it.

Maybe he's just found out he's got a disease.

Oh dear. He's got three months to live.

That's terrible. He's dying.

Tom tottered into the kitchen.

Tom: "I give you kiss from my kiss bucket. I got ten for you."

Eliza bent down and scooped him up and gave him a massive kiss on his cheek.

Tom: "No gerroff! I do kissing. My bucket. Yours empty cos they wet."

Eliza: "Ok, sorry darling. Get kissing then. Where do you want me?"

Tom: "Arm."

Eliza: "Please."

Tom: "Gimme arm. Please."

Eliza pulled up her sleeve and bent down whereupon Tom looked down into his imaginary bucket which was held in the crook of his arm and grabbed a handful of invisible kisses, pretended to eat them, then proceeded to kiss up and down her arm.

Tom: "Special one on knobbly bit. Look odd."

Eliza: "That's my elbow."

Tom: "Not nice. Look old."

Oh charming.

Eliza: "Yes alright. Come on you, time for bed."

Eliza set about the bedtime routine and when Tom was settled happily, she went into the bathroom and stared at herself.

Right. I'd best make myself presentable.

Oh, and put some moisture cream on my elbows.

At half past eight on the dot there was a gentle knock on the door.

Eliza opened it and there stood a tired looking Lewis.

Lewis: "I knocked quietly as I didn't want to wake Tom."

You could drop a piano down the stairs once he's gone off, he sleeps so heavily. You see, you wouldn't know that as you've not been here.

Eliza: "It's ok, he's out for the count. Come in."

She held the door wide and kept a safe distance.

I'm not sure how I feel about all this. I've not seen him in the flesh since we sold the house. That was months ago and that was on neutral territory.

He looks tired. That'll be the shock of his imminent death.

Eliza: "Cup of tea?"

Lewis: "Yes please. The cottage looks nice. Very homely."

Yes well, you've not visited before, have you? I've painted the walls twice since I've moved in. You might have liked the last colour scheme too.

He's trying to be pleasant. He's definitely gravely ill.

Eliza busied herself with the cups and realised she was shaking.

Don't let him see.

She offered him his cup of tea and suggested they sit in the lounge.

She sat opposite him and looked at him carefully.

He looks nervous. He wants to tell you. Brace yourself.

Make it easy for him.

Eliza: "So, how long have you got?"

Succinct.

Lewis: "Probably an hour or so."

Shit! He's come here to die.

That's you all over, isn't it? Leave me to sort the mess out.

A dead body in the lounge. How am I going to explain that to the neighbours?

I'll be on the local news and all sorts.

Eliza: "Bloody hell. That's not long. Are you sure?"

Lewis: "Well, perhaps a couple of hours, at a push. I don't want Geraldine to know."

She'll know soon enough when I have to explain that the corpse of her boyfriend is in my cottage.

That's got to be very bad chi. My life force will be severely affected by this.

I'll have to feng shui completely.

Eliza: "Ah, so you don't think she will take it very well then."

I feel a sense of power in some warped way. I win the dead man. When the going got tough he came back to me.

Lewis: "To be honest, I don't know."

He looked despondently at his hands.

Ooh ooh, I sense trouble. How marvellous.

Maybe he caught something virulent off her.

Oh, how brilliant would it be if she had it too?

That's the bad fairy talking. Shut up.

Do I really want them both dead?

Not really, just a little bit, perhaps. Not completely dead.

If I wished them completely dead, my karma would be shot forever. I'll definitely be designated a life full of cats and no sex.

Eliza: "How is she?"

Lewis: "She's been laid off her job, which couldn't come at a worse time in all honesty."

Eliza: "I bet. There'll be things to pay for."

Funeral expenses.

Lewis looked up unexpectedly and stared into her eyes intently.

It caught Eliza completely unaware, and she felt extremely awkward and diverted her gaze to the standard lamp, quickly.

Don't stare at me. I don't like it. Your eyes are what got me into this pickle in the first place.

Lewis: "Yes, you're right, a lot of things. You forget how much."

Forget? No one in your family has died. Well, mad old aunt Beryl came a cropper after the toaster incident a few years ago, but your mum sorted that out.

Eliza: "Well, you've not really had to deal with it before, have you?"

Lewis looked sadly at her and shook his head.

Lewis: "I know Eli, I've let you and Tom down."

Oh stop right there. Don't try and right your wrongs just because you've got a few hours to live.

I'll have a word with my mum and see if she can talk to her contacts in the ether and make sure you go to heaven. Years of dedication to the pixies; she must be able to pull a few strings.

Eliza: "It's ok. I don't hate you. We're both fine."

Now we're ok. We weren't, but we are now. Time truly does heal.

Hang on, pay attention. He's still staring.

Do I see tears? No, surely not.

How do I feel about seeing him with emotion?

A bit detached actually. Oooh, that's good.

Chapter twelve of "Moving on with your Life" had the "feeling detached" paragraph in it.

Ah, but I don't like to see him sad.

Eliza: "Are you crying? It's understandable of course, but why have you come here? Surely you should be with Geraldine at a time like this."

Best to send him home. Let her deal with it.

Lewis: "I can't cope with her at the moment."

Eliza: "You're together now. You should be sharing this. This is a big thing. Actually, the biggest thing."

Death. Doesn't get much more final than that, honey.

Lewis: "You're right. It's not what I expected and, if I am honest, wanted."

Eliza: "Of course, it's not what you wanted. But it is a part of life. You should be with your new girlfriend and family."

Lewis: "I wanted to tell you in person."

Eliza: "That's thoughtful. If there's anything I can do, just let me know. I'll be there as a support."

You'll be dead. You won't know if I fall a bit short in certain areas, but it shows I'm noble. It'll look good on my karmic sheet.

Eliza felt a sudden wave of sadness wash over her.

You see, now you've made me care again. I'm upset. That was you looking at me in that way, that did that.

Eliza: "Are you ok?"

Lewis stood and went over to where she was seated, he crouched down and held her hands tenderly.

Lewis: "Can I hug you?"

Uh oh. Physical contact.

Zip up the anti-emotion flak jacket.

Eliza: "Yes, of course. It might be the last chance you get."

She stood, awkwardly, and he held her. Like he had countless times previously. She felt him rest his chin on her head and he nuzzled her hair and breathed in deeply. The familiarity was too overwhelming, and she stood back quickly.

Eliza felt a lump in her throat.

Don't cry. Save that for when he can't see it.

Lewis: "Please don't say that. This has made me realise a lot of things. I will make it up to you and Tom. I promise."

Eliza: "How? Will you let me have your car?"

Lewis: "Eh? Well, I should probably think about a bigger car, the two-seater won't be practical. It would be ideal for you and Tom, actually. Ok, I'll see what I can sort out."

Bigger car? Are you thinking of a hearse?

Eliza: "You're thinking in a very pragmatic way. It's very brave of you."

Lewis pulled Eliza into another embrace and this time she relaxed into it and rested her head on his chest.

My beautiful, useless soon to be deceased ex-husband. Not Geraldine's. Mine.

Lewis: "Geraldine says I need to man up."

She's a harsh cow.

Eliza stood back again and stared up at Lewis.

Eliza: "So do you know what you've got?"

I'm hugging him. Make sure it's not contagious. If it is, I'll go and wipe myself all over with an antibacterial wipe.

Lewis: "It's a boy. We had the scan yesterday."

Eliza felt a rushing of blood in her ears and felt her legs give way.

I need to sit down!

She extricated herself from his arms and flumped back on the chair.

Eliza: "A baby?! You're having a b-b-baby?"

I'm stuttering. I cannot form words properly.

They know the sex – she's had the twenty-week scan. That's most definitely pregnant.

Lewis: "Well yes, I thought you'd guessed from the way you were talking."

Eliza: "No, I thought you came here to die."

Lewis: "Pardon?"

Eliza: "I thought you'd got a life ending disease. This is much worse."

Lewis: "Pardon?"

Shit. How do I feel? I don't know. I need to assimilate this information.

He needs to leave.

He needs to leave, immediately.

Eliza, quickly: "Right then, I consider myself informed of developments. Thanks for that, most thoughtful."

Lewis: "Are you ok. You've gone a bit odd. You thought I was dying?"

Eliza: "Absolutely. Right then, you need to go. We can't have the mother-to-be getting stressed as to your whereabouts."

Lewis: "Erm, ok. I'm pleased I came to see you. I've missed you, Eli."

Out! Now!

Eliza: "Have you now? Well, you've another offspring on the way to not look after now. Good luck with that."

Caustic. Do I care? No. No I don't.

Lewis: "You're angry at me, I understand that. Please let me make it up to you."

Eliza, raising her voice: "How? How do you think you can do that, hmmm?!"

I'm hollering. God I'm mad.

Lewis: "Don't shout you'll wake Tom."

Eliza, fuming: "Do not dare tell me how to act with regard to Tom! For your 'not involved in any flip-flopping way' information, you can hire a one-man band to play at the end of his bed and he'll not wake up."

Lewis: "Flip-flopping?"

Eliza: "Yes, flip-flopping."

Lewis: "I should go."

Eliza: "Yes, you should."

Lewis: "I'll ring tomorrow and will arrange to sort out seeing the pair of you, if you're happy with that?"

Eliza: "You want to spend time with me and Tom?"

This is a new development on top of the embryo development.

Lewis: "Yes, I would like to be a proper father to him and be a support to you, if you'd let me?"

Erm, how far does this support extend?

Eliza: "Do I still get the car?"

Lewis: "Yes."

Just checking.

Eliza: "Just go now and let me digest this information. I'll text you tomorrow."

Lewis: "Ok Eli. Thank you."

Eliza ushered him out the door and closed it promptly behind him and leant her back against it.

She slid down the door and sat on the floor cross-legged. Ellington wandered up and started licking her face.

Eliza: "Get off, dog."

Ellington climbed on her lap and tried to get comfy.

Eliza: "You're far too big to sit on me. You've got doggy dysmorphic disorder. Stand easy."

Ellington clambered off and flopped beside her with his head on her lap and she stroked his ears, absentmindedly.

How do I feel? I don't know. I have too much swimming around in my head.

A lot of the thoughts are not good. It must be said.

Uh oh, they're forming. Close your ears karma fairy. They're coming out, unhindered.

I hope her ankles swell.

Oh, and that she puts on three stone and can't shift it again.

Ever.

Oh, and her ever so straight hair goes frizzy and she gets acne.

Actually, I think I preferred it when I thought I was going to have to deal with a stiff in the lounge.

Bed. I shall go to bed and forget about this evening.

Let my brain sort it all out whilst I'm asleep.

Eliza stood, picked the cups up and lobbed them in the kitchen sink.

Eliza: "My bedchamber awaits, Ellington. You are in charge. Keep watch."

She grabbed Norris on the way past and lobbed him into his basket and went up to bed.

Status: *"What we've got here is... failure to communicate."*

Chapter Eighteen

Affirmation for the day: *I have positive mental images.*

Eliza awoke to find Tom dressed in a policeman's outfit over the top of his pyjamas, standing beside her bed.

Tom: "Allo, allo, allo."

Eliza: "Morning PC Plod."

Tom: "Not Plod. PC Tom. I catch cwooks."

Eliza: "Have you found any?"

Tom: "Found a mummy in bed."

Eliza: "The highest crime imaginable. It's a fair cop. Put me away for twenty years. In fact, just leave me here. I'll settle for that."

Tom: "What?"

Eliza: "Pardon, not what. What time is it?"

Tom: "Pardon time is it, not what. Can't tell time. Tummy rumbly."

Eliza rolled over, the clock said half past five.

Eliza: "Tom! Way too early!"

Tom's chin started to wobble and his bottom lip shot out. He rubbed his stomach.

Tom: "Tumbly rumbly. Need food mummy."

Eliza: "Ok, ok. Don't get all emotional on me. I'm getting up."

Eliza dragged her dressing gown on and shuffled downstairs to be greeted by an exuberant Ellington and stretching Norris.

She set about her morning routine and went to fill the kettle up. Whilst doing so, she looked out of the window to the garden, whereupon she saw a welly wearing Philip. Bedecked in his saggy pants, he was wandering down from her overgrown vegetable patch. She'd not got round to doing anything with it since she'd moved in as it was full of old brambles and weeds.

Eliza: "Allo, allo, allo. What's going on here? As PC Tom would say."

She instinctively stepped back, switched off the light and watched him from the side of the window.

She could make out, in the half-light, that he was walking down her path carrying something. She peered harder to see what he had in his hand.

Well, flipping flip-flops, he's carrying a spade!

She stopped breathing and watched as he stopped for a moment, looked around furtively, then quickly stepped over the ridiculous boundary and back into his garden.

What is a man doing in pants and wellies at a quarter to six in the morning, with a spade in his neighbour's garden?

It's like Cluedo – Mr Hargreaves, in the vegetable patch, with a spade.

Am I sleepwalking?

Perhaps, I'm not actually awake.

Eliza turned the light back on.

Eliza: "Tom, come here and pinch me."

Tom looked up from his porridge and shook his head.

Tom: "Not good to hurt, mummy. You say that."

Eliza: "Yes of course. Sorry. Good point."

Tom: "I can bite you if you want?"

Eliza: "No it's ok. I'll just hit myself instead."

Tom: "Funny mummy."

Indeed.

What do I do now I've witnessed that?

Has he buried someone in my garden?

Yesterday, I would have been quite grateful of his services when I thought Lewis was dying. That would have cut out the funeral costs.

As it is, Lewis is just a prolific fatherer of children he's incapable of looking after, so Philip, your services are not required.

Shall I just go into denial?

I can't. I'm too inquisitive.

I need to know what he's doing at the end of my garden.

What if I actually find a dead person? That will really upset neighbourly relations.

I've heard about things like this over Leylandii trees.

Cups of tea and pleasantries one day. Lawsuits and six-foot fences being erected the next.

It's a cautious approach I need to take.

Obviously highly dubious if it has to be carried out under the cover of darkness.

It's definitely a dead person. What other explanation could there possibly be?

I mustn't let Ellington out for a wee for a good half an hour. Philip mustn't know I'm aware of activities occurring.

****

Later that morning, the sun was out and she'd decided she'd had enough of being cooped up inhaling paint fumes. Pottering in the garden allowed Eliza's mind to clear and always soothed her soul. It also provided ample opportunity to attend to the borders and, whilst at it, survey the hastily made grave in her back garden. She was on her knees yanking out weeds from her overflowing borders and stole a glance to the end of the garden. She'd not ventured up there yet for fear of what she may uncover.

I'm having a week of it.

First, Lewis becoming an unwilling father with Geraldine.

Now a dead person in my garden.

I'm sure Claudia Schiffer doesn't have this sort of trouble.

I am rooted to my weeding spot. I daren't go up there.

She looked over her shoulder. Tom was sat in the middle of his sand pit with his tractor. He was busy scooping up front loads of sand and pouring them over his podgy little legs. He was explaining to Ellington that he was Bob the Builder. Ellington looked suitably impressed and was proffering him a slobbery tennis ball which he spat out onto Tom's lap.

Tom: "Urgh. Spit ball. Gerroff! I build road."

He picked up the ball and threw it over arm and it landed approximately two feet away. Ellington bounded on it with great zeal and subsequently did a victory lap around the garden with it in his mouth.

Norris was curled up in the flower bed having a snooze in the sunshine. Eliza turned her attentions back to the weed infestation and her mind wandered to an objective look at where her life was now. She often thought of her life as a film. She had the leading role, but she hadn't bothered to read her lines properly and didn't know what she was meant to say or her cue and as a result was permanently adlibbing.

She analysed how she felt about Lewis becoming a father again and she had to confess the overall feeling was ambivalence. It was an initial shock as she had completely misunderstood the nature of his visit. She'd thought it was a life-ending, but it was actually the start of one. Yin and Yang. All in one evening. The resulting knowledge had pulled her up short and made her realise his life had moved on but also that hers had too. She actually felt sorry for Geraldine which is an emotion she thought she'd never possess towards that woman. Eliza had first-hand knowledge of Lewis' uselessness and, by his own admission, it was another child he didn't feel ready to cope with. But, at least, it might mean a new car, which was a bonus.

On a personal level, she acknowledged she was feeling hopeful. She felt a level of happiness which she'd not thought possible just some months before. Her new life suited her. She had adjusted and regained control of her life. She felt more in charge of her own destiny. The despondent days were becoming much less and soon she'd start to see a financial return from her furniture upcycling venture. She had to concede that the natural flow of the business had fallen into Lydia buying the pieces and dumping them in Eliza's lounge and then Eliza doing just about everything else from stripping, painting, distressing, and distressing herself whilst bashing her shins on them for weeks whilst they languished in her house as she finished them off. Lydia then wafted in to get 'a little man' to take it down to the shop. This 'little man' was invariably Mr Hicks who also ended up predominantly running the shop instead of Lydia, as she found it boring. He didn't accept payment, so they paid for his utilities in his flat instead. It worked well apart from the fact every piece of furniture sold came with six crusty rolls and a cottage loaf. It also resulted in customers being served by a dishevelled, toast eating man wearing pyjamas if they turned up before twelve on a weekday. That aside, Eliza conceded it was appearing to work out.

Eliza also noted that Lydia renovated one unit to her three, but she didn't mind so much. It kept her busy, it was generating income and it meant she was flexible with regard to Tom.

I am concerned about the level of furniture the business has bought to furnish Lydia's home though.

I need to sit down with the bookkeeper and see where we're at.

The feeling of discord rumbled in her stomach. Her musings were interrupted by a rough paw scraping her thigh.

Ellington spat the ball out beside her and bounced about, excitedly.

Hmmm, I see a plan hatching.

Eliza stood and stretched, ostentatiously.

She picked up the ball, did a little pirouette and lobbed it down the garden to the end where the suspected dead body was. It landed in amongst the foliage.

Eliza, over brightly: "Oh dear! Silly me! Haha! What a rubbish throw Ellington. Let me help you find it."

Ellington had charged off to find the ball.

Eliza, shouting: "Stand easy boy! I'll get it."

Suddenly there was violent banging on the window from Philip's house.

Eliza heard Philip coughing and shouting from his open kitchen window. She looked over to his cottage.

Oh shit! It's the gravedigger!

Philip: "Yoooo hoooo!"

I would have got away with it too if it hadn't been for them pesky neighbours. Tut.

Philip: "Eliza, my dear lady! Would you partake in a beverage with me?"

Philip was pointing to his kettle wildly and over emphasising the words as if she was three miles away.

Foiled. I shall have to wait until he's out. He's definitely guilty of a very big misdemeanour.

Eliza: "That would be lovely. I'll have a cup of tea, please."

Maintain an air of ignorance. Not hard to achieve, to be fair.

Eliza wiped her hands on her jeans.

Philip, hollering: "Normal, decaff or something else?"

Laced with Arsenic?

Eliza: "Normal, please."

Philip: "I like a caffeine fuelled filly. Coming right up!"

Ellington came charging back with the ball and dropped it at her feet. He had very muddy feet. She looked at him carefully.

What have you seen, boy? Anything?

Go and sniff if there's any juicy bones to dig up. If you come back with a femur, I'm calling the police.

A couple of minutes later, Philip came out into the garden with a tray full of chocolate chip cookies and a pot of tea. She recognised the china as the same pattern her grandmother had owned. He had matching cups and saucers.

He stepped over the fence and plonked them down on her bistro table.

Philip: "Very noble of you, my dear Eliza, tending to the weeds. I have a strimmer. We could always just reduce them to an inch of their lives and go and do something more interesting. Would you care to borrow it?"

Eliza: "That would be most helpful. Thank you, Philip. I've got to sort out these pots too."

She gesticulated towards some rather wilted pansies.

Philip: "Yes, my dear Eliza. They are, what we call in the trade, fooked. We can go down to the garden centre and get some more. I want to look at the tool section, I need an axe. An excursion for you, me and the little person. What do you think?"

An axe?

At that point, Tom, who had finished road construction, came over.

Tom: "Biccy wit please."

Eliza handed a biscuit to him and he wandered back to the sandpit with it.

Eliza: "Perhaps, I'll see how I'm fixed for time, Philip. I'm absolutely rushed off my feet today."

Barefaced liar.

"Tut tut" the fib fairy will say.

Philip: "I do beg your pardon, my dear Eliza. I presumed because you were doing the gardening you had a lull in the renovation proceedings for today."

Eliza: "Yes well, drying you know. Stuff like that."

Philip: "Ah, yes of course. You have a different world to mine."

Indeed. I don't feel the requirement to dig up my neighbour's garden in the dead of night for starters.

Eliza: "What is your world, Philip?"

Apart from moonlight burials, a penchant for berating random people on the phone and walking about in your pants.

Philip: "I work in research."

That's vague.

Eliza: "What sort of research?"

Philip: "Don't you worry your pretty tousled head about such things. It's nowhere near as interesting as your little lifestyle."

Patronising. Lovely.

Eliza: "Anyway, tea break over. I'll get back on with my gardening then. Thank you."

Philip: "No problem at all. I'll whip my strimmer out for you."

I bet.

Eliza: "Thank you."

With that, Philip cleared the tray of tea and biscuits and went indoors.

Don't think I'm finished with you Mr Gravedigger Saggy Pants.

I'll choose my moment and I will prevail. I will look in my vegetable patch. Oh yes.

Status: *"I'll be back."*

Chapter Nineteen

Sub Affirmation for the day: *I relish the idea of new opportunities.*

Eliza stood in the kitchen, looking out of the window towards the garden and rang Lydia.

Eliza: "Hello, how are you today?"

Lydia: "Hi darling, currently mainlining tea and Jaffa cakes. How are you?"

Eliza: "Oh you know, the usual. Lewis has unwillingly impregnated the perfect Geraldine and my neighbour has buried a body in my vegetable patch."

Lydia: "When did this happen?!"

Eliza: "Which bit? The impregnation about twenty weeks ago. They had the scan the other day. It's definitely a baby."

Lydia: "Crikey. How do you feel about that? Poor unborn baby. A crap father like Lewis. It's not fair. People desperately want children and he goes round willy-nilly with his willy making women pregnant."

Eliza: "Can I be honest?"

Lydia: "Of course."

Eliza: "I don't really care."

Did you just tut then Lydia?

Lydia: "Oh. Really?"

You sound disappointed.

Lydia, you love drama.

Eliza: "I'm concerned how it will affect Tom in the future but, to be honest, it's just been him and me for the past year so it's not like there's any great shift for me. Lewis came over and hugged me."

Lydia: "Did you smack him in the face?"

Not quite.

Eliza: "No, I hugged him back."

Lydia let out a sigh.

Lydia: "Don't do that again. It'll get confusing. Stick to disliking him. He's in a place where you can get on with your life then."

She has a point.

Eliza: "You're right, but isn't hate an emotion that uses energy? Isn't it better to just not care?"

Lydia: "You and your bloody self-help, hippy stream. If it uses extra energy, have another Hobnob to up the deficit. You mark my words. Don't let him back in. You'll get hurt."

Get off the Lewis subject.

Eliza: "Do you hate Roy?"

Lydia: "I love and hate him in equal measure and it kills. My rational mind doesn't understand how I can love someone who damaged me mentally and physically but love isn't rational is it?"

Eliza: "No. Can you make yourself fall out of love with him?"

Lydia: "Believe me, I've tried. I'm hoping that if I find someone else who's kind and takes care of me then I will be able to move on. I think that's why I serial date. The Mighty Sword might do the trick."

There was a pause on the end of the line.

Lydia: "Sorry, hang on. Did you say your neighbour has buried a body in your vegetable patch?"

Ahh, that nugget of information has filtered through to her consciousness.

Eliza: "I tried to get a look at it earlier but he distracted me on purpose with offers of his strimmer. I will go back and have a look."

Lydia: "I'll come over and help you. Ooh, I wonder who it is."

Eliza: "Probably a man from the council. He was hollering at one the other day on his phone about the potholes in the road outside his house."

Lydia: "Shall we do it tonight?"

Eliza: "What about the children?"

Lydia: "I had a call from Brian earlier and he wants to pop over and see us later, see how we are. How about we come to yours and he can watch the children whilst we investigate?"

Eliza: "Oh flip-flop, I haven't got a date yet. He'll ask for a progress report."

Lydia: "He was very giddy about his 'do'. You know what Clive and he are like; they love a good old get together."

Eliza: "I'll call Bland Man. I'll go out with him, ascertain he can chew food, doesn't have a fake set of teeth and doesn't have stalker tendencies and will drag him along. How bad can he be?"

Lydia: "Exactly. He just looks like a man. Innocuous."

Eliza: "Ok. A plan then. Come over with Brian at about six and when it gets dark, we'll go out and have a look what's down there."

Lydia: "Okidokes. I'll ring Brian and you ring Bland Man. What's his name?"

Eliza: "Neville."

Lydia: "I've not had one of them. I wonder what Nevilles are like. See you later. I'm off to watch daytime TV."

Uh oh, it's a workday.

So says I, who spent the morning digging up weeds.

Eliza: "How about stripping that chest of drawers we've got an order for?"

Lydia: "Tomorrow. I'll do that tomorrow. I can't face manual labour today."

Eliza: "Ok, they've called about it so we do need to get on with it."

Lydia: "Don't be a nag darling, it's frightfully unbecoming."

Eliza: "Ok. Ok. But tomorrow, yes?"

Lydia: "Yes, yes. Now see you this evening."

Eliza: "See you later."

Eliza picked up her mobile and texted Bland Man.

Eliza's text: "Hello. How are you? I'm very sorry I cancelled the other night. Perhaps we could rearrange sometime. Eli."

Send.

He knows it's me. Why sign my name? I'll be writing "Kind Regards" next. I'm so not a natural at texting.

Her phone pinged.

Oh, he's replied.

Neville's text: "Hi Eli, that would be lovely. Are you free tomorrow or Friday evening? Neville ☺"

Eliza texted Lydia and asked if she'd look after Tom on Friday evening. A reply came shooting back as a yes so she replied to Neville.

Eliza's text: "I'm available on Friday evening. Shall we go for a meal?"

Neville's text: "Yes ok. We can meet in town if you like and then go to a club after. ☺"

A club? Bloody hell, it's been years since I've been to a club and last time I did I fell asleep at half eleven with a pile of coats over my head to the lyrics "What would you look like with a chimney on your head."

Eliza's text: "A club. Lovely. Do you go clubbing often?"

Neville's text: "A fair bit. I love to dance. Do you?"

No. I'm all happy hands and mad feet. I dance as if I'm enduring some sort of seizure.

Eliza's text: "Oh yes, you can't beat a good old dance."

Liar liar, crap dancing pants on fire.

Neville's text: "So shall we meet at 8pm outside Milliman's? We'll grab some sushi then go for a dance."

Sushi. Oh, my giddy aunt. I like my food cooked.

Eliza's text: "Sushi. You like sushi?"

Neville's text: "I love it. I have it loads ☺"

You're meant to be bland. Your face belies this side of you. It's misrepresentation of goods. This is all far too exotic for me. Uncooked fish and clubbing.

Eliza's text: "Lovely. 8pm on Friday then. Enjoy the rest of your week. Eli."

Neville's text: "I'm looking forward to it. See you Friday ☺"

Status: *"Fasten your seatbelts. It's going to be a bumpy night."*

Chapter Twenty

Sub Sub Affirmation for the day: *My decisions are always well judged.*

There was much knocking on the door at six o'clock. Ellington woofed a single woof, looked at the front door then at Eliza and flopped back down in his bed.

Tom was watching television and without glancing up hollered.

Tom: "Door bang bang. People wanna come in mummy."

Eliza: "You are both so helpful. I'd be lost without you."

Eliza opened the door to Lydia, Freya and Brian and they bustled in.

Freya instantly sat down next to Tom and started to watch television with him.

Brian: "Hello poppet. How's my favourite little divorcee?"

Lydia pinched Brian on the arm.

Lydia: "Oi, I'm divorced too."

Brian: "Yes, but you have chaps on the go all the time. Eliza's a proper divorcee. She's always single, pining after her lost love."

That's just lovely, that is. Eli the saddo.

Lydia: "You're right about that, but she's working on it. She's got a date with a bland man on Friday."

Eliza took their coats whilst Brian and Lydia fussed about with Tom, Ellington and Norris. Eliza walked back into the lounge.

Eliza: "He's not so bland, actually, he eats sushi and dances."

Brian: "Ooh, an adventurous palette. He'd be a good judge for the menu launch."

Eliza: "If he's anywhere near normal, I'll ask him, ok? I've met a couple of other guys but they were barmy."

Lydia turned to Brian.

Lydia: "Eliza met Jesus last week."

Brian: "Really? It's all that meditation you've taken up, poppet. I heard about a man who found god when he walked out of his garden gate one morning. He just stopped right there and then and had an epiphany. It can hit you at any time, by all accounts. He still went to work, though, as he had to pay the gas bill."

Eliza: "He wrote me a lewd poem."

Brian: "Are you sure that was Jesus? I don't think that was in the Bible."

Lydia: "It is not that which entereth into the mouth defileth the man; but that which proceedeth out of the mouth, this defileth the man. Matthew 15:11, I think you'll find."

Both Brian and Eliza stopped and stared at Lydia for a moment with their mouths open.

Okaaay.

Lydia: "Sorry, convent upbringing. Bugger those bloody nuns."

Eliza and Brian shook themselves slightly.

Brian, clapping his hands: "Anyway, I do believe you need to find a stiff."

Eliza: "We do. Under the cover of darkness. I don't want Philip to know. He'll never lend me his strimmer again if he's aware I'm onto him."

Brian: "I can see how being responsible for his imprisonment for manslaughter by proceeding to dig up the evidence would damage relations."

Eliza: "You see my dilemma. You need to keep watch. On the children and on his back door. Ok?"

Brian: "I can multitask. I vacuumed and spoke on the phone the other day. Couldn't hear a bloody word the man said, though. I think I agreed to a timeshare in Alicante."

Lydia: "I have my outfit in my bag. I'll just get changed."

Eliza: "Outfit? You have a body digging up outfit?"

Lydia: "Well, I didn't wander into Miss Selfridge, go up to the sales assistant and say "I need something that looks good with a shovel" but I have dark clothes and wellies. They're a bit different though as I wore them to that festival last year. I was working the "festival chic" look."

Eliza: "Ah yes. The Trench Foot incident."

Lydia: "Never again. I'm not comfortable in that level of mud and other people's close proximity to me. One thing I learned though; I have a very strong bladder. I didn't know I could hold it for so long. Those skanky bogs taught me that."

Brian: "Go and put on your togs then. How exciting! I've never seen a dead person in real life."

Lydia dashed off with her bag of clothes to the bathroom.

Tom: "What's a dead person, mummy? People never dead really. You said."

Eliza: "No one, darling. People don't die they just come back as other things."

Brian, whispering to Eliza: "What's this you're filling his mind with now? Last week, it was pixies and fairies ruling the cosmos."

Tom: "I come back as butterfly or Power Ranger."

Eliza, whispering to Brian: "Reincarnation."

Brian: "Indeed. I'm going to come back as the Queen, Tom."

Tom: "You will wear a pretty dress and a crown."

Brian: "I do that already, poppet."

Lydia came back into the lounge in a black Lycra, tight fitting catsuit and a black beanie hat with her hair tucked in.

Brian: "Crikey! You're not grave robbing, merely seeking evidence of foul play."

Eliza: "Flip-flop! That outfit has never seen a natural fibre!"

Lydia: "Shut up, just because you're at one with cheesecloth."

Eliza: "I feel rather underdressed in my jeans and sweatshirt. Shall I go and find a stocking to put over my head?"

Lydia: "Very funny, come on let's get cracking. It's dark enough now."

Eliza: "Right then, I only have one torch but I have a lightsaber which emits a bit of light. I also only have one big spade. I have a trowel though, so I'll have that, ok?"

Eliza and Lydia crept out of the back door armed with a lightsaber, a torch, a spade and a trowel.

Brian watched with amusement and turned to Tom and Freya.

Brian: "It's like The Chuckle Brothers. How this will end is anyone's guess. Want some crisps, kids?"

They both hollered "Yay!"

He grabbed a bag of crisps, threw a load into a bowl and plonked himself on the settee with the pair of them. He addressed Freya and Tom.

Brian: "Who is this please? I need information on what I'm watching."

Tom pointed at the screen.

Tom: "He Mr Tumble. He friend of Justin. He a clown."

Brian looked closely at the programme for a minute.

Brian: "He is Justin, isn't he?"

Tom: "Don't be silly Bwian. He Mr Tumble. Justin friend."

Brian shook his head and said to Freya.

Brian: "He must be the same person. Surely, they aren't employing two of them. That's reckless abuse of TV licence funds otherwise."

Freya: "There are two of them. One wears jeans and stands up, the other one wears a waistcoat and falls over a lot."

Brian peered at the screen for a few moments longer and shook his head.

Brian: "I give up. Pass us a crisp."

Meanwhile, Eliza and Lydia had made it to the vegetable patch.

Lydia: "Where do you think it is?"

Eliza: "How about that bloody great mound there?"

Eliza pointed with her lightsaber to a pile of freshly turned over soil.

Lydia: "Oh. Derr. Ok. I feel a bit odd. Should we be doing this?"

Eliza: "Of course we should. We need to see what he's capable of."

Lydia: "Perhaps, he's just planting potatoes at night."

Eliza: "Oh yes, because Gardener's World always advocates midnight vegetable digging in your neighbour's plot."

Lydia: "Come on let's choose a spot and get digging. How about I position the lightsaber and torch on the compost heap and we can both dig. First one to find the head."

Lydia positioned the light sources and they started digging.

A few minutes later they stopped, stood and looked at each other. Eliza put her hands on her hips and Lydia wiped her brow with muddy hands.

Eliza: "Found anything yet?"

Lydia: "Not even a finger."

Eliza: "Me neither."

Lydia: "Maybe, it's six feet down. That's the optimum burial depth, isn't it?"

Eliza: "You're right. Let's carry on."

Brian got up from the settee.

Brian: "Drinks and chocolate?"

Freya and Tom cried again in unison: "Yay!"

He wandered into the kitchen and looked out of the window to see the faint shadows of Lydia and Eliza bent over at the end of the garden. He could make out them talking to each other and gesticulating. He watched as Lydia jumped onto the top of the spade, lost her balance and fell over in the soil.

Back up at the vegetable patch, Eliza stood and looked at a sprawled-out Lydia.

Eliza: "What in god's name are you doing, woman? It's not a pogo stick."

Lydia: "I wanted to go deeper. I'm not used to spade work. Pull me up! I'm not happy to be lying on top of a dead person."

Brian smiled as he watched Eliza in the distance yank Lydia up.

Brian: "To me... to you... Oh shit!"

He spotted the distinct outline of Philip stepping over the low boundary. He was holding something.

He looked closer to see the barrel of a gun glinting in the dim light as Philip strode up Eliza's garden path.

Brian: "What the fu...?!"

Brian hollered in the direction of the lounge at Freya and Tom.

Brian: "Stay there watching the television. Do not move a muscle. I will be back when I've diverted another couple of burials!"

Brian shot out the back door

Brian: "Yoo hoo! Philip!!"

Back at the vegetable patch, Eliza stopped in her tracks when she heard Brian's voice.

Eliza: "Shitting flip-flops! We've been rumbled!"

Lydia: "Assume crash positions!!"

Eliza: "What?!"

Lydia dropped her spade and threw herself on the mound of earth, face down.

Eliza: "Oh ok."

She promptly followed suit and threw down herself beside her.

Further down the garden, Philip had stopped and turned to face a very red-faced Brian who had grabbed him by the arm.

Philip: "Eh? Who are you? Oh, you're the food chap. Hello. We've got blasted looters in our midst!"

Brian looked up at the garden and hollered.

Brian: "Oh my, Philip, you have a gun!"

Lydia, face down in the soil: "Shit, he's armed Eli!"

Eliza from beside her, also face down in the soil: "We're mothers, he can't kill us. I didn't know he was mental. I just thought he was eccentric."

Lydia: "Do you think we should have thought about this a bit more carefully?"

Eliza: "Yes, I do believe you could be right. I should have vetted the neighbours prior to moving in. It's your fault, you said this was a lovely little village."

Lydia: "I meant digging up the garden at night, you stupid cow. We should have thought about it a bit more."

Eliza: "Oh, sorry, yes. If we don't die, I think we should make a pact to consider our plans more before action, in future."

Lydia: "Pact sealed. What shall we do? Just lie here?"

Eliza: "In the absence of any other ideas, yes."

Back down the garden, Brian was still grabbing hold of Philip by the arm.

Brian: "Looters? What do you mean? This is Eliza's garden. Why are you in here with a gun?"

Philip: "Ah well, my dear man. Someone must have caught wind of the kitty. I'm protecting it."

Brian very loudly towards the end of the garden: "Ohhh I didn't know you had a cat."

Back at the vegetable patch on the mound.

Lydia: "Eww, we're lying on top of a dead cat."

Eliza: "Why would he bury his cat in my garden? I didn't even know he had a cat."

Back down the garden.

Philip: "My dear boy. Not in a feline capacity."

He removed Brian's grip from his arm and strode expeditiously towards the vegetable patch holding his gun ready for action.

Brian, shrieking: "He's coming down the garden!! He's armed and walking with purpose!"

Eliza and Lydia: "Shit!!"

Eliza and Lydia sprang to their feet in unison and Eliza seized the lightsaber and Lydia grabbed the spade.

Philip strode up to them then stopped in his tracks as they jumped up.

Philip: "What the…?!"

Eliza: "Philip! What on earth are you doing?! For goodness' sake! Put that gun down this instant!"

Philip lowered his gun.

Philip: "My dear girl! I didn't know it was you up here. I would never have caused you any upset had I been aware you were here."

Eliza: "It is my garden."

Philip: "Yes. Yes, I know. I sincerely apologise."

Brian had joined them and was brandishing a watering can in the vague direction of Philip.

Lydia: "What are you doing with a gun? Isn't that illegal?"

Philip: "Is that you, my dear Lydia? I can't tell in this light and under all that mud. Good Lord! That's a very racy little number you're wearing. Pass me the torch, I need a closer view."

Philip reached over to the compost heap and grabbed the torch and shone it on her catsuit.

Philip: "I say! Very nice indeed!"

Lydia: "Answer the question. Why have you got a gun? I could report you."

Philip: "I understand your dissension, but it's merely a pellet gun. It looks more alarming than it is and it's perfectly legal. I shoot pigeons with it."

Eliza: "You'd better not shoot my Winky or I'll be having words."

Philip: "Winky? Have you been drinking, my dear Eliza? Why are you up here in the dark?"

Think fast.

Eliza: "I'm planting potatoes. Monty Don suggested it. Makes them taste lovely. He's never had mash like it, apparently. Moonlight ones are the best."

Lydia: "Yes, everyone knows that."

That's my explaining over with. Now your turn.

Eliza: "Why are you up here, Philip?"

Philip: "Ah well, you see. That's a bit tricky to answer."

Thought it might be.

Eliza: "Who is it? You may as well be honest, the game's up."

Philip: "Yes, I do feel it may be. Only if you promise to keep it to yourselves for the moment."

Brian: "Just tell us and quickly. I've left two children unattended with a remote control in there. They could be flicking around the porn channel. I need your assurance you're not going to shoot them."

Philip: "Of course I'm not going to shoot them my dear boy. Attend to your charges."

Eliza: "Go on Brian. Go back indoors and put the kettle on. We'll be in shortly."

Hopefully.

Brian waved the watering can at Philip with a final flurry then put it down and ran off back down the garden and into Eliza's house.

Lydia: "Go on then, Philip. 'Fess up. Purge your soul."

Philip leant on his gun and sighed heavily.

Philip: "Well, my dear ladies, I have been reading up about this chap who found a load of Saxon gold in a field. It's worth millions. I have been fascinated and enraptured by the discovery. I bought a metal detector online and I've been looking for hidden riches ever since. My garden didn't reveal anything other than an old shed key but yours, Eliza, produced some interesting finds. I must confess; I've been venturing into your garden during the twilight hours in search of treasures. Now you have planted potatoes, I shall cease for the remainder of the season. Perhaps, you'd consider moving the beans down the garden a bit though, so I can still dig up that bit over there?"

He pointed to an overgrown patch of land in the corner. He continued.

Philip: "I'll share with you, my dear Eliza, any revenue received from such finds. I am aware, though, that your house is rented and I am reluctant to inform the owner, hence the subterfuge. I was going to inform the relevant authorities I found the relics in my garden. Your landlord is a miserable old bastard to be perfectly blunt and has quite enough money as it is. He also works for the council. I can't abide those people. They have yet to rectify the pothole issue outside my house."

Eliza: "So you've been digging up not digging in?"

Philip: "I have been retrieving from the soil my dear Eliza, yes. Gifts bestowed to us by our ancestors."

Eliza: "You've not buried a dead person then?"

I said that out loud, didn't I? It's the gun. I'm in a state of alarm.

Philip: "I beg your pardon?"

Lydia: "It's ok. She's been drinking. That's why she's coerced me into planting potatoes in the dark. She goes a bit barmy when she's had a few."

Thank you for saving the situation, Lydia.

Lydia did a loopy brain sign beside her head.

Lydia, warming to her theme: "I've told her to become teetotal but does she listen? She'd drink morning, noon and night if she could get away with it."

Whoah, steady on missus. He'll think I'm a dipso in charge of an underling.

Eliza: "Anyway Philip, how marvellous to know I may be thrown a few pounds thanks to some old artefacts, especially as they're in *my* garden. Lydia, you need to get out of those muddy clothes and have a cup of tea."

Lydia: "I do indeed. Come on. See you later gun-toting neighbour. For the record, I feel ill at ease with you shining a torch on my tits."

Philip: "I am dreadfully sorry, my dear Lydia. I was somewhat transfixed, I do concur. I shall bid good evening to you both. Please accept my heartfelt apologies again for causing alarm."

Lydia put down her spade, took the torch off Philip and dragged a saber holding Eliza by the arm and strode off with her, back into the house.

They walked into the kitchen and burst out laughing with relief.

Lydia: "You're a stupid cow, Eli. We could have got a blinking pellet between the eyes!"

Eliza: "I know. I'm concerned, Lydia, I have a fixation with death at the moment. When Lewis came over, I thought he was dying but he was pregnant and then I was convinced there was a dead body in my garden but it's ye olde gold. Am I drawing these grim reaper thoughts towards me, unwittingly?"

I need to read more on the chapter about cosmic ordering. Maybe, I ordered death when I wasn't concentrating.

Lydia: "Nah, they come in threes, don't they? You'll probably witness someone get run over by a bus tomorrow. A trio of deaths. Then you'll be done with it for a while and it won't cross your mind for a year or so."

I do subscribe to the "run of threes" theory.

Eliza: "Oh, fair enough."

Lydia hollered in the direction of the lounge.

Lydia: "We're alive, Brian!"

Brian came running in and hugged them both.

Brian: "Thank god! What was it all about?"

Eliza: "He's found some treasure in my garden and I think he wanted to keep it but considering he's now found me lying on top of it, he feels compelled to share it with me."

Brian: "Goodo. Worth nearly getting shot for, with a bit of luck. I'm afraid something occurred in our absence."

The three of them walked into the lounge to see Tom's faced covered in Eliza's make up.

Eliza: "What's going on? Tom! That's my new lipstick smeared all over your chops!"

Freya: "He said he wished he was Mr Tumble so I made him like him."

Tom: "I am Mr Tumble. I can fall over."

Lydia: "Freya, you mustn't rifle ('scuse the pun) through Eli's make-up drawer without asking. Ok? She needs that to make herself look acceptable to the world."

Oh charming.

Eliza: "Yes, thank you Lydia. Oh blimey, it's everywhere. Right Tom, you need to fall into the bath. Everyone else do whatever you want."

Brian: "I'm going to head off. Clive wants to try out the new wine bar in town and I've had quite enough excitement for one evening. You must tell me how the bland man is, ok?"

He collected his coat and gave everyone a hug and, on the way out of the door, turned to Eliza.

Brian: "Thank you for an interesting evening. It's never dull around you, is it? You probably want to go on tablets or drink yourself into a stupor regularly. Something to calm that overactive mind of yours."

Eliza: "Well, I've got the delight of sushi and dance on Friday. I think I may well have to imbibe to get through that."

Brian: "Definitely. Get very drunk and have the best fun. Bye my little darlings."

Eliza closed the front door, scooped Tom up and left Lydia and Freya trying to wipe lipstick off the cream leather settee.

Twenty minutes later, Tom had been bathed and was in bed. Eliza walked into the lounge to find Freya and Lydia curled up fast asleep on the settee together. She flopped down next to them and pulled a blanket over them all and she too drifted off with a parting consideration.

I probably do need some sort of external assistance. My synapses don't quite meet.

It's probably not wise to attempt to carry on through life without some form of crutch.

Find a vice. Cake isn't cutting the mustard.

Status: *"Well, here's another nice mess you've gotten me into!"*

Chapter Twenty-one

Affirmation for the day: *I am confident with my choices.*

It was 6 o'clock on Friday evening and Eliza was in the full throes of a clothes crisis. Tom was sitting on the floor layering himself up with scarves and was putting a pair of tights on his hands. Norris was curled up snoring on the bed, on top of a very expensive dress and Ellington was flumped on the floor beside Tom watching proceedings.

Tom: "Oooh tights. Like tights. They soft."

Eliza: "Gerroff them! You'll ladder them."

Tom: "I don't see no ladders. Fireman Sam don't use no tights for fires."

I don't see no ladders, fool. Quit your jibba jabba.

Eliza: "Just give them to me, please. I'm enduring a clothes trauma. I need your help."

Tom: "Ok mummy."

Eliza took the tights off him and Tom looked up, dressed in his myriad scarves to be faced with a pant and bra wearing Eliza.

Tom, scrunching his nose up: "Don't wear that, mummy. See tummy. Not good."

Eliza: "Oh, that's just charming that is. For your information, scarf boy, I'm wanting advice on what to cover the offensive tummy with, not general heckling."

Tom: "I like tights. Put them on."

Eliza: "You're only three. What's with the tight thing?"

Tom: "Nearly four. Put them on."

Eliza: "Alright, alright bossy boots! I'll wear a skirt then."

Eliza then put on a posh voice and said in a dramatic fashion.

Eliza: "One always wears a skirt for sushi, darhhhling."

Eliza stepped into the tights and pulled them up.

Tom, nodding: "Cover tummy. Good. Like them."

Eliza patted her tummy and looked in the cheval mirror.

Eliza: "Holds any saggage in quite adequately, I do agree. What skirt then chaps?"

I must think about a fitness regime. I'm skinny but under no stretch of the imagination am I toned. I have wobbly bits. I need to become like Madonna. All sinewy and 'grrrr'. I'll do sit ups. I'll start tomorrow and I'll lift up some baked bean tins. That'll do it.

Eliza ferreted around and pulled out two skirts and held them out to Tom and Ellington.

Tom hit the grey one and Ellington put his paw on the red one.

I prefer the red one to be honest. Hmmm.

Eliza: "Ellington wins the skirt round."

Tom's bottom lip shot out and he started to pout.

Tom: "He dog. I Tom. I win. I want grey one."

He started to whine and assumed his snivel face.

Eliza: "Don't start Tom. It's a democracy, I agree with Ellington. I'll let you win the next round, ok?"

Tom: "Ok."

Tom put another scarf on.

Tom: "I hot."

Eliza: "I'm not surprised. Can you breathe? I haven't got time to go to Accident and Emergency this evening. I've got raw fish to eat."

Tom: "Why are you going to eat raw fish, mummy?"

Eliza: "A very pertinent question Tom and one to which I haven't got a credible answer, except I subscribe to the 'try anything once" theory. I need to tick this off the list."

Tom: "Will it have its head on?"

Eliza: "Oh, I hope not. I think they wrap it in leaves."

Tom: "What his head? Urgh. Will you eat his eyeballs?"

I feel quite queasy. Change the subject.

Eliza: "Let's just stick to the clothing matter in hand, eh? I won't be going anywhere if I don't get a wiggle on. By the way, Tom, I'll be doing that later too."

Tom: "Wiggling? Like The Wiggles do?"

Eliza: "In a fashion. I'll be dancing."

Tom, gravely: "Oh no mummy! Don't do that!"

Out of the mouths of babes.

Eliza: "Oh, that's just blinking lovely that is! What's the matter with my dancing?"

Tom shook his head and looked sombre.

Tom: "Not good mummy, very silly arms. It a bit scary. You hit persons."

Eliza: "I've only ever hit you in the face once Tom and that was your fault. You should have seen that I was doing a spin and had lost my bearings. You should have stepped back."

Eliza went towards the wardrobe and pulled out two jumpers. She decided on the black one, so proffered this to Tom and waved a stripy one vaguely at Ellington.

Tom hit the one nearest him.

Eliza: "An exquisite choice, Tom. You are a fashionista."

Tom looked at a bored Ellington.

Tom: "I won. Ner ner ne ner ner."

Eliza dragged the black polo neck over her head and looked in the full-length mirror.

Eliza: "Ooh, I'm rocking the sixties look. Block patterns and all that. Where's my black patent boots? That'll look awesome."

She crawled down to search under the bed. Ellington got up and started licking her ear.

Eliza: "Get off dog! That's disgusting! I've just washed them."

She wiped his dribble off and he dejectedly flopped back down beside Tom.

Eliza: "Oh, don't get the mards on. Come here."

Ellington got back up and she gave him a cuddle.

Eliza: "Flip-flops. I've got dog fur all over my black top. I'm getting a designer dog next time. One that's manufactured not to moult. A Schnoodle or whatever they're called."

A Schnoodle factory. I'll go there and buy one off the shelf.

Eliza rummaged about under the bed and threw out one boot and hit Ellington with it. He made a hasty retreat to the other side of the room.

Tom: "Say sorry mummy. Hit doggy wiv boot."

Eliza, muffled from under the bed: "Sorry Ellington. Can you come under here and sniff out the other one?"

Ellington stayed where he was.

A few minutes later, a dishevelled Eliza crawled out from under the bed.

Eliza: "Got it! Finally! I also found Postman Pat, Tom. We've been looking for him for ages."

She held a boot and Tom's Postman Pat toy aloft, victoriously.

Tom: "Postman Pat! Ohhh, I missed you! Jess will be so happy!"

Tom stood and promptly tripped over his scarves. Eliza gave him Postman Pat and he staggered back and plonked himself back down, whilst kissing Postman Pat, profusely.

She pulled on her other boot, straightened herself up and looked in the mirror.

Her hair had gone wild, she was red faced and had dog fur all over her top.

Eliza: "Ok, not so much the sixties look now. More I look sixty."

Sticky tape.

Eliza: "Stay there everyone, I need to get the fur removal tool."

She shot downstairs, retrieved the tape from the kitchen drawer and raced back upstairs.

She wound a load of tape around her hand and patted herself all over her top with it. She then wound a fresh batch around her hand and patted Ellington with it. He looked up at her with a bemused expression. Tom looked at her with a mirrored expression.

Tom: "Mummy, you a bit mad."

Eliza looked across at him from the random dog grooming exercise.

Eliza: "Succinctly put Tom. Lunacy is very liberating. It means you never have to explain yourself. If you go doolally when you're older, I'll support you in your life choice."

Tom: "What's lunacy?"

Eliza: "It means you howl at the moon."

Tom: "What?"

Eliza: "Pardon, not what. Nothing dear."

Eliza threw the tape in the bin.

Eliza: "I need to attend to the face. In the absence of my new expensive lipstick, I'll have to wear the old muck."

She shot Tom a stern look.

Tom, shaking his head: "That not me. That was Freya. She naughty. Tut tut."

Eliza: "Ooh, I'll go all cats' eyes, shall I? Proper sixties. Did they eat sushi in the 1960s?"

Tom: "You eat cat and fisheyes. Bleugh. Eat spaghetti hoops. Nice they are."

Eliza: "I'm exhausted already, Tom. I do agree with you, spaghetti hoops on toast would be a preferred meal."

Tom: "Don't eat Norris eyes. He walk into fings."

Eliza: "I have no intention of eating any eyeballs. Norris' or otherwise."

She did her make-up and showed Ellington and Tom.

Eliza: "What d'ya think? Look at the left eye, that's the best one by all accounts."

Tom: "Oooh, pwetty mummy."

Quit whilst there's a compliment on the table.

Eliza: "Right then chaps. I need to throw all these clothes back in the wardrobe. Oi, Norris! Wake up. Tom, I need to get your bits ready for Lydia and you need to prepare for house watch, Ellington."

Eliza sorted everyone out, threw on her coat and put Tom into the car. She drove to Lydia's house, left the engine running and hurtled Tom up the path.

Lydia opened the door.

Lydia: "Hello darlings. Ooh, who have you got there, Tom? Postman Pat? You look beautiful Eli. I love this look. Very Twiggy."

Eliza: "I'm running late."

Lydia: "Why break the habit of a lifetime? Are you driving?"

Eliza: "I've decided to drink. I need it to eat the fish, so I'm driving there and leaving the car. I'll book a taxi home."

Lydia: "Good choice. Become a lush. All the best people do. I might join you. We could have matching hip flasks. I want you to text me as soon as you can. I need to know he's bland and not a nutter."

Eliza: "I will, as soon as I can. I need to get a wiggle on."

Tom: "Mummy's going to wiggle later. She going dancing."

Lydia's eyebrows shot upwards.

Lydia: "God help anyone within a twenty-yard radius."

Eliza: "Not you an' all. I've had quite enough from the little person here."

Lydia looked down at Tom.

Lydia: "My Tom, that's a lot of scarves you have on there. Are you expecting a blizzard?"

Eliza: "Descarf him will you? I think there's pyjamas on underneath. I'm off to the great bland unknown. Wish me luck."

She gave Tom a massive kiss and hugged Lydia.

Lydia: "Good luck, he'll love you. Have a brilliant time!"

Tom: "Bye mummy. Don't eat the eyes."

Eliza: "No eyes. Gotcha. I love you."

Status: *"Insanity runs in my family. It practically gallops."*

Chapter Twenty-two

Sub Affirmation for the day: *I am in total control.*

Eliza parked the car and breathed deeply.

This is the last time I'm doing this. It's not good for my health. I am enduring a mild panic attack.

Hippy breathing. In for ten, hold for ten, out for ten. Oh ok, out for two.

Whatever. Just don't faint.

She locked the car and strode towards Milliman's.

She saw him as she approached and he turned to greet her.

There he is. He looks like a man. Just a man. A walk past the street man.

What's the word I'm looking for?

Dull.

Is that my level? Distinctly average?

What does he do for a living? Oh yes, accounts. Just about sums it up really.

I'm generalising. Give him a chance. He may have hidden depths. He eats raw fish for a start. Surely, not many accountants do that.

She reached him and he leant forward for a hug and kissed her on the cheek.

Bland Man: "Eliza, lovely to meet you. You look beautiful."

Ooh, immediate flattery.

Eliza: "Hello. And you. Not beautiful, obviously. You're normal looking. The other bit, I mean. The meet bit."

Shut up, you verbally incontinent woman!

Bland Man: "Haha! Come on, it's chilly. Let's go inside and get a drink."

Yes drink. Now. Good plan.

Eliza: "Excellent idea. I could do with a drink ahead of eating. I think, I'd like to have a couple before I eat."

Cease any more wordage. Be brief and to the point. What is the matter with you?

It's the fear of sushi.

Bland Man: "Yikes! You like a drink, do you?"

I sense a concerned undertone to your questioning. I can fully understand why. I've effectively just told you I'm an alcoholic.

Eliza: "Oh, not generally. I've just taken it up. Tonight's the first night."

I'm mental. It's official.

Bland Man: "Haha! Lucky old me then! Come on gorgeous. Let's get sloshed."

Sloshed. Now that's not generally a word used by under fifties. Maybe they teach accountants to use words like that when they study.

Year two, under the heading 'How to deal with clients who lose receipts'. Your record keeping is shot to bits; you may as well go and get sloshed'.

Neville took her by the arm and steered her into Milliman's and towards the bar.

Bland Man: "What can I do you for, Eli?"

Eliza: "Vodka and coke, please."

Bland Man: "Coming right up, m'lady."

He went towards the bar and Eliza looked at him.

His own teeth? Check.

Hair? Not too bouffanty? Check.

Looks like he sees daylight? Check.

Would his face make a replica of the Turin shroud if he fell asleep under a tea towel? Nope. Check.

Just enjoy it, Eli. Let yourself go,

Stop talking to yourself in the third person. He's fine. Perfectly plain and perfectly normal.

She took her phone out and surreptitiously sent a text to Lydia.

Eliza's text: "Normal, friendly. No axes in back pocket and has own teeth. Looks like it might be ok. Kiss for Tom. Love you xx"

Send.

Neville came back with two drinks and they found a table in a corner.

They took off their coats and settled down.

Oooh, that's a very green outfit. Sage t-shirt and olive trousers. All that's missing is a lime cardigan.

Eliza: "My, that's a green ensemble you've got going on there."

Bland Man: "Ha! Indeed. It's my favourite colour. All the best superheroes are green."

Is he joking? He's smiling. He must be.

Eliza: "Quite."

Bland Man: "I've booked the table for half an hour. Plenty of time for you to get some alcohol flowing through your veins."

Make amends for your earlier idiocy.

Eliza: "It's only because I've never eaten sushi."

Bland Man: "Then let us embark on new things together Eliza. It'll be fun."

Eliza: "Ok. Have you ever eaten pigs' trotters?"

Bland Man: "In all honesty, probably yes."

Eliza: "Oh."

Bland Man: "Haha! You sound so disappointed. I only say yes, as I love sausages and they're sure to have some old pig's feet in 'em."

Eliza: "Ah, so you've never had ones on a bed of chocolate?"

Bland Man: "Definitely not. That's a meal I'm sure I'd remember."

Eliza: "Well, if I survive the sushi you can embark on one of your firsts and join me in a menu launch with some friends, if you'd like?"

Bland Man: "I'd like. Thank you very much for inviting me."

You're the best of a bad bunch in all honesty and I'm running out of time. I'm prepared to look past your dubious green food inspired clothing choice.

To be fair, my outfit was chosen by a dog and a three-year-old, so who am I to judge?

Eliza: "My pleasure."

She downed her vodka and coke.

Oh yes! I needed that! I don't know why I didn't turn to drink years ago. I missed a trick there.

Bland Man: "Crumbs! Sushi really does put the fear of god up you! Haha! I'll get you another."

Neville got up and went to the bar.

He says the words 'yikes' and 'crumbs'. He's a comic strip character.

Eliza studied him at the bar and watched him paying for the drinks.

Neville came back to the table with two more drinks.

Bland Man: "I got you another vodka and coke. When you've finished that, you should be ready to face the food!"

I need to slow down a bit; keep my wits about me. And I must stop thinking of him as Bland Man or I'll end up confused when pissed.

The waiter came up to them and informed them their table was ready.

Neville: "Are you ready to face dinner?"

Eliza: "I am. I laugh in the face of fish."

Neville smiled.

Neville: "Come on then, gorgeous, let's eat."

They were shown to their table and they sat down as the waiter presented them with a massive menu.

Eliza looked at it.

Yikes, as Neville would say, there's loads on here and all of it in words I don't understand.

Neville: "How about we just go for a whole range of numbers and you can try them all."

Be still my beating heart.

Eliza: "Ok. That sounds nice."

Do I really subscribe to the 'try anything once theory' or do I just say that to make myself appear more exotic?

I can honestly say that when I'm in an old people's home and my carer asks, "so crazy Eli, did you ever eat sushi with a random man wearing a somewhat ill-chosen green outfit?" I'd not care if the answer was, "No."

Neville assumed control and made a list of dish numbers on his phone. He occasionally interjected with "you have to try this." And "this one is ace."

Eliza caught the eye of a passing server.

Passing server: "Ready to order, guys?"

Neville: "I'm not. Eli, did you want her?"

Eliza: "A vodka and coke, please."

Passing server: "No problem. Back in a tick."

Eliza leant over the table to Neville and whispered.

Eliza: "I think she's from Australia."

Neville looked up from typing the number for Oshinko Small Maki into his phone.

Neville: "I don't think just because they sell sushi, they have to have corresponding ethnic groups employed."

How disappointing. I think it should be law.

Eliza: "They missed a trick there."

Not very authentic, is it?

Neville looked at her, smiled slightly then went back to his mammoth sushi list.

The server returned with Eliza's drink.

Please stop, Neville. Your list is extraordinary long. I can't eat all those numbers.

Eliza: "I think we're ready to order, thanks."

Neville looked up mid-number punch.

Neville: "Oh, ok. Here you are then. We'd like that lot."

He showed his mobile to the server and she made a note of all the numbers on her pad.

Passing server: "No worries, bear with us a whilst we get it all sorted for you, ok guys?"

She left them to it.

Small talk time. What day is it?

Friday.

For normal people, a workday.

Eliza: "How was work today?"

Neville: "So so. I hate my job to be honest."

Eliza: "The place you work or the actual job?"

Neville: "Both."

Eliza: "Why do you do it then?"

Neville: "It's what I trained in."

Eliza: "Did you always want to do sums?"

Neville shook his head.

Neville: "Haha. Sums. Not really. I kind of found myself going into it and that's been my life ever since."

Eliza: "Why don't you do something else then?"

Neville: "It's not that simple, is it?"

Eliza: "Isn't it? If you don't like it, train in something else."

Neville: "I like your view on life. It's very simplistic and refreshing."

Is it? Seems like common sense to me. Life is short, my friend.

We are but a sneeze in time.

Eliza: "So what would you like to be?"

Neville: "I'd like to be a superhero."

Eliza spat out her vodka and coke.

Waste of a perfectly good drink, that.

He's joking now, he has to be. Check the face. Oh, he looks quite serious with it all.

Quite contemplative.

He's looking into the middle distance. Hmmm.

Eliza: "Quite a career shift from accountant to superhero."

Neville: "Clark Kent went from newspaper to superman. It can be done."

Okaaay.

Eliza: "I think you'll find that was made up."

Neville: "But achievable and believable all the same."

Really? How myopic would you have to be to believe that?

Eliza: "To be fair, I always suspected Lois Lane to be a bit thick. Nobody looks completely different just by donning a pair of specs. Unless, of course, they were mahoosive and covered their whole face."

I just used the word mahoosive! How many have I had?!

Neville: "It'd be the best way ever to earn a living."

I cannot disagree there.

Eliza: "Beats sums, I grant you. I don't think they do a degree in "How to be a Superhero". If they did, my son would be the first to sign up."

Neville: "It wouldn't surprise me actually if they did. They do degrees in all manner of arbitrary subjects these days. At least this would be of assistance to humankind."

I quite like you, you're a bit deranged.

I haven't the faintest idea if you're serious or if you're just very droll but I'm quite enjoying myself. I do believe alcohol is aiding in this merit, but I care not.

Eliza: "When you graduated, you'd not wear a mortar board and gown, you'd be given your superhero outfit. Just imagine how cool the graduation ceremonies would be for that?!"

I've warmed to my theme. I could go on all evening now.

Neville: "Haha! Only a few special people would graduate, though. Only the chosen few can be superheroes."

Eliza: "Of course. Can't make it too mainstream. There's only so many superpowers people possess."

Neville: "What would your superpower be?"

Making sushi disappear?

Being in the knowledge of how many drinks I need to drink before I fall over?

Knowing how tonight will end?

Yes, probably that one.

Eliza: "Time travel. You?"

Eliza picked up the remainder of her drink and put it to her lips.

Neville: "I'd have the world's longest tongue, so I could take you to heaven and back."

She promptly spat out the mouthful of drink across the table.

Hahahaha! Shit! I've turned into Dicky boy. It's catching!

Eliza: "Hahahaha! Sorry. That one was your fault. I wasn't expecting that reply."

Neville: "Haha! It's ok. I quite like the thought of your spit on me. I'd prefer to be naked, though."

He wiped his green top and smiled at her.

Oooh, I've not had enough to drink for this sort of carry on.

Eliza: "Where's that Australian? I need her."

Neville caught their server's eye and gestured for two more drinks.

Neville: "You'd make a brilliant Princess Leia in my opinion."

Erm...

Eliza: "If I was to do plaits, I'd look more Hurdy Gurdy, running down the daisy laden hillside, than her."

What's her name? Heidi. That's it.

Neville: "In Austria, you mean? Like a goat herder?"

Eliza: "Yes, more European than Intergalactic. I can yodel, actually. Would you like me to show you?"

Neville: "Perhaps later. We'll save that for when it's just you and me. I'd like to make you yodel."

Hahahaha!

I can talk about any subject and he brings it round to nooky. That's quite a talent.

He's wasted on numbers.

Eliza: "I don't yodel on the first date."

Neville: "Glad to hear it. How about a quick rendition of Edelweiss?"

Eliza: "I might be able to sing that. Let's see how dinner goes."

Neville: "Excellent. Ooh, drinks and food is up."

The server brought their drinks and was followed by a waiter carrying myriad plates with various dishes.

Eliza: "In the words of Dangermouse, 'Good Grief!'"

Once all the plates had been distributed on the table, he backed away and wished them an enjoyable meal.

Just being alive at the end of it will suffice.

Neville: "You need to try this one first. It's like a doughnut with custard in."

Eliza: "For main food, not a pudding?"

Neville: "Yes, just eat it. You'll love it."

Eliza took one from the bamboo dish and dropped it promptly.

Eliza: "Urgh, it's hot and squidgy! Doughnuts don't feel like that."

Neville: "Ah yes, take it steady, they are a bit warm."

Eliza peeled off the paper from the bottom of one and bit into the white doughy ball and a yellow paste came oozing out.

Dear Lord, that's not custard. It's a weird, gritty consistency.

If I served that up on apple crumble, there'd be serious repercussions.

Neville: "What do you think? They're simply divine, aren't they?"

Eliza: "Divine? You're cuckoo. It's grim!"

Eliza plonked the half-bitten ball back into the wooden bowl.

Neville, laughing: "Perhaps, an acquired taste. Try that one."

He pointed to a circle of food on the plate.

Eliza: "That looks like smoked salmon in cream cheese. What's that round it?"

Neville: "It's seaweed."

Eliza bit into it and, finding she couldn't bite through the seaweed, stuffed it all into her mouth.

That tastes like the beach.

Eliza: "That's like taking a bit of seaweed out of your bucket at the seaside and plonking it in your chops. That's quite acceptable."

Like everyone does that on a day trip to Brighton.

Neville: "Try this one. Dip it into the smallest bit of this."

Neville pointed at a green paste at the side of the plate where the dishes were presented.

Eliza, buoyed by her previous mouthful, picked up a rice parcel and swiped it in a gung-ho fashion across the paste.

Neville: "Whoah there, Eli! That's dead hot! This restaurant does the real deal!"

Ha! How hot can it be? I can eat a chicken korma; I can do spicy.

Eliza threw it into her mouth and started chewing.

Neville stopped eating and gawped wide-eyed, with concern.

Eliza stopped chewing and put her hands around her throat and gasped.

Eliza: "Jesus! Mother of Flip-flops and all that is sacred! What the devil is this stuff?! I need to spit it out! I think my ears are going to bleed!"

Neville: "Spit it out! Spit it out!"

Eliza got her napkin and spat her mouthful into it and downed her vodka and coke.

She paused. Shook her head and took his drink and downed that as well.

Eliza waited and her eyes started watering.

Neville: "Shit Eli, are you alright?"

Eliza: "I don't know. I think I've cleared out every tube in my body in one foul swoop."

Neville: "I'd like to clear out some of your tubes."

Time and a place Neville boy, time and a place.

I've nearly just killed myself by way of a toxic paste.

Eliza gave him a look.

Neville: "Sorry, poor timing. You're alive, that's good and your eyes aren't watering so much now, which again, is good."

Eliza: "Yes, I'm quite relieved I didn't keel over at the table. That's frightfully bad form."

Neville: "That's wasabi. It's quite hot. It's a member of the Brassicaceae family."

Eliza: "Don't introduce me to his relatives, I'm not overly enamoured."

I am not hungry in the slightest now.

This is the answer to obesity. No more gastric bands required. Just have this delivered. People would be shedding stones overnight.

I can see the pages of Chat magazine now, "Yes, I lost twenty stone in two weeks, it was all part of the Wasabi

Diet. I took three spoons a day and now I can never eat again as all my pipes have disintegrated."

They picked their way through the rest of the meal with Neville eating ninety percent of the dishes. Eliza opted for a liquid dinner and made her way through another vodka and coke.

How many have I had? Dunno, I feel a bit woozy. I expect that's the paste, though. It's made my brain melt.

After dinner, they paid the bill and made their way to leave.

Neville: "Are you up for some dancing, Eli?"

In a word, no.

Eliza: "Yes, that would be lovely."

Neville: "Brilliant! There's a bar I know that is great fun. Come on gorgeous, let's let our hair down."

Eliza: "Ok."

At least I can tell the care worker at the home that actually "yes" I did eat sushi with a man top to toe in green and never did again as a result of such folly.

Neville tucked Eliza's hand into his pocket and guided her across the road towards their next venue.

Status: *"I'm melting, mellllting!"*

Chapter Twenty-three

Sub Sub Affirmation for the day: *I am beautiful and smart and that's how everyone sees me.*

They walked into Vertigo and Neville manoeuvred her towards the bar.

Hello, what's occurring over there?

Eliza tugged at Neville's jacket and he looked down at her.

Neville: "What's up, gorgeous?"

Eliza: "Is that a pole?"

Neville: "Yes."

Pole dancing?! Not ten miles from Pilkington on the Moors? Heavens.

Does Lydia know about this? She can't do or she would have definitely said.

Eliza: "As in dancing up and down a pole?"

Neville: "Yes."

Hence Vertigo, I presume. Go too high up the pole and they get a forklift to come and retrieve you.

Eliza: "Do you pole dance?"

Neville: "I dated a pole dancer for a while so I can, yes. It's quite strenuous you know."

He dated a pole dancer? Accountants aspiring to be superheroes don't date pole dancers.

Eliza: "What was her superpower?"

Neville: "She could do the flag. She had a very strong inner core."

That's not a superpower. That's too much time on your hands.

Eliza: "Fair enough. Was she called Saskia and have a penchant for leopard skin?"

Neville gave her a bemused look as he handed Eliza her drink.

Neville: "No, she was called Emily and was a solicitor."

Eliza: "Crikey, they've lowered the bar. Haha! Bar. Sorry."

I have the voice in my head piping up. My behaviour has roused my subconscious into raising the yellow flag of concern.

I shall drown her out.

I'm not listening, little voice of reason. I have chosen to ignore you.

I am in a pole dancing club. I believe it is illegal to be sober in such circumstances.

Neville looked at her quizzically as he led her towards a quieter corner of the bar.

Neville: "Are you ok Eli, you seem a bit tipsy."

Eliza: "I'm fully facultied up, thank you. I could even pole dance if I wanted."

Neville: "Really? Can you pole dance? You little dark horse, you."

How hard can it be? If Emily can do it, I can.

Eliza: "Of course I can. I have a marvellous core. Both inner and outer."

Neville took her drink off her and placed it on a shelf beside them and pulled her closer to him.

Ooh, someone to support me. My legs do feel a bit unsteady. Lovely.

Neville started kissing the top of her head then dipped down to nuzzle her ear and started nibbling it.

Oooh, that's nice. Hang on, that's the Ellington ear. It's got dog slobber on it.

Ah well. Never mind. He seems happy enough.

He's better at it than Ellington too. I won't tell Ellington though; it'd hurt his feelings.

Hello. I feel a bit of a twinge in my lower regions. Is your ear bone connected to your pelvic bone?

I'm sure that wasn't in the song. I'd have remembered that as a ten-year-old.

We're in public. I'm not very comfortable with displays of affection in public.

I'll add that to the list of "AOB" when I hold the summit with mum and dad about my upbringing. I'm publicly inhibited.

Should I do something? I'm a bit stuck to be fair. I'll just stand here.

Do normal people have all this going on when they're having their ears nibbled or do they just zone out?

I'll Google that later.

I need to distract him. I can't indulge in this sort of shenanigans in full view of others.

Eliza: "Shall we dance?"

He stopped nibbling and kissing her.

Neville: "Hey yes! Come on!"

He let go of her and she nearly fell over.

Ooh, I was very reliant on him for ballast.

They headed off towards a section of the bar, where people were dancing.

Call that dancing lady? You of the incredibly dark marker pen drawn on eyebrows and massive cleavage? Flailing more like. I feel at ease. I can dance better than this lot.

Eliza started moving to the beat and watched Neville as he started dancing the correct moves to the music.

Ooh, he's learned them. Where did he do that? In his lounge on a Sunday afternoon?

That's a bit disconcerting. A grown man practicing moves in front of the television.

Eliza, hollering at Neville: "Can you do the Macarena?"

If he says yes, call a taxi.

Neville, hollering back: "Don't think so, show me it."

Phew.

Eliza bumped into marker pen eyebrow girl and accidently grabbed one of her ample bosoms to stabilise herself.

Marker pen eyebrow girl: "'Ere watch where you're grabbing. Gerroff me tits."

Eliza: "I'm so frightfully sorry, they were in steadying distance. I'll move over there."

Marker pen eyebrow girl: "Yeah, get out me way."

Try and be polite, she's an aggressive sort.

Eliza: "If it's any consolation, they're very nice."

Marker pen eyebrow girl: "Piss off, you lezza."

Oh, very ladylike. I bet you get all the men.

Neville stepped up to her and moved her towards the pole.

Neville: "Come on sexy, flaunt your moves."

Oh shit.

Eliza: "I don't know if my core is ready for it at the moment."

Neville: "My core is more than ready. Come on. Show me what you've got."

Eliza waited for the current girl to leave the pole and took a deep breath and grabbed hold of it.

You can do this Eli. It's a metal pole.

Now then, what do you do with a metal pole?

I do feel very peculiar. I could just grab on to the pole for grim death to be frank.

Eliza hooked her leg around it and swung a bit whilst holding it with her left arm.

A bit too Jungle Book, I think.

"I'm the King of the Swingers yeah, the Jungle VIP."

No. Not alluring.

What would Fireman Sam do?

Eliza grabbed hold of the pole and started to shin up it.

Neville looked around and then back at her with some confusion.

Neville: "Eli, what are you doing?"

Don't interrupt me, it's slippery, I'm struggling to maintain purchase.

Eliza: "I'm getting to the top so I can slide down."

Neville: "Why?"

Eliza: "I can't slide from the bottom, can I? Silly boy."

Eliza gripped the pole between her thighs as she attempted to climb up it.

She hollered to Neville.

Eliza: "See Neville, I have thighs that could crack nuts. Not your nuts, specifically. That wouldn't be good. Walnuts, I was thinking. I don't think I could do Brazil nuts, they're notoriously hard and they're difficult to get these days due to overharvesting. I bet hard core Emily didn't have nut cracking thighs."

She carried on attempting to climb the pole.

Neville: "Please get down Eli, people are looking."

Ooh, I sense a pleading tone to his voice.

She looked down from her vantage point to see a group of revellers watching her with unabashed amusement.

They're impressed by my thighs. I am too actually. I didn't know I had it in me.

If Tom could see me now, he'd be so proud.

Right, one more pull and that'll be enough for me to slide down.

Flip-flop, this is hard work. Hats off to Emily. I couldn't even go half-mast let alone a full flag.

Eliza pulled herself up the pole further with one almighty surge of energy.

Yay!

She let go with one hand to do a victory fist in the air and started to slide rapidly down the pole.

Oh shit!

Eliza, shrieking: "Oh buggering bollocks!"

She tried to regain grip on the pole and landed in an ungainly heap at the bottom.

To which the surrounding group cheered and whooped.

Neville rushed over and grabbed her arms.

Neville: "Bloody hell Eli, you're bonkers! Are you alright?"

I think I may have broken something.

Eliza: "Fine. Just fine. Anything Fireman Sam can do; I can do better."

Uh oh, I feel decidedly dodgy.

Eliza: "Do excuse me, I need to find the ladies pronto. I need to powder my nose."

Eliza ran off to the ladies and just made it into the cubicle before being very sick.

Dear me. I don't feel very good. I think the wasabi disagreed with me.

Maybe I'm allergic.

Eliza left the cubicle and looked in the toilet mirror.

My face isn't swollen and I haven't developed a fever. I do look very red, though.

Marker pen eyebrow girl walked in.

Marker pen eyebrow girl: "Your geeky boyfriend asked me to check if you're alive."

Eliza: "He's not geeky, he's going to be a superhero. Anyway, I only met him tonight and he's gone as far as nibbling my ear where the dog did so he doesn't qualify as a boyfriend yet."

Marker pen eyebrow girl: "I'll tell him you're alive, but still a moron."

Marker pen eyebrow girl went into a cubicle and Eliza tapped on the closed door.

Eliza: "Can I ask you something? You know your eyebrows? Are they trendy? Please don't hit me when you come out, I'm just wondering. I don't get out much."

A few minutes later marker pen eyebrow girl emerged from the cubicle.

Marker pen eyebrow girl: "Do you mind? I was having a wazz. They're swank, innit. You're old. Yours are way too plucked, lady."

Eliza: "I am old, I do agree. I feel remarkably old at this very moment. I'd be concerned about drawing them on in case I did one in a permanent state of surprise."

Marker pen eyebrow girl: "You get a template wiv 'em."

Eliza: "Really? That's fantastic. Like those ones you have for borders on your wall. What a marvellous idea. You can choose eyebrows to suit your mood. I'd adopt 'quizzical' so people would always think I was pondering something. You could go mad and use any template, like a bunch of grapes or something. Think of the possibilities."

Marker pen eyebrow girl was looking at Eliza with her lip curled.

Marker pen eyebrow girl: "You know you said you don't get out much. I think that's a good thing. Do you want me to take you back to the superhero?"

Eliza: "Thank you very much. That's very kind of you. I'm not a lesbian, by the way, but if I were you'd be on the list."

Marker pen eyebrow girl: "I am a lesbian, but you're most definitely not on the list."

Eliza: "Oh."

Marker pen eyebrow girl presented Eliza back to Neville.

Marker pen eyebrow girl: "Here she is. She's just chundered everywhere so you probably don't want to kiss her."

Neville thanked her and she drifted off back to her friends at the other side of the bar.

Neville: "Come on, I think you've had quite enough excitement for one night. Let's get you home, little lady."

Eliza: "I'm dreadfully sorry. I think it was the wasabi that did it."

Neville smiling: "Definitely. We'll save Edelweiss and yodelling for another time."

Eliza: "You mean you still want to see me again?"

Neville: "Of course, you're wonderful. Without any doubt you're utterly bonkers, but gorgeous."

Eliza: "Grand. Trotters it is."

Neville: "Indeed. Trotters it is."

Neville hailed a taxi and put Eliza into it. Eliza slumped into the back, gratefully.

Neville: "What's your address, Eli?"

Eliza recited it. Neville looked at the taxi driver.

Neville: "How much for that?"

The taxi driver told him and Neville handed over the money.

Neville: "Text me when you get home, gorgeous - before you pass out. I'll see you soon."

Sleep, I need sleep.

Oooh, spinning things when I close my eyes. Not good.

Eliza mumbled, gratefully.

Neville tapped the top of the car and waved a comatose Eliza off.

Status: *"Neville, what the fuck is going on? She's supposed to be sliding down the pole, not climbing up it."*

Chapter Twenty-four

Affirmation for the day: *I focus on breathing and grounding myself.*

Eliza could hear banging and an occasional bark. Then it stopped.

What?! Where is that? Is it inside my brain or external?

She lifted her head slightly off the pillow,

Oh no! That's bad. Way too adventurous.

Pills. I need copious amounts of pills.

She reached her arm out to her bedside table and floundered about a bit until she popped out two paracetamol and knocked them back with a glass of water.

Water! I need more water. I'm parched.

The banging started up again.

I need bearings. Who am I? What day is it? What time is it?

Eliza sat up, rubbed her eyes and looked at her bedside clock.

Eliza: "Shit! I mean flip-flops! Eleven?!"

What day is it?

Brain, work.

Erm. Saturday.

Thank you, brain.

Saturday?! God! Where's my child?! Eliza, you bad mother.

Eliza threw back the covers and tried to sit up swiftly.

Don't move quickly, you'll probably die.

Eliza practically fell out of bed and threw on her dressing gown. She slid down the stairs on her bottom, gingerly stood and promptly tripped over Norris as he greeted her at the bottom step by winding himself around her legs.

Eliza: "Norris, piss off. Can't you see I'm dying here?! I can't be doing with you creeping round me."

He yowled at her in dismay and stalked off towards the kitchen to wait for his breakfast.

Ellington was looking at her and then the door, torn as to which one deserved more attention. In the end, they received equal and he just bounced about eagerly looking between the two.

Eliza: "It's the door. That's the banging. It's the social services come to inform me they've removed Tom from my care."

Eliza unlatched the door and swung it open.

She was greeted by Lydia in full make-up regalia, a mummified Tom back in all last night's scarves and a bacon sandwich eating Freya.

They swept past Eliza and Freya lobbed a bit of bacon at a jubilant Ellington.

Eliza: "Urgh. Bacon. Freya would you mind eating that out in the garden or at the very least, facing the wall? I can't look at it at this moment in time."

Freya shrugged and carried on eating it in front of her.

Lydia: "Good afternoon, my little stop out. Nice to see you're not face down in a ditch. He's not here, is he?"

Lydia put Tom down and he staggered towards the television.

Eliza: "I'm so sorry, Lydia. I had a nasty reaction to some green paste and passed out."

Lydia: "You've got to watch that green paste. Was it sold by the unit and come in a glass?"

Tom: "Mummy Tom wants mummy to put telly on."

Eliza: "Lydia, put something sedate on for him, can you? I need to put the kettle on."

Lydia: "Of course. Then I need to hear all about it."

Eliza shuffled off into the kitchen and filled the kettle and lined up three cups with tea bags in. Two for her and one for Lydia.

Ellington and Norris were around her legs, tripping her up at every turn.

Eliza: "Gawd creatures! Alright! You'll not keel over just because your brekkie's a bit late. Look at Lydia, she fasts for days on end and can still nearly function. Some days it's rather tenuous I grant you and she needs to sniff on a jelly baby to get through the afternoon."

Lydia wandered into the room.

Lydia: "Who are you talking to? Your imaginary friend?"

Eliza: "The animals. They're complaining I've not fed them yet."

Lydia: "They're probably scared. Have you seen the state of yourself?"

Eliza: "No and I'm not ready to at the moment. I'll drink my teas first. Tom still recognised me, so I can't be that bad."

Lydia: "To be fair, his vision is somewhat impaired due to mummification. So, tell me how it went."

Eliza: "Oh, you know, the usual. I nearly melted all my tubes by way of a red-hot condiment, grabbed a lesbian's tit, slid down a pole thinking I was the living embodiment of Fireman Sam and threw up in the bar's toilets. Your average Friday night soiree in town."

Lydia: "Oh."

Eliza: "Indeed, oh. I don't think drinking's for me. I don't think it's my recreational pleasure of choice."

Lydia: "Whose pole did you slide down? Neville's?"

Eliza: "No, Vertigo's. You wouldn't get Fireman Sam sliding down another man's pole. Elvis would set on him with his jaws of life if he did that sort of thing. It's a pole dancing place."

Lydia: "Vertigo? Is that the place in town? It's a pole dancing club? Bugger me, I never knew that. Mrs Hestington-Charles will be horrified. I'll tell Freya and she can tell Hermione at school. It'll get back to her then."

Eliza: "Yes, I can imagine her telling mummy that over the dinner table."

Lydia: "She'd start a petition. Or even better, move."

Eliza: "You don't like her very much, do you?"

Lydia: "She looks at me disapprovingly. I think it's because I'm a single mother. She thinks I'm letting the village down."

Eliza: "I'm a single mother too but she doesn't look at me disapprovingly. The real reason she gives you 'the look' is because of that day when you said right in earshot of her in the playground that you'd received a message off multitudeofmates from a guy who said that when he looked at your picture, he wanted to dump his load. I had to pretend he worked in aggregate, in order to rescue the situation."

Lydia: "Ohhh yes, I forgot about that. Well, she shouldn't have been eavesdropping."

Eliza: "She was stood behind us! You have no spatial awareness woman!"

Lydia: "Whatevs. Anyway, bland man. How was he?"

Eliza: "He's not bland, he wants to be a superhero."

Lydia: "Excuse me?"

Eliza: "He seemed very nice in an odd sort of way. I must be honest, I got so out of it, I wasn't in the coherent mind set to make a fully informed opinion. He ensured I got home safely, so that's good."

Lydia: "Yes, he didn't take advantage of you which is a merit point. You need a bath, you reek of puke."

Eliza: "Thank you. I seem to recall he's agreed to come to Brian's do. So that's that job sorted. God, I feel awful, I need more tea."

Lydia: "I'll make you another couple whilst you plonk your bones in the bath. I'll watch the kids."

Eliza: "Ah, thank you."

Lydia: "Shall we go to Dave's after for a fry-up?"

Eliza: "Ok, I think I might be able to face one by then."

Eliza shambled upstairs and, on the way, picked up her mobile.

Crikey, how many messages?!

Ohhh bugger, I think I was meant to text the superhero that I'd got home safely.

Eliza replied to the ten messages received from Neville.

Eliza's text: "Hi Neville, so sorry for the late reply. I passed out. Thank you so much for looking after me last night. I'm very sorry for my behaviour, I don't do condiments very well. Eli x"

Send.

I'll creep a bit and add a kiss as I need him to come next Saturday.

Eliza went and ran the bath and stole a look at her reflection in the mirror.

Shit! I look about a hundred and forty!

That's nice, a dribble mark on my chin. Most attractive.

When did I start getting pillow folds in my skin that don't uncrease? How long will I have to endure a folded right hand side of my face? I hope it's not permanent. That would bugger my man chances good and proper.

Don't look any more, Eliza, you'll just upset yourself and consider Botox.

Her mobile pinged. She shuffled over to it and saw she'd received a message from Neville.

Neville's text: "Thank goodness Eli. I was dead worried about you. Hardly slept a wink. Hope you're ok. You did drink a lot of condiments. ☺ x"

Eliza sighed.

I did indeed. I'm back on the wagon.

Eliza stripped off and clambered into the piping hot bath, recalling the previous night as she lay back.

I climbed up a pole and slid down it; I'm such a fool.

I did this in public, in front of a man I intend seeing again.

Interesting about the eyebrow templates, though. I'll have to ask Lydia about them. She knows about all things make-uppy.

Eliza sank under the water with just her nose exposed in order to breathe.

I could quite cheerfully stay here all day. It's like a floatation tank. Maybe all the toxins will leach out of me and the water will turn a muddy brown.

Some time had elapsed when there was a hammering on the bathroom door.

Lydia: "Come on, Flipper! Some of us are hungry."

Eliza shot up out of the water.

Crikey, I think I dropped off! I could have drowned in my toxin bath.

Eliza: "Sorry! Just coming!"

A few minutes later, Eliza hurried downstairs and downed the now cold cups of tea Lydia had made her.

Eliza: "Right then, I'm ready for my public."

Lydia: "You've not got any make-up on."

Eliza: "I'm not bothered; it's only Dave's."

Lydia: "What if you see people?"

Eliza: "Do I honestly look that hideous without make-up?"

Lydia: "A bit pasty. You look like a magnolia wall that needs a picture hung up."

Eliza: "That's nice. Shall we go?"

Lydia: "Ok, fair enough."

They went into the lounge and rounded up the children.

Eliza: "Come on kids, let's get a late breakfast but don't make any loud noises as I feel a bit ropey."

Tom looked up at Eliza.

Tom: "Mummy, you look poorly."

Eliza: "I just need a picture hung on my face, darling. It's all fine; I'm under control."

Lydia: "I'll drive, you're probably still a zillion times over the limit."

Eliza: "Ok, but I removed the toxins by way of osmosis in the bath."

Lydia: "What was in that paste? I wouldn't have that again if I was you. Tell me more about superman."

Eliza: "He's more Hobgoblin than Superman. He has an unnerving affection for green. His whole outfit was green."

Lydia: "Mental people get obsessions like that; you want to be careful. Take it as a warning. I read an article about it. I read about a man who had to have everything orange. Before he knew it, he was incarcerated for his own protection as he was caught hugging a traffic cone. He got quite violent when they tried to take it off him."

Eliza: "Why did they try to take it off him? He wasn't harming anyone."

Lydia: "He was on the third lane of the M1 at the time."

Eliza: "Oh, good call then. You can make up your own mind as to his mental state when you see him on Saturday."

Lydia: "Indeed, I will. I've not seen you with anyone since Lewis. It'll be quite interesting."

Eliza: "He's not love's young dream, Lydia, but he's nice enough. Plus, he didn't run a mile after I slid down the pole and threw up, so he is caring. I'm a bit immune from forming natural feelings. I'm a bit of an onlooker to it all, to be honest."

Lydia: "Of course you are. I'm the same. When you've had your heart trampled on, it's hard to let the barriers down. 'Ere, maybe he's one of these guys that takes on the parent role and you'll have to call him 'daddy'."

Eliza: "I do hope not. As long as it stops with the green attire, I can cope."

They pulled up outside the Merrythought and wandered into the condensation riddled café.

Dave looked towards the door and hastily dropped a plate of pancakes in front of a customer.

Dave: "Oh oh, hello Eliza. You look, erm, erm..."

Eliza: "Alive. Yes, that is about the limit of it."

Lydia, whispering in Eliza's ear: "You see, you must look shit if Dave can't even find an adjective."

Dave: "Are you sickening? Please don't tell me you're ill. What can I do to put some colour in your cheeks, Eliza?"

Lydia: "What's your remedy, Dave? A wet J-cloth wafted across her pasty brow or are you going to cure her with your special sausage?"

Dave: "Do you have to accompany her everywhere?"

A look of animosity crossed his face as he looked at Lydia.

Lydia: "Yes, actually. I'm her carer."

I feel a bicker brewing. I feel a bit tender to be coping with it today.

Eliza: "It's self-induced I'm afraid to say, Dave, but thank you. Any chance of a table out of the way, please, so I don't upset too many customers?"

Dave: "Yes of course, give me a moment. There's one over here in the corner."

Dave hurried over to where Belinda, the waitress, was sitting, reading a magazine and drinking a cup of tea.

Dave: "You girl. Get up and go somewhere else please, there's a table over there that needs clearing."

Belinda: "I'm on me break, Dave."

Dave: "Well sit in the kitchen or something. Now get up."

Belinda grumbled and shot a look at Eliza and Lydia.

On the way past, she hissed loudly at Eliza.

Belinda: "He pervs at you."

Dave: "I heard that, Belinda. Get in the kitchen!"

Dave blustered back and ushered them to the table.

Dave: "I'm so sorry for her insubordination, Eliza."

Lydia: "What are you going to do, Dave? Dock her a slice of toast?"

Dave ignored Lydia and directed his question to Eliza.

Dave: "What can I get you all?"

They ordered their brunch and drinks and Dave hurried back to the kitchen.

Eliza: "Poor old Belinda is in for a tongue lashing."

Lydia: "Nah, he's saving that for you."

Eliza: "Urgh, must you Lydia?"

Lydia: "Soz. Tom are you ok?"

Lydia diverted her attention and looked concerned at Tom who was pulling a pained expression.

Tom: "Yes Wydia, I try out my angry face."

Lydia: "Oh ok. Not bad."

Tom: "I going to use it on mummy when she doesn't do as she's told."

Lydia: "We'll be seeing that quite a lot then."

Eliza: "I am here you know."

Lydia: "Barely."

Dave returned to the table and fussed about them with their food. Eliza looked at her plate and her lip curled involuntarily.

Eliza: "Oh dear, I feel a bit queasy."

Lydia: "The impending mastication of Dave's special sausage is enough to make anyone feel a bit dodgy."

Eliza: "Must you use the word mastication? You know it makes me feel a bit peculiar. It's like the word suckle. That's another word that makes my innards squirm. What's your word, Lydia?"

Lydia: "Work. That leaves me feeling very uncomfortable."

Eliza: "Haha! Yes, it's a four-letter word alright. Talking about work, I need to have a closer look at how things are moneywise. We're a bit behind with the renovations. Have you finished that chest of drawers yet?"

Lydia: "Not yet. I haven't been in the mindset."

Eliza: "What mindset do you need to be in to paint a cupboard? It's hardly Tracey Emin stuff we're achieving here."

Lydia: "I have been thinking, darling. I don't know if the whole sanding and repainting gig is fulfilling me. It's a bit, well, boring."

Uh oh. She's gone off the boil. Reel her in.

Eliza: "You what? This is our business. Anything that becomes a business has an element of repetition and boredom about it. I can't sand everything down and prime it ready for you to do a flurry of hand-painted doodles on it; we have to share it. Anyway, I don't have the room to have it all."

Lydia: "Do you think we should get a small unit? Shove the stuff in there. We could employ a couple of people to do all the tedious bits."

She's serious. She has zero business acumen. This is alarming.

Eliza: "Do you know how much a unit costs to rent per month plus business rates, extra utilities and people will want paying and kept in tea and biscuits. We don't have the money, Lydia. We've only got Mr Hicks as he's been institutionalised to stand beside a till. I had a call from Mrs Ashton the other day, when she opened her new chest of drawers it was full of scones."

Lydia: "Oh, ok ok. Stop getting all serious. It was just a thought. I'll try and finish the thing this week."

Eliza: "No, we must finish it this week. It's late already. The woman is waiting to put it in her renovated barn."

Lydia: "Yes, yes pasty, naggy pants. I'll do it. Now masticate your banger."

Tom: "Massicate Nanger, special nanger!"

Eliza: "I feel seriously dodgy."

Oh heavens, I don't feel right. It's the plateful of lard in front of me.

I need the toilet. I feel hot and cold in equal measure.

Oh no, please don't throw up on the plate.

Lydia: "God, you've gone minus pale. Are you going to hurl?"

Eliza: "Dunno. I need to get up. I'm stuck. MOVE!!"

Eliza struggled to get out of the corner and past the chairs.

Eliza: "Sorry Tom, Freya, everyone. Move please!! Now for your own safety! I'm not confident of my faculties."

Eliza tripped over her handbag on the way past and landed on her knees.

Eliza: "Bollocking flip-flops!!"

Freya: "Ummm, she said the word bollock."

Lydia: "She did, it's where the bangers come from. Bullocks. Also in her defence Freya, she did just fall flat on her face."

Freya: "Can you say bollocking if you fall over?"

Lydia: "Only in the face of impending doom."

Tom: "Bowwocking dooooom!"

Eliza shot a "sorry" look at Lydia as she scrambled up from the floor and shot towards the toilets.

Dave came out of the kitchen carrying a plate of poached eggs on toast and Eliza thundered into him and he dropped it on the floor.

Eliza: "God! Sorry Dave!"

Lydia, laughing: "How does your customer like her eggs, Dave? Fried, scrambled or over easy off the floor?"

Dave shot a look of concern at Eliza.

Dave: "Eliza! Get to the toilet! I have health and safety watching me at the moment after the last visit. I can do without puke on me tiles."

Lydia: "Oooh, so masterful Dave. You man you."

Dave shot a look at Lydia.

Dave: "Shut up."

He hollered over his shoulder towards Belinda who was looking on in amusement. As was the rest of the café.

Dave: "Belinda, stop gawping and clear up these eggs!"

Belinda: "Yeah alright. Keep your wig on."

She mooched over towards the pile of food on the floor and languidly made an attempt at clearing it up.

Dave: "For heaven's sake, get out of my way, you useless girl. What did they teach you at school? What's your O level in? Texting and idleness?"

Dave took the J-cloth out of his belt hook and proceeded to tidy up the spillage.

Belinda: "What are O levels?"

Meanwhile, Eliza rested her head on the cold wall tiles in the Merrythought Café toilet and stood there waiting for her body to inform her which major organ was going to give way on her.

She found out rapidly enough, it was all her internal organs, as her bottom exploded in a spectacular fashion.

Oh, heavens to Betsy, Dave will be closed down for his!

Please don't anyone else come in for at least ten minutes.

I am never ever ever having sushi again.

Jesus, my bottom is on fire!!

Who needs colonic irrigation when you can have that stuff?

A quarter of an hour later, Eliza emerged to be faced with the whole café staring at her.

Oh shit. How thin are the walls?

Lydia: "Well?"

Eliza: "Yes, thank you. Just a bit of wind. All fine now."

Lydia: "Okaaay. We saved your breakfast."

Eliza: "I'll pass if that's ok, I'll just have a cup of tea please, Dave."

Eliza directed her request towards a concerned looking Dave.

Dave: "Certainly, certainly. Are you sure there's nothing Belinda needs to attend to in there?"

He nodded towards the toilets.

Feign ignorance. It's the only way to save face.

Eliza: "I don't know what you mean. It's all perfectly fine, I just needed a bit of quiet time."

Dave: "Good ok. I'll fetch you a pot of tea."

He turned his head and shouted.

Dave: "Belinda! Tea for the lady."

Belinda: "I'm right in front of you, no need to shout. And she ain't no lady from what I just heard."

Oh great.

Dave: "Do you want a formal warning?"

Belinda: "Another one? How many do I get before I get a certificate?"

Dave: "Such insolence. I'll be having a word with your mother."

Belinda: "Like she's bothered."

Dave, almost begging: "Just go, now. Kitchen. Please!"

Belinda turned on her heel and stuck her tongue out at his turning back as Dave switched his attention back to Eliza. Dave shook his head forlornly.

Dave: "You take on these youngsters, think you're doing a good thing, giving them a step up onto the working ladder and this is their thanks."

Lydia: "Yeah, because clearing up poo is something you'd proudly put on your CV."

They all heard. Shall I just die now?

Eliza: "I'm so sorry, Dave."

Dave: "It's alright. I've got bleach. They made me get some at the last inspection."

Eliza: "You might need to purchase some more. Add it to our bill."

Eliza slumped down on the nearest chair and put her head on the table whilst Tom delicately placed bits of bacon in her hair.

Tom: "There you go, mummy. You can save it for later and eat it when you're not so poorly."

Eliza, muffled from the depths of the Formica table: "So thoughtful, my little gift from the heavens. Lydia, take me home please."

Status: *"Nobody puts baby in the corner."*

Chapter Twenty-five

Affirmation for the day: *I am safe and sound.*

It was Saturday night and the day of Brian's menu try out had arrived. Eliza had arranged with Neville to be picked up at hers and her mother had very excitedly come over to babysit Tom.

Eliza: "Come on... Come on man. Where the devil are you?"

Eliza's mother: "What time's he meant to be 'ere, Sparrow?"

Eliza: "Twenty-five minutes ago."

Eliza's mother: "Ooh, tardy time keeping. I can't abide that love; it shows a lack of respect. Time is the most precious of all commodities."

Eliza: "Indeed mum and I'm starving."

Eliza's mother: "Would you care for some pine nuts? I've got some in me pocket."

Eliza: "Er, no thanks, mum. Why do you have them in your pocket? In case you meet any passing squirrels?"

Eliza's mother: "They're nutritious, I learnt all about them on last week's course."

Eliza: "What was that one called?"

Eliza's mother: "Food for your chakras."

Eliza: "Which one do the pine nuts fix?"

Eliza's mother: "Do you know love, I don't know. They didn't cover that in the course. Maybe, they mend a bit of all of 'em."

Eliza: "Go on then, I'll have a handful. My chakras could probably do with a bit of a sort out."

Eliza's mother: "Do you want me to Reiki you? Ahead of all that peculiar food you'll be having to stomach? "

Eliza: "No thanks, mum; I'll stick to the pine nuts."

There was a knock on the door.

Eliza's mother: "Ah, here's the tardy timekeeper."

Eliza: "Hmm, now mum he's nice, I think, but to be honest I can't remember much about him. Don't go thinking he's the next in line after Lewis, ok?"

Eliza's mother: "Of course, dear."

Eliza went to open the front door and overheard her mother whisper to Ellington who had perked up at the knock "how exciting Ellington, we get to see her new beau."

Eliza: "Hello Neville."

Neville: "Hi Eli, I'm so sorry I'm late, I had to finish a level on my game."

Eliza: "What game?"

Neville: "On my Xbox."

You were late because you were playing a computer game?

That's not real life.

Me standing here waiting for my dinner, whilst eating pine nuts to clear my chakras, is real life.

Eliza: "Right. Fair enough. I'll just get my coat."

Eliza's mother stepped into the lounge.

Eliza's mother: "Hello, you must be Neville. I'm Eliza's mother, Mrs Turner. Delighted to make your acquaintance."

Her mother had put on her poshest accent and extended her hand.

Mum, you're cockney. You sound ridiculous.

Neville did a peculiar little curtsey and took her mother's hand and kissed the back of it.

Neville: "Delighted, Mrs Turner."

Have I wandered back into the 1800s?

Will I look out of the window and see Mr Darcy dismounting his horse?

Eliza's mother: "Ooh, charmed and such a delightful ensemble you're wearing. Where did you buy it?"

Mother, are you kidding me?

It's another green effort. Oh, hang on, that's not green. That's red. Very red.

He probably bought it in Primary Colours R Us.

Neville: "I frequent many stores in order to maintain my image."

Yes, I expect you're known in every charity shop in a radius of fifty miles.

Enough of this ye olde conversation, we're late enough as it is.

Doff your cap, old bean and we'll be on our way.

Eliza: "Right Neville, I'm ready to rock and roll. Let's go."

Neville swept his gaze at Eliza.

Neville: "You look gorgeous, Eliza. Mrs Turner you have a simply wonderful daughter, you must be very proud."

Creep.

You'll be saying we look like sisters next. Then I'll have to hit you.

Eliza's Mother: "My husband and I are. She's never been a minute's trouble."

Liar

You choose to forget the manic postnatal depression and divorce incident.

Oh, and the cutting of the dog's hair with the pinking shears.

I was ten at the time though, so I can be let off that one.

Anyway, stop this chit chat.

Eliza: "Mum, you have my mobile number, just text me if you want me at all, ok? I won't be late."

Eliza's mother: "No problem, Sparrow, you two kids have a lovely time."

Kids? I'm thirty-five, mother.

Neville: "I look forward to meeting you again, Mrs Turner."

Eliza's mother: "Likewise, Neville. Perhaps, you might make it on time on the next occasion."

Ooh, you had to get it in didn't you mum?

Neville blushed the same colour as his outfit and held the door open for Eliza to walk out first.

Neville: "Oh, yes. I'm dreadfully apologetic about that. It won't happen again, Mrs Turner."

He turned his attention to Eliza.

Neville: "Your chariot awaits m'lady."

Yes, yes alright. Calm down with the chivalry now.

Don't think I've forgotten that your ex was a pole dancer and you want me to yodel.

I wonder what car he's got. Probably the bat mobile.

Eliza didn't have to wonder for long as Neville directed her to a green Skoda.

Oh, how frightfully dull.

He is an accountant. He just has delusions of superheroness.

Don't mention the car, it's a material possession. It doesn't matter.

Eliza: "You have a Skoda."

Thank you mouth for completely letting me down, yet again.

Neville: "Yes, it's marvellous on fuel economy and has a massive warranty. They are made by VW now, it's truly a car of dreams."

Oh, I stand corrected.

He held the passenger door open for her and guided her in. He then ran round to his side and sat beside her.

Neville: "Right then gorgeous, where are we off to?"

Eliza: "Brian and Clive's restaurant. It's called Manners."

Neville: "Oh, I've heard of that. That's very swanky. I've always wanted to eat there but Emily wasn't very adventurous on the old food front."

Eliza: "Emily, the hard-core solicitor?"

Neville: "Yes, I've only really had one girlfriend, if truth be told. She broke my heart, actually."

He stared out of the windscreen, lost in the memory.

Gawd, I've only just got in the car.

Don't go all maudlin on me.

Eliza: "That's a shame. All part of life's rich tapestry. What doesn't break us, makes us stronger."

Any more clichés to throw in there or are we done?

Eliza: "The path of true love never doth run smooth."

Oh ok, there's more in the tank.

Stop now, you sound like you've swallowed a box of fortune cookies.

I blame mum. She's always drip feeding me these pearls of wisdom.

It's only natural I spout forth when there's the opportunity.

They're all stored in my brain, waiting for a chance to flow out.

Platitudes of piousness.

Eliza looked across at Neville, still lost in thought.

Come back to me Hobgoblin. Earth to middle earth, are you receiving me? Over.

Eliza: "Shall we start the car?"

We? What am I going to do? Get out and turn the starter handle?

Neville: "Yes, yes, sorry Eli, of course. Let's go."

Neville brought himself back into the present and started the car then carefully pulled out of her lane.

He's a cautious driver.

Neville: "Which way, gorgeous?"

Eliza: "Left."

Neville signalled left and looked numerous times left and right before pulling out.

Definitely just passed his test. His hands are 'ten to two' as well.

He spotted a gap in the traffic and promptly shot out of the junction at a neck wrenching speed with a wheel spin to top it off which took Eliza completely by surprise.

Bloody hell, I think I just hit G force.

He sped up to sixty miles an hour then slammed on the anchors until he was at thirty miles an hour again.

I could have just swallowed my teeth then. Not cautious, he's a nutter!

Eliza calmed herself and stared across at Neville.

Breathe Eli.

Eliza: "Blimey, Neville! What's with the speed thing?"

Neville: "It's a built-up area, I have to do thirty miles an hour."

Have you got short term memory loss?

Eliza: "Indeed, but what about the sixty bit before that?"

Neville: "It was just acceleration from the junction."

If you're a rally driver, yes. Not a Skoda driver.

My life is in his crazy, Need for Speed Xbox playing hands.

Please let me make it to Manners in one piece.

Ok ether, if the next light we come to is green then that means I will make it alive.

They got to a set of traffic lights as they turned to red.

I'm toast.

Neville continued driving.

Flip-flops!!

Eliza, panic stricken: "STOP!! The lights are red!!"

He slammed on the brakes, skidded to a halt and her seat belt yanked her back in her seat.

Neville: "Oh, I'm so sorry Eli! Are you alright? I struggle sometimes as I'm colour blind. I mix up my reds and greens. The medical term is protanopia."

I'm doomed. The ether has decreed it. I'm going to meet my maker in a Skoda.

It's too tragic for words.

I can't die today; I've got odd socks on.

I promise karma fairy, I'll not think any bad thoughts for at least two weeks if you let me live.

Neville continued.

Neville: "Colour blindness is a bit tricky when your favourite colour is green. I used to rely on Emily to tell me the difference when we went shopping together."

The lights turned amber and he was off like a horse out of the starting gate.

And he looks so innocuous.

Neville looked across at Eliza who was gripping onto the sides of the passenger seat.

Neville: "You ok Eli? You look a bit pale."

Eliza: "I'm not accustomed to dying. I'm coming to terms with the inevitability of it."

Neville: "Eh?"

Eliza: "Your speed is rather, erm, erratic. Have you had many crashes?"

Neville: "Only a couple recently. To be fair, I'm not used to passengers. I passed my test a couple of years ago. Took seven attempts. I haven't the faintest idea why. Before that, I used to take my skateboard to work."

A grown accountant taking a skateboard to work?

That doesn't sit very well with me. It's not very cool, is it?

How can you take a man wearing knee pads talking about profit and loss seriously?

Eliza: "Did you wear a helmet and have padded elbow pads?"

Neville shot her a sideways glance.

Keep your eyes on the road man!

Neville: "No, of course not! Superheroes don't wear protective padding. Well, if they do, it's part of their costume and built in."

You're so crackers, it's concerning and quite endearing at the same time.

I strongly feel the concerned feeling will overtake the endeared one quite quickly, but for now I can stomach it. That's if I live, of course.

Eliza: "How many superheroes drive Skodas?"

Neville: "Apart from me? I don't know."

Eliza: "You know the clothes you're wearing tonight? Did Emily choose them for you towards the end of your relationship by any chance?"

Neville: "Huh? Yes actually. It was the day she dumped me. We'd been clothes shopping and we went to Costa for a coffee afterwards and she told me she never wanted to see me again. How did you figure?"

Oooh, hard core Emily has a wicked streak. I quite like her.

Eliza, shrugging: "Just a lucky guess."

He continued to drive with intermittent bursts of breakneck speed with Eliza calling out the traffic light colours until they pulled into Manners car park.

Thank you, karma fairy, I'm alive.

Granted, I've visibly aged ten years in the space of twenty minutes, but I'm alive.

I'll do my best to be pure in thought and deed for a fortnight.

I'll eat pine nuts to keep my chakras clear of any unwanted ethereal debris.

Neville: "Blimey, you're out the car sharpish, Eli! What are you doing? Have your legs given way?"

Eliza had thrown her bones out of the passenger door and had dropped to her knees.

Eliza: "Kissing the ground. Come on, let's go and meet my friends."

Eliza stood, brushed herself down and waited for Neville to finish checking all the doors, including the boot. He patted the top of the car and informed it they wouldn't be long.

Superhero, my arse.

Oh crap, I lasted less than a minute with the karmic agreement.

I'll nip to the health food shop in town. What's it called? Mother Nature, that's it. She'll sort me out. I'll get a bag load of nuts by way of recompense.

Pureness starts tomorrow.

Status: *"I feel the need, the need for speed."*

Chapter Twenty-six

Sub Affirmation for the day: *I can control my emotions effortlessly.*

They walked through the heavy swing doors of Manners to be greeted by a very excited Brian. He grabbed hold of Eliza and gave her a massive hug in the doorway.

Brian: "Hello! You look a bit wide-eyed and dangerous. Are you alright? Let me get you a drink."

Eliza: "Hello Brian. I'd love one, please."

Brian hollered over his shoulder towards Giles, the resident server, to get Eliza a vodka and coke.

She shot a look at Neville.

Eliza: "I'll only have the one, you're ok. I won't be in the same pickle I was last time."

Neville smiled and gently rubbed the small of her back. She turned her attention back to Brian.

Eliza: "Brian this is my, er, friend, Neville."

Neville extended his hand by way of greeting and Brian warmly accepted it.

Brian: "Hello, lovely to meet you. I've heard all about you. How marvellous to have one of the Incredibles over for dinner."

I'll kill Lydia.

Neville: "Hello Brian. It's very nice to meet you too. You have a lovely restaurant. I've always wanted to pay a visit but my ex wasn't very experimental."

Oh yes, let's hoist full flag Emily out in the first sentence, shall we?

Giles wandered over and gave Eliza her drink and looked enquiringly at Neville for his order.

Brian: "Oh, you'll not have that problem with our Eli. She's up for all sorts!"

Brian!!

Neville: "Really? Well, that I look forward to. She does strike me as a bit of a dark horse. A lager shandy for me, please. I'm escorting the good lady tonight."

This situation needs to be rescued!

Eliza: "He means food-wise. Sushi aside, I'm quite open to things."

Neville: "I like open, the more open the better."

Dear lord.

Brian's eyebrows shot up and he went slightly slack jawed for a moment before collecting himself.

He leant forward conspiratorially and whispered loudly.

Brian: "Lydia's here and she's brought a chappy with her. He's quite the dish. If I didn't have Clive, I'd snaffle him up myself!"

Eliza looked over Brian's shoulder to see the rear of a slightly built man with brown, closely cropped, wavy hair; the curls resting gently on the collar of his pale blue shirt. He was leaning slightly over the bar, accepting a drink from Giles.

Lydia said she was bringing The Mighty Sword.

Ooh, he is quite broad shouldered.

Brian shouted across to the bar.

Brian: "Yoo hoo, Jude!"

The Mighty Sword turned round, beamed at Brian and wandered towards them.

Oh crap! My knees have gone. That smile! That face!

It's like the world has freeze framed.

What's happening to me?

Everything else has drifted into soft focus and he's the only one with any clarity.

What's occurring? I can't breathe properly.

Maybe, I've found god and I'll have to spend the rest of my life spreading the word in the town centre.

Or, maybe, I'm having a stroke?

Is this what happens when you have a stroke? I'll move my face, see if it works.

Eliza formed an 'O' shape with her mouth and stretched her face to test that her face worked.

It moves. What are you looking at, Neville?

Maybe, it's a delayed reaction from the near-death experience in the car.

Brian: "Eli... Eliza?"

Brian was shaking her arm and looking at her enquiringly. She was transfixed on Jude.

He's flip-flopping gorgeous.

Eliza: "Huh? What? Sorry?"

Brian: "Are you ok, poppet? What's with the facial contortions?"

Eliza gathered herself and realised she was trembling.

Neville: "Do you need to down your drink and I'll get you another?"

He definitely thinks I have drink issues.

I need to get a grip.

Eliza: "No, er, it's ok. I'll be alright. I thought I might be having a stroke but I'm fine."

Stop staring at him.

Blink for god's sake woman.

Oh shit. He's probably the most perfect man I have ever seen.

I want him.

Neville looked at Eliza completely bemused.

Neville: "A stroke?"

Eliza glanced up at him.

See him, Neville? He's a superhero if ever there was one. There's Superman, right there.

Lydia never said he was perfect, she just said he had a big willy.

Oh no, perfect and a big willy. God was having a good day when he made him.

What on earth is Lydia doing even thinking about petrol pump Clarke as back up when she has him?

She doesn't deserve him.

Eli! Did you just think that? No. The jealousy fairy thought that.

Lydia has had a bad time with Roy, she needs a lovely boyfriend. You should feel happy for her.

Yeah well, at this moment, I don't.

Oh, oh, he's approaching me with an extended hand. I get to touch him.

Oh, that smile.

Jude: "Hello Eli. I've heard lots about you. It's lovely to meet you."

Eliza: "Hello The... I mean, Jude. Sorry about the face thing just then, I was just testing to make sure I wasn't having a seizure. I had a bit of a journey here and thought I was going to cock it."

What?!

Eliza: "CARK!! Cark it, I mean! Not cock it. Sorry."

Brian let out a guffaw. Neville continued to look somewhat perplexed at Eliza and Jude laughed.

Shut up, Eli.

You moron. A Freudian slip if ever there was one.

Oh, that laugh.

It's wonderful.

She held out her hand, tremulously, and he went to grasp it.

As their fingers touched, she jumped and Jude took a sharp intake of breath.

Flip-flop! Was that static? I hope not. I have enough trouble taming my hair as it is.

She shot an alarmed look at Brian as she whipped back her hand and his eyes widened.

Brian darted a look at Neville, then at Jude who was looking slightly baffled whilst inspecting the fingers of his right hand. Brian then looked back at Eli before clapping his hands together and hurriedly announcing.

Brian, hurriedly: "Neville, this is Jude. Jude, Neville. Right well, we can't be standing here all night now, can we? Let's go and say hello to the others."

I sense a raised, blustering tone to Brian's voice. He's rescuing the situation.

He hastily ushered the three of them towards the others who were at the far side of the bar.

Jude went over to where his drink was and took a slug from it.

He knows I've had a moment.

A life-changing, brain and body giving way moment.

That's just bloody typical that is.

The most perfect man in the world and he's going out with my best friend.

Thank you very much.

Karma fairy. You and I are going to have some serious words over this.

Brian: "Neville, me lad, go and collect yourself that shandy off the bar. I've some news I must catch Eli up on, if you don't mind me having her attention for one intsy minute?"

Neville: "No, no, not at all. I'll get you another one, Eli. You look like you need it."

Great, another night of shinning up a pole awaits.

Jude made his way back to his spot at the bar.

Brian hustled Eliza towards a corner of the restaurant and hissed in her ear.

Brian: "Oh. My. God! You've had a thunderbolt! How marvellous! You only hear about these in the movies."

Everyone noticed. I'm so unsubtle.

Eliza: "I'm not dying then? That's a relief. I could do without being resuscitated before me dinner."

Brian: "I don't think you're going to cock it."

Eliza: "Don't."

Eliza rolled her eyes.

Eliza: "I'm such a plank."

Brian: "Are you alright? Are you going to cope with the evening ok?"

Eliza: "I don't know, Brian. I feel completely pole-axed. He's beautiful."

Brian: "Yes, he is indeed, but without wishing to piddle on your strawberries, he is also Lydia's at present."

Eliza: "I know. How completely pants is that?"

Brian: "A spanner in the works, I do agree. Maybe, it's just a kerpow meeting thing. He might smack his lips when he eats and fart at the dinner table. Let's hope he has some bad habits, eh?"

Eliza: "Yes, here's hoping he's out on parole."

Brian gave her a warm hug.

Brian: "We won't tell anyone; our little secret. Now we must mingle; I'll look after you."

He went to guide her back towards the rest of the group and she grabbed his arm earnestly and pulled him back.

Eliza, whispering: "He felt it too, Brian, didn't he?"

Brian looked at her square in the eyes and nodded.

Brian: "Yes, poppet, he did."

That's awful and yay at the same time.

I can't have him.

Maybe Lydia will tire of him and offer to let me have him.

I'll try and persuade her to date petrol pump Clarke.

Yes, because that's very likely. Not.

Why is there some friendship law where you can't go after your best friend's boyfriend? Hmmm.

Bloody archaic unwritten moral code.

Brian: "Come on. Let's join the others."

He patted her hand and hooked her arm in his as they wandered towards the group at the main bar and Clive came over to Eliza.

Clive: "Hello, my little tatty head. I met your fella; he's getting you a double vodka. Pretty set on getting you tanked up by the looks of it, so keep your hand on your ha'penny."

He gave her a wink.

Clive: "Brian, we're needed in the kitchen. Carlos is starting to panic. His jus isn't playing ball, by all accounts."

Brian: "I can't be coping with him screeching like a banshee. Do excuse us, poppet."

Eliza: "No problem, I'll go and get quietly sozzled."

Brian gave her a kiss and ran off after Clive towards the kitchen.

Eliza looked around and saw Lydia in the corner of the bar playfully flicking Jude's nose.

Please don't flick him.

I must not think like this. It's destructive. It's not her fault.

If only I'd seen him first. Why, oh why, did she have to meet him before me?

I feel very wobbly. A bit faint.

I must have really upset the chi wagon for this to happen.

Lydia turned, caught sight of Eliza and waved. She excused herself from Jude and ran over to where Eliza was standing. Neville left the bar with their drinks at the same time and they bumped into each other, with him rescuing the drinks, just in time.

Lydia: "Oof! Who are you? Santa's little helper?"

Neville: "Eh? I'm Neville. Who are you?"

Lydia: "Lydia, Eli's best friend."

Neville: "Oh, I don't think she's mentioned you. Hello."

Lydia: "Charming. Hello."

A great start I must say. Step in, Eli.

Eliza: "Hi Lydia. It's not actually a red outfit, it's supposed to be green."

Lydia: "Fair enough. Hello darling! I missed you coming in. I was in the loo reapplying my lippy. How are you? You looked a bit lost then."

Neville was looking down at his jumper and trousers, intently.

Neville, non-plussed: "Is my outfit red?"

Lydia looked at him with derision.

Lydia: "As a pillar box."

Neville looked crestfallen and shook his head sadly.

Neville, muttering: "She could be quite cruel, you know. I had no idea."

Eliza felt a bit sorry for him and patted him on the arm. Neville looked down at her and smiled.

Neville: "Ah well, I've got you now, gorgeous. You're utterly bonkers and drink like a fish but you don't strike me as unkind."

Put like that; I am quite the catch.

Eliza: "She has to have a ruthless side, Neville. She's a solicitor; it's in her blood."

Lydia looked disinterested and waved her hand dismissively.

Lydia: "Anyway, less of whoever."

Lydia leant in towards Eliza and hissed excitedly.

Lydia: "What do you think of The Mighty Sword? Bit of alright, isn't he?"

Neville looked puzzled at Lydia.

Neville: "The Mighty Sword?"

Oh flip-flops. That's not for others' ears.

Think fast.

Eliza: "Yes, he erm... collects knives. Whopping big 'uns."

Situation rescued – slightly.

Neville visibly perked up.

Neville: "Really? That's wonderful! I have a great interest in them too. I wonder if he's into Warcraft. I also collect the figures. I have them all around my bedroom."

Lydia and Eliza shot each other a look.

He's a dweeb. I don't think I've ever dated a real, live dweeb before.

Lydia has a Greek god and I have a geek god.

Marvellous.

Lydia: "Yeah Neville, ask him if he collects dolls. He'll love that."

Neville: "I don't think they fall under the category of dolls. Some fetch a fortune online, you know, as they're really rare. Collectors' pieces."

At that point, Brian and Clive flew out of the kitchen, both very red faced.

Brian clapped his hands and spluttered, slightly hysterically.

Brian: "Right guys! Pick a seat, we must crack on and try out the menu. It's just at the point where it could be rendered inedible, so we have to get it in our chops sharpish."

Clive wiped his brow and sighed heavily.

Clive: "Carlos is a bit stressed."

Lydia waved at Jude to join them.

Lydia: "Come on let's treat ourselves to trotters."

Eliza watched Jude approach them.

I'm captivated. I know I mustn't stare but I can't stop myself.

I want to remember every freckle and line on his beautiful face.

Jude looked at her cautiously, smiled briefly and diverted his attention back to Lydia, who was dragging him to a table.

Neville grabbed Eliza's hand and held it, proprietarily.

Assess the situation.

I can't have him. I have a guy who accepts I'm barmy but likes me anyway.

He's not perfect, by any stretch, but he's pleasant.

Is pleasant enough?

For tonight, it'll have to be.

Status: *"... I wish I had never met you. Because then I could go to sleep at night not knowing there was someone like you out there."*

Chapter Twenty-seven

Sub Sub Affirmation for the day: *I deserve the best in life.*

Later that evening, an exhausted Eliza was standing on the doorstep of her house after enduring, what can only be described as, the most emotionally draining evening of her life. Worse than childbirth, she had to concede. At least at the end of that, she had a human being.

She rested her head gently on the front door and sighed.

As she leant, the door swung open and she fell over the threshold onto her mother.

Eliza's mother: "Blimey Sparrow, hello! Are you alright? I thought I heard you approaching. Have you lost your key?"

Eliza regained her balance by grabbing onto the coat stand and looked at her mother wearily.

Eliza: "No mum, I was just taking a moment."

Eliza's mother: "Darling, are you alright? You look wiped out. Where's whatshisname?"

Eliza: "He's gone home. What an evening. How was Tom?"

Eliza's mother: "Tommy's a treasure. A proper little star for his grandma. Come on, take your coat off and tell your old mum all about it. I'll make you a hot chocolate."

Eliza smiled. It was good to see her mum, with her familiar ways. Eliza took her coat off and threw it on the armchair. She ran upstairs and checked on Tom then came down and flumped on the settee with her feet up on the coffee table.

A few minutes later, her mother returned with a tray of biscuits and a hot chocolate for them each.

Eliza's mother: "Feet off the table. Come on then, spill the beans. What happened?"

It's my house, mum. I can swing off the chandelier, by my pants, if I so choose.

Eliza took her feet off the coffee table, took her hot chocolate and sighed.

Eliza: "He's beautiful, mum. Probably the most perfect person I have ever met."

Eliza's mother: "Really? That's lovely. They say it's what's within that matters. It's nice to see you with some emotion back and moving on from Lewis. How was the food? Do you need to detox for the next few days?"

Eliza: "I need to detox for the next millennia probably, mum. The food was so rich. By the way, I forgot to tell you, Lewis is pregnant."

Eliza's mother: "No!! Really? How did he do that?"

Eliza: "Via the usual way, I should imagine. I don't think Geraldine used a syringe or anything."

Eliza's mother: "Oh I see, they're having a baby. How do you feel about that?"

Eliza: "Alright, I think. I was a bit shocked at first but I feel a bit sorry for them now. She's lost her job, has a useless boyfriend and she will get fat ankles."

Eliza's mother, huffing: "Save your sympathy, she split up your family and he's an appalling father and husband. Michael and I are quite disappointed in him. To think the amount we spent on that wedding. Makes you blanch, it really does. You're not going to marry this one, are you? Only we're thinking of a cruise."

Eliza: "No, mum, I don't think I'll be going down that route again."

Eliza's mother: "Good, I fancy the Med. I must pop down to the travel agent this week, after yoga."

Eliza: "You've taken up yoga?"

Eliza's mother: "Yes. You know Marjorie, down at number twenty-four? She swears it's done wonders for her, erm, love life. Woken all her wherewithals up."

Alrighty then. I think this is where we stop this conversation and I go to bed.

Eliza: "Thanks mum, for looking after Tom. I'm whacked, I think I'll turn in."

Eliza's mother took her cue, downed her drink and went to get up.

Eliza's mother: "No problem, Sparrow, you get your sleep, I need to be getting off, I've got a pottery class in the morning. It's called 'Expression through clay.' You open your kundalini to the universal energy and see what comes out. If I make a nice pot, I'll bring it round. Are you wanting to come round for Sunday dinner sometime soon?"

Eliza: "Yes, soon mum. I've got upbringing matters to discuss with you and dad. I'll let you know."

Eliza's mother: "Alright. Sleep well my darling child."

Eliza felt a tear well up.

Eliza: "I love you, mum. Thank you for being there."

Eliza's mother waved her away.

Eliza's mother: "Don't go all daft on me."

Eliza's mother put her coat on, kissed Eliza on her cheek and stood in the doorway.

Eliza's mother: "Night night, Sparrow."

With that she was off into the night. Eliza shut the door and stood there for a moment, thinking.

Ellington wandered up to her and wiped his nose on her leg.

Eliza: "Oh Ellington, the penny's dropped! She thinks I have fallen for the hobgoblin!"

No wonder she thinks I was drunk.

She flumped back onto the settee and Norris meowed on his way into the lounge. Ellington sensing a detractor from the potential ear tickling, clambered on top of Eliza's lap to stake his claim ahead of Norris.

Eliza: "Must you? You're not a lap dog. Oh right, now you're getting in on the act, Norris."

Norris climbed aboard the lap and perched on top of Ellington and started kneading Ellington's fur with his long claws.

Ellington let out a whimper and leapt off Eliza's lap and Norris snuggled in for a cuddle on Eliza's knee.

Eliza: "Very clever move there, Norris. Blimey guys, I've had a very taxing night. Do you want to hear about it?"

Norris purred loudly and Ellington rested his head on her knee and looked up at her with his expressive, brown eyes.

Eliza: "You're a captive audience. Well, I met the most perfect man ever. I mean gorgeous. Problem is, he's with Lydia. I know. Uno massivo problemo. We could incant a spell that makes her forget she ever met him so I can have him. Always supposing that is, he wants me, of course. I'll make a spell for that, whilst I'm at it. What's that Ellington? Wasn't I with a man in a bright red outfit who drove like a maniac? Well, yes I was and he's nice enough. I do have a few issues regarding him, though. He collects dolls. Which, in itself, is a bit creepy but to make it slightly worse, he leaves them in the boxes. He doesn't even play with them."

She stroked Ellington's ear, absentmindedly.

Eliza: "Another issue I have is, I drink a lot in his company. If I stick with him, I might end up at AA. I don't want to sit in a circle with a bunch of strangers. I'm sociable, but I don't think I can go down the 'bare your soul' route. Another problem is, he thinks he's a superhero yet he drives a Skoda, very badly I might add. I don't think that's quite normal. He also uses a hanky. I can't date a man who has a hanky."

Ellington continued to rest his head on her lap and Norris continued his purring and kneading.

Eliza: "He wanted to come back for a coffee. Hmmm, Ellington, that old chestnut. He doesn't even drink coffee, so I knew that was a ruse from the outset. I shall hold off on yodelling for a while, I don't think he's worth it. It's been a while, you know, on the old yodelling front. What if I've forgotten what to do? They say it's like riding a bike. If that's the case, Lydia must be in the Tour de France with the rate she's racking them up."

Eliza sighed and continued rambling at Ellington and Norris.

Eliza: "Anyway, I took the bus home. I haven't been on public transport for years. A man nearly threw up on my shoes. Most unpleasant that was. I only just moved my legs out of the line of fire in time. But it was preferable to being killed in a misjudged traffic light collision. You see, that's another thing against him, I'd have to drive everywhere as he's a liability behind the wheel. What if we want to go on holiday to the seaside?

Hours, I'll be driving. That falls into man territory, that sort of driving. A bit like shelf putting up and putting the bins out. Man jobs. And yes, I know I'm stereotyping. I'm allowed in my own house. Anyway, I could have got a lift with Lydia and Jude but I didn't want to make a fool of myself in such close proximity, so I refused. I think I may have upset Neville a bit because I said no to his request for coffee and then informed him I was taking the bus home. I didn't create a very good impression, probably. Ah well, I'll remedy that tomorrow. I'll call him and say I don't want to see him again. If nothing else, Jude has shown me I need to raise my expectations, somewhat."

Eliza stretched and yawned.

Eliza: "Right then you two, it's time for bed. I'll let you do your ablutions and then we're lights out."

She stood and carried a floppy Norris to the back door and let them both out whilst she set about switching the lights off. Whilst doing so, her eye was caught by the calendar. She looked at it and then did a double take.

Hang on, what date is it?

Oh no, already?! I need to sort out Tom's birthday party and sharpish.

I've been so preoccupied with Brian's meal and finding a man to take I've lost track of time.

Eliza pulled the calendar off the wall and put it on the work surface as a reminder to set to it first thing in the morning.

She let Ellington back in and called for Norris but he was nowhere in sight.

Eliza: "Looks like you're sleeping solo tonight Ellington old boy, much like myself. We can both lie like starfishes and snore happily without getting an elbow, or paw in your case, in the ribs. Night."

She kissed him on the top of his head and wandered upstairs to bed, stopping off at Tom's door to listen for his gentle, rhythmic breathing. She blew him a kiss and went to her room.

Ahh my baby, four years old in a few weeks.

What sort of party shall we have then?

Star Wars.

Oh yes, brilliant idea.

Now then. Tomorrow I must get rid of Neville and go back on multitudeofmates and find an available one.

It's a plan. Now bed.

Status: *"That's just the trouble with me, I give myself very good advice, but I very seldom follow it."*

Chapter Twenty-eight

Affirmation for the day: *I am in charge of my own destiny.*

Eliza picked up her mobile and called Neville's number.

Neville, cautiously: "Hi Eli. How are today? I take it you made it home ok on public transport."

Deep breath and do it.

Eliza: "Hi, yes apart from puke near my pumps. Neville, I've been thinking. I don't feel we're very, erm, matched. Do you?"

Neville: "In what respect?"

Eliza: "Sort of, every respect."

There was a pause.

Neville: "You do have a point. I was hoping for a girlfriend who could ski."

Hahaha! That was unexpected.

Eliza: "Oh? Why's that then?"

Neville: "Emily left her ski stuff when she dumped me and I'm loathed to sell it on eBay. The posting and packaging would be extortionate. She's got salopettes and a snowboard. I wouldn't know how to start packaging up one of those. I was hoping I could find a girlfriend to make use of it."

Eliza: "Maybe do it 'buyer collects'?"

Neville: "I never thought of that! Oh Eli, you're quite bright underneath it all."

Such a giver of the backhanded compliments.

Eliza: "Thanks."

Neville: "Can we still be friends? You are jolly gorgeous even though you're bonkers."

Eliza: "Of course."

I'm not lying. We can be friends; just ones that never interact again.

Neville: "Take care, Eli."

Eliza: "And you."

Goodbye.

It would never have worked.

I only know the first two lines of Edelweiss.

Eliza hung up and exhaled. One down... How many more before I meet my own Mighty Sword?

The phone rang the instant Eliza disconnected the call.

Eliza: "Hello?"

Lydia: "Hello. How are you this morning? I feel shocking! My innards are playing havoc after last night. I'll have to have a word with Brian about it."

Eliza: "Hi, I'm alright. I think it's because your body isn't used to food."

Lydia: "You may have a point there. It's the village fête in a couple of Sunday's time. Are you going?"

Eliza: "That's come around fast. It was quite good last year, wasn't it? I was rubbish at throwing a welly up a drainpipe, though. I'll not attempt that again."

Lydia: "I'll take Jude. Freya's at Roy's. She likes it there now and asks to go every weekend. It's since *she's* been there. Anyway, Mrs Taylor told me they've got a "Whack the Beaver" stall this year. I simply must have a bash at a beaver!"

Indeed. An opportunity not to be missed.

Everyone should have a bash at a beaver at some point in their life.

It should be on a pre-determined bucket list.

Ohh Jude... Jude... The lovely Jude.

Eliza: "Oh? Jude's coming?"

I did nonchalant very well then. Well done me.

Just saying his name makes me feel a bit faint.

Lydia: "He's working away but he said he'll try and make it back. Training or something."

Eliza: "Tom and I will go."

Lydia: "What about the Caped Avenger or is he playing with his dolls?"

Eliza: "No, I've got rid."

Lydia: "Oh when? Jude said you didn't seem very well suited."

Did he? Jude had an opinion towards me.

Eliza: "Well, Jude was right. I rang him this morning. He didn't mind because I can't ski."

Lydia: "What?! He should have put that in his dating profile then. 'Need a girl who can slalom'. Anyway, he's definitely not good enough for you. Find yourself one that doesn't wear head to toe crimson and who doesn't lick his plate."

Eliza: "The crimson wasn't his fault to be fair but I do agree he's got a few too many foibles for me to cope with. The licking of the plate was completely uncalled for. I don't care how tasty a meal is. In public, you don't shove your face in it. No manners in Manners. Brian and Clive were appalled and rightly so."

Broach the party.

Eliza: "I've got to sort out Tom's party. Invites and all sorts. I've decided to go for a Star Wars theme. Will you nip to the shops with me to get all the stuff?"

Lydia: "Yes, of course. No problem. You're not inviting Lewis, are you?"

Eliza: "Yes. He's trying a bit harder now."

Lydia: "No he's not. He's just offered you his car."

Eliza: "Yes well, whatever. I must go. I can see Norris trying to catch a mouse."

Lydia: "No problem. Catch you later, darling."

Eliza hung up and from her vantage point in the kitchen could see Norris batting a terrified mouse around, nonchalantly. Eliza ran out of the back door.

Eliza: "Oi Norris! Leave it will you?!"

Norris looked up and ran over to her with his tail up, quivering. Eliza picked him up and cradled him like a baby and he purred loudly.

The mouse lay prone for a few seconds, then realising imminent danger had ceased, scuttled off towards the hedge.

Eliza looked up towards the garden to find Philip knee deep in a hole in her vegetable patch.

What now?!

Philip, hearing her presence, looked up. He wiped his brow and waved at her. She walked along the winding garden path up to him.

Philip: "Ahoy there, Eliza dear! Don't worry, I've steered clear of your spuds, but I have to be honest, I haven't come across any yet. Have you planted them really far down?"

Eliza: "Yes, six feet."

Philip: "Crikey! I don't think it says that on the packet. Anyway, I've found a bit o' treasure me ole hearty!"

I don't think a village cottage vegetable patch could be misconstrued as the mighty seas but he's happy so indulge.

Eliza: "Oooarr, What you be 'aving there then, my old luvver?"

Philip: "I don't believe that's a pirate's voice, dear Eliza. I think you'll find that's more West Country."

Ok, don't indulge. Just ask.

Eliza: "What have you found in *my* vegetable patch then?"

Philip: "A bit of a metal. Look at that!"

Philip held, triumphantly aloft, a muddy, twisted rusty bit of metal.

Philip: "There could be more. It looks like part of a fork."

Be still my beating heart.

Eliza: "Indeed. Maybe a whole canteen of cutlery."

Eliza left Philip to his digging and went back, with a cradled Norris, indoors.

She checked on Tom who, dressed in a skeleton costume with a sombrero on top of his head, was peacefully playing with his stickle bricks in the lounge.

Eliza: "Hello darling. Who are you? An underweight Mexican?"

Tom: "I'm a scary skellington. Whoarhhhh! Mummy, when I hit stickybrick on face, it hurt."

Eliza lifted his sombrero to find his forehead covered in a square of minute red dots.

Eliza: "Can I suggest you don't do that again, love? You'll end up looking like a colander."

Tom: "What's a colander?"

Eliza: "It drains your lettuce."

Tom: "I don't like letters. I not do that again."

Eliza: "Good lad. Are you happy there building things with Cheddar Chicken? I'm just going to do some important work on the computer."

Tom: "Yes mummy, we happy. I going to be Bob the builder when I grow up. Kiss head before you go, please."

Eliza kissed the imprinted dots on Tom's forehead, replaced the sombrero and wandered into the dining room towards her computer and flicked it on.

She went onto her blog:

As you have probably noticed, I've not been on much lately. This is due to the fact Jesus found me via Google.

As you can imagine, this alarmed me rather, so I've decided to stick to less frequent, personal and rambling monologues from now on. To be fair, I feel considerably more chipper these days. Still mental but it's one I can cope with. I've adjusted to my mind imbalance, I think. It's become part of my personality. I've stopped trying to like everyone. I find it too much like hard work. It's quite the revelation to start to understand yourself and realise what you can and can't put up with.

I must tell you. I had a complete epiphany last night. I thought I was having a stroke but it turns out I just had Eros thwack me with his arrow. It's a bit of a bugger actually, due to current circumstances, I can't have him. I am going to have a chat with the karma fairy about it but, in the meantime, I mustn't let this throw me off track so I'm going to try and find me a man that is available. Maybe, he has a twin. No... I think he is probably a one off.

She posted the blog and sat there, pondering for a moment.

I wonder what sort of pot mum's kundalini is making.

I'm actually interested. Oh! When did this shift happen? Mum will be so pleased; I'm nearly a fully-fledged new ager. I've emerged from the ashes of being a world hater to a tree hugger.

I'll be taking in homeless hedgehogs next and building them their own runs. That actually sounds very noble. I'll ask mum how many karmic points that would gain me.

She penned a quick email to her mother for when she returned from her pot making course and flicked off the computer.

Right, I can't sit here all day; I have a Mexican skeletal child to attend to.

Eliza went back into the lounge and a flyer dropped through the letter box.

She read the notice:

Pilkington on the Moors Annual Show
25th August
The Cake Competition!

To commemorate the 370-year anniversary of the Battle of Pilkington, when three quarters of the village perished, we will be holding a cake competition where you are all invited to bake your best cake for sale during the show *

All cake contributions to be presented to Mrs Hestington-Charles' front lawn (No 48, next to the Post Office) on the eve of the show.

ALSO!!

On display, during the show, will be re-enactments of the battle staged by the Pilkington Re-enactment and Theatrical Society (PRATS) who we are delighted to announce will bring their own pikes.

AND!!

For the first time ever, we will have a mortar display!

This has kindly been built by Mr Regis and we'd like to thank him for his efforts. We'd also like to thank the community for their understanding regarding the damage caused by some of the trial runs.

On behalf of the Pilkington on the Moors Show organisers we look forward to seeing you there!

*All cake proceeds will go to the Mortar Compensation Fund

Yes, because everyone celebrates the wanton death of innocents with a slice of cake.

'On the anniversary of your husband being blown up by a roadside bomb, I have made you a tiramisu. Enjoy.'

Eliza: "Tom, do you want us to make a cake for this year's village show to mark the Battle of Pilkington?"

Tom looked up from his stickle bricks and lifted his sombrero to look at Eliza.

Tom: "Can we eat it?"

Eliza: "No. We have to leave it outside Mrs Hestington-Charles's house."

Tom: "Why? Fox eat it if we do that. I not make choccy cake for fox to eat."

Eliza: "What if we make a cake that foxes don't like? We ought to make the effort, Tom, what with mummy having a shop in the village. Anyway, I'll put it in a tin."

Tom: "Ok. Make two. We keep one."

Tom pulled down his sombrero and continued playing whilst Eliza looked at the leaflet again.

I wondered how that hole occurred in the boathouse verandah.

Never in a million years would I have said it was a mortar bomb.

Status: *"I love the smell of napalm in the morning."*

Chapter Twenty-nine

Affirmation for the day: *I am non-judgemental.*

The phone rang and Eliza put down her paintbrush. She saw Lydia's number flash up.

Eliza: "Hi Lydia. Have you managed to get your end away yet with The Mighty Sword?"

Lydia's phone: "Er, hello Eliza."

Shit! That's not Lydia!!

Eliza: "Jude?! Is that you?"

Lydia's phone: "Yes."

What's he doing calling me on her phone?

What did I just greet him with? Oh, bugger.

I must just say 'hello' in future.

Hang on, he sounds a bit upset.

Eliza: "Is everything ok? Why are you calling me on her phone?"

Lydia's phone: "She's otherwise detained. I'm calling to tell you she needs some, er, assistance."

Eliza: "Assistance? In what way? Is she injured? Why can't you help her?"

Lydia's phone: "I'm calling you, so you can go and sort her out."

Eliza: "Sort her out? What?! Where is she?"

Lydia's phone: "She's upstairs in her bedroom. You can't miss her, she's the one shackled to the bed. Have you got a house key or shall I leave the front door on the latch?"

Eliza: "Shackled?! Did you do that?! I'm appalled at you!"

Well, I'll be buggered.

I never had him down as a bondage freak.

Lydia's phone: "No, I found her like it. I evidently surprised her when I turned up, unannounced. I have no wish to hang around if it's all the same, Eliza. I just felt it right to get help for her."

I've just accused him. I'm a stupid cow!

Eliza: "Right, of course. Sorry. Thank you for telling me. I'll go and rescue her; I have a key."

What's the silly bint gone and done now??

How could she upset The Mighty Sword?

She must be deranged.

Loopier than me, and that's quite something.

Lydia's phone: "Ok, thanks Eliza. Sorry to disturb you."

He's well-mannered even though he's just found his girlfriend in flagrante delicto.

Eliza: "No problem. Oh, Jude, I'm sorry."

Lydia's phone: "It's not your fault."

There was a pause.

Lydia's phone: "You seem very different, you and her."

To blinkin' right we are.

She doesn't appreciate a good man when she sees one for a start.

Eliza: "We are."

There was another pause.

What are you thinking?

Are you going to ask me out instead?

Please!

Lydia's phone: "It was good to meet you, Eli."

He used my name shortened.

My heart just skipped a beat.

Eliza: "Yes, and you Jude."

There was another pause.

What are you thinking?

Lydia's phone: "Goodbye Eli."

That's very final - goodbye.

That's that then.

Eliza: "Bye Jude."

The line went dead and Eliza stared at it for a moment and sighed. She then went in search of her keys.

She found them ten minutes later underneath Tom's giant Mr Tickle toy. She was grateful that he was at nursery. This was the last thing she needed him to see.

She jumped in the car and shot down the road to Lydia's house.

She banged on the front door and let herself in.

Eliza, hollering: "Lydia?!! It's me! Are you upstairs?"

Of course, she's upstairs.

She's not bleedin' Houdini.

She heard a muffled shout and ran two steps at a time to Lydia's room.

She swung open Lydia's bedroom door and was greeted by a stark-naked Lydia handcuffed by her arms and legs to the bed, she had one of her G strings in her mouth.

Eliza: "Fuck, I mean flip-flop, me! Have you been burgled?! What's gone on?!"

Lydia mumbled something.

Eliza: "Eh?"

Take the pants out of her mouth, Eliza.

Eliza: "Sorry, I'll remove your pants."

Eliza leant over the bed and gingerly pulled the green, lace G string out of Lydia's mouth.

Lydia spluttered.

Lydia: "Oh darling!! Thank god you're here! It was Clarke!"

Eliza: "Clarke? Tiger token Clarke? Has he done something to you?"

Other than the whole stripped naked and cuffed to the bed thing.

Eliza: "I'll bloody kill him!!"

Lydia: "I'm not injured in any way. It was consensual. I just had no idea Jude was going to turn up. Clarke even opened the effing door to him."

Eliza: "I need to know what's kicked off. Jude called me from your mobile."

Lydia: "Ah, that's thoughtful. He is a lovely man. Would you mind terribly, darling, unlatching me, I can't really hold a conversation with the wind billowing up my fanny."

Eliza: "Oh, of course, sorry. Where's the keys?"

Lydia: "On the chest of drawers, by the window."

Eliza got the keys and attempted to unlock the handcuffs without, at any time, looking at a stark-naked Lydia.

I could never be a lesbian.

I feel quite uncomfortable in such close proximity to a naked woman.

When Lydia was unlatched, she did a massive cat like stretch and massaged her wrists and ankles.

She got up and wrapped her dressing gown around herself.

Lydia: "A cup of tea is in order, I think, don't you?"

How frightfully British.

Eliza: "Too bloody right. Where's Clarke?"

They went downstairs together and Lydia put the kettle on.

Lydia: "He scarpered when Jude came thundering up the stairs. He shoved his kecks on and left. He didn't even have the courtesy to say goodbye, the coward. He opened the door to Jude with a stonking great riser which didn't help matters."

Eliza: "Poor Jude. What on earth were you playing at?"

Lydia: "I need to get my oats somehow, darling. It's all very well him being polite and charming but I need my sex. If he's not going to give it to me, I need it from someone else. He's far too gallant. Clarke's very saucy. He understands my needs."

Eliza: "Jude probably wanted to get to know you and have a proper relationship"

Wait a moment. What day is it?

Eliza: "Hang on. Why aren't you in the shop? You're meant to be in there today."

Lydia flushed slightly.

Lydia: "Mr Hicks wanted to make some petit pains so I let him be in charge."

Eliza: "Lydia! You hardly ever do anything these days to do with the business. I'm doing all the renovations and you're busy having deviant sex with a pump attendant instead of marketing the business and manning the shop."

Lydia: "I'll try harder, darling. I promise. I'm not used to work, that's all."

Eliza: "You must. Mr Hicks has taken to tumble drying all his pants instead of putting them out on the washing line by way of recompense for the amount of time you put him in the shop."

Lydia: "Ok ok, I'll do at least four days a week. Promise. Biscuit?"

Lydia offered her the biscuit tin and Eliza took two.

Eliza: "What are you going to do about Jude and Clarke? I had no idea you were knocking him off on the side."

Lydia: "I knew you wouldn't approve. You're quite moral, so I didn't tell you. Anyway, having Clarke made me less desperate towards Jude. It's good to have back up, you should think about it."

Eliza: "How about I find one decent one? I like him, he likes me. End of?"

Lydia: "It's not that simple, sweetheart. If it was, none of us would be divorced."

Eliza: "I think you've blown it with Jude. He seemed very upset."

Can I have him? I'll look after him.

Lydia: "I'll have a word with him. We never said we were exclusive."

Eliza: "What the hell does that mean? Do you have to spell out the boundaries of your relationship so you both know the score?"

Lydia: "Yes darling, you do. Until you actually have a conversation about such things, anything goes."

I was not aware of this.

Eliza: "What if you catch something?"

Lydia: "God, I've seen the state of Clarke's soft furnishings, I make him wear a condom. It's quite likely he's got something. Shocking taste in furniture being one of them. Half of his stuff looks like it's been fished out of a skip."

Eliza: "So you're going to stick with him then?"

Lydia: "He's very thick, but I quite like that. It gives me the upper hand. I do like Jude a lot though, he's more boyfriend material."

Eliza: "He deserves better."

Lydia: "He's a man Eli. He's nice but still a man and as such, prone to bouts of complete stupidity and profoundly irritating behaviour. All men end up at the same point eventually, no matter what place they start from."

Eliza: "You don't like men very much, do you?"

Lydia: "I blame Roy."

Eliza: "I blame Roy too."

Eliza sighed.

Eliza: "Right, I need to go now I've ascertained you've not been raped and pillaged in broad daylight. I need to finish that cupboard for Mrs Fallows at number twenty-two."

Lydia: "Eli. Thank you. I feel a bit foolish to be honest. I think I might try and spend a bit less time on sex and a bit more time on work. I'm sorry."

Eliza: "Good. Can you go and relieve Mr Hicks from duty?"

Lydia: "I'll whip some clothes on and head down there."

Lydia went to go back upstairs.

Lydia: "Clarke's into them, too."

Eliza: "What?"

Lydia: "Whips. He's frightfully M and S."

Eliza: "S and M. I don't think Marks and Spencer's sell gimp masks."

Lydia: "They ought to. Their takings would shoot up."

Eliza went towards the front door and turned to Lydia.

Eliza: "I hope you sort things out with Jude."

Lydia: "I'll call him later, when he's cooled down a bit."

Eliza got back into her car and tutted.

I'd lay money on that being the last time we ever see him.

Thank you pain in the arse fairy.

You literally wave my ideal man in front of my face and now you say "That's your lot. One glimpse. Now go and try and find one similar."

I've never had a thunder bolt before. Not even with Lewis. That was more of a slow burn.

I overlooked his preoccupation with instructions and rules as I loved him.

Jude was something else.

An instant 'kerpow' moment.

If nothing else, I suppose when I'm a bitter and twisted old hag in the old people's home, I can tell my carer that in the intervening period between melting my innards with a sushi condiment and lunacy, I had what I thought was the onset of a stroke but was actually love at first sight.

I can tell the carer that it does happen in real life and it's not just the stuff of romantic novels and Hollywood films.

They'll just up my pills, but I'll know the truth.

To think, I was happy to remain married oblivious to the fact this could even happen.

How does that make me feel? Better or worse?

I suppose I'm living now. Experiencing all life has to offer. With Lewis, I would have remained in my neat little house, bringing up Tom, reading instruction manuals and cooking chicken and chips on a Thursday.

I wouldn't have my business.

I wouldn't be able to sit about in my pants all day on a Sunday eating cake and drinking tea.

I wouldn't be able to hang pictures in random places.

I wouldn't be able to meet the man of my dreams.

Oh.

There was a banging on Eliza's car window. It was Lydia. Eliza wound down the passenger side.

Lydia: "You still there darling? Won't it start? Maybe, you ought to get the new one from knob chops sooner rather than later."

Eliza: "No, I was just thinking. I got a bit distracted."

Lydia: "You do that. You live in a world of your own half of the time. I blame the hippy books. But, whilst you're still there, can you drop me down to the shop, please?"

Eliza: "Of course, hop in. Nice to see you with your clothes on."

Lydia jumped into the passenger seat and fastened her seatbelt.

Lydia: "I'm sorry about that. Did I look alluring like that? Clarke says I'm the best he's ever seen."

Eliza: "I don't think being butt naked, emulating a manacled starfish with a pair of pants in your chops, can be called alluring, Lydia."

Lydia: "I don't like being on top. I can't do it in case when I look down at him, all the folds on my face age me another ten years. I've looked down at a mirror, I know what happens. I look like a Shar Pei, darling. I need to angle myself in such a way I look like a nubile teenager with no excess saggage, whatsoever."

Eliza: "Why don't you find a man who's happy with you the way you are?"

Lydia: "You're so adorably old school, Eli. Do you know how many single women our age are out there now? It's worse than when we were in our twenties because we've developed droopy bits and bad habits. Look at me - I can't leave the house without unplugging all my electric goods and turning the lounge light on and off three times for fear of an electrical fire reducing the house to a cinder. That never happened to me in my twenties. I'd cheerfully go on holiday to Spain with the television left on standby without a care in the world. The older we get, the weirder ways we adopt."

Eliza: "We're here."

Eliza had pulled up outside their shop. The little hand painted sign "Illusions of Grandeur Crafts – Open" swayed in the breeze.

Eliza: "I'll come in with you, say hello to Mr Hicks."

They both got out and the bell rang out as they entered the shop. There was no one in evidence.

Lydia: "Mr Hicks! It's us! Yoo hoo!"

Nothing.

They both shouted out but received no response.

Eliza: "Brilliant. Eight thousand pounds worth of unattended stock."

Lydia: "He must be in the kitchen. He must be kneading some dough."

They went through to the back of the shop and both stopped in their tracks.

Lydia: "Jeezus Mother of Mercy! Cover your eyes, Eliza! You're too pure to witness this!"

Eliza stood rooted to the spot.

That's not kneading dough!

Flipping Flip-flops! That's Mrs Hestington-Charles' naked arse!!

What on earth is she doing on her knees like that? With her head in Mr Hicks's crotch.

Oh, dear Lord! Bleugh!

Near the bread ovens too!

Lydia: "Well looky here! Good afternoon, Mrs Hestington-Charles. Lovely day for it."

Mrs Hestington-Charles yanked her head away from Mr Hicks's nether regions.

Urgh. Really?!

I'm appalled at you Mrs Hestington-Charles.

Am I the only one not indulging in sexual activities on a Wednesday afternoon?

It's like a club I didn't know existed.

Mr Hicks zipped up his flies and let out a yelp as he caught his foreskin in the zip.

Mrs Hestington-Charles grabbed her cashmere cardigan and scrambled to her feet. She was naked except for her pearls and pop socks. She hastily attempted to cover her almost naked body.

Lydia: "Nice pearl necklace you've got there."

Ok, Lydia is enjoying this too much.

I need to step in.

Eliza, haughtily: "Good afternoon. We're very sorry to interrupt such passion but I think perhaps there's a time and a place for such activities and our shop is not it. Especially during opening hours."

How frightfully pious.

Well done me.

Mr Hicks found his voice, about an octave higher than his usual, but found it all the same.

Mr Hicks: "I'm so dreadfully sorry, Eliza. Bunty and I are very sorry, aren't we?"

Mrs Hestington-Charles looked adoringly at Mr Hicks and nodded.

Bunty Hestington-Charles: "Yes Big Bear, we are."

Lydia, muttering: "Big Bear? Shit me."

Eliza shook her head and sighed.

Mrs Hestington-Charles gathered herself slightly and addressed Eliza and Lydia.

Mrs Hestington-Charles: "I wonder if you'd mind terribly if we just kept this between these four walls, only relations at home have been strained recently, since Sebastian's management buy-out failed."

Poor Sebastian, him of the ever-present blazer with elbow patches. First business problems and now his wife's having it off with a dishevelled ex-baker.

Lydia: "It'll cost you."

You what?!

Eliza: "Lydia!! Be quiet!"

Mrs Hestington-Charles: "How much?"

She looked Lydia square in the eye.

Lydia: "The big Welsh dresser we painted in country cream."

Mrs Hestington-Charles: "How much?"

Mr Hicks and Eliza looked on at the exchange with their mouths slack.

Lydia: "Fifteen hundred."

Eliza: "Lydia!! Stroll on! It's only up for eight fifty!"

Lydia and a near naked Mrs Hestington-Charles were still squaring up to each other.

Mrs Hestington-Charles: "If I buy the dresser for fifteen hundred pounds, do you promise this will go no further?"

She waved her hand at Mr Hicks.

Mr Hicks, Lydia and Mrs Hestington-Charles all stared at Eliza.

She shrugged.

Eliza: "I wasn't going to say anything anyway. I'm a bit speechless to be honest and who would I tell? I don't think it's the sort of conversation to be having with Tom over his spaghetti on toast. By the way Tom, you'll never guess who I saw giving Mr Hicks a blow job in the shop today..."

Lydia turned her attentions back to Mrs Hestington-Charles.

Lydia: "We promise. Fifteen hundred and you get your own man to collect the dresser this week."

Mrs Hestington-Charles: "Done."

Lydia: "Done."

Mrs Hestington-Charles: "For the record Lydia, I don't find you to be a very pleasant person."

Lydia: "Careful Bunty or you'll be buying a chest of drawers an' all."

Mrs Hestington-Charles: "But you do have nice taste in clothes."

Lydia: "That's better."

I've witnessed quite enough human discomfort for one day, thank you.

Eliza: "Come on Lydia, let's allow Mrs Hestington-Charles to get dressed and Mr Hicks remove his purple foreskin from his flies."

Lydia: "Ohhh, alright."

Eliza guided Lydia out of the kitchen and into the main shop.

Lydia, hissing: "I was enjoying that."

Eliza: "I noticed."

Lydia: "Flogged that dresser, which is good news, and I didn't even have to stand behind the counter!"

Eliza: "Genius indeed. We could just blackmail the entire village to buy our stock."

Lydia: "Stop being all worthy. They shouldn't have been doing that in our shop and, as you said, eight thousand pounds worth of stock was sitting there unattended."

Fair point.

Eliza: "You have to be in the shop, that's all there is to it, Lydia; he can't be trusted. Lord only knows what shenanigans have been going on whilst he's been on watch. And all the while, we've been paying his bills for the pleasure of his pleasuring."

Lydia: "Oh alright, if I have to. I'll get myself a laptop and surf the web all day."

Eliza: "Why would she do it? With Mr Hicks, I mean."

Lydia: "Probably the same reason I do it. I'm hoping it'll be good for my complexion."

Eliza: "Not oral sex, you stupid tart. I mean why would she go with him? They've always looked very happy together, her and Sebastian. Anyway, I must get back. I need to finish that cupboard. Stay there until five and do not, under any circumstances, blackmail Mrs Hestington-Charles into buying any more stock. Promise me?"

Lydia: "Cross my heart. darling."

Lydia swiped her hands over her chest.

Eliza: "Good. Ok then, I'll speak to you later."

Lydia: "Laters taters."

Lydia muttered under her breath as Eliza walked out of the shop.

Lydia: "Nothing promised about holding Mr Hicks to ransom though."

Eliza, shouting over her shoulder: "I heard that!!"

Lydia: "Crap."

Status: *"You seem somewhat familiar. Have I threatened you before?"*

Chapter Thirty

Affirmation for the day: *I attract friendship, love and romance to my life.*

Eliza logged on to multitudeofmates.com.

I've not been on for a week or so, I wonder if I've got any messages.

Blimey, I've got loads!

She clicked on the top one – a message from SILVERFOX1968.

SILVERFOX1968: Hey sexy. You look and sound fun. Please read my profile and let's chat. #coolbananas

A grown man using a hashtag cool bananas. Hmm.

Let's look at your profile then, Silver Fox.

Eliza clicked on and noticed seven selfies, all with exactly the same pose.

One would have sufficed really; all that's different is your shirt.

Profession: Sales.

Hobbies: house renovation, the arts, hed kandi, red wine, walking on the beach, sitting by a fire.

Hed kandi? What the flip-flop is that?

Eliza Googled it.

He's thrown that in just to be hip.

A man in his forties, trying to be street by using hashtag cool bananas and says he's into hed kandi.

Can't be doing with that.

Next!

Eliza clicked on the next message. This one was from LARRYLAMM.

LARRYLAMM: Hi. I laffed out loud when I red your profile. Your dead funny and cute. Please meet me. Lots of Love Gavin xxx

Bit over familiar with the old kisses there, Gavin.

You really ought to spell check your messages before sending them out.

You've a nice face which is a bit unfortunate as I'll have to have a closer look now.

Let's see what you do.

Eliza clicked on his profile.

Profession: Plummer.

Absolutely not.

Bradley Cooper doppelganger he may be, but under no circumstances can I date a man who can't spell his own profession.

Next!

Eliza clicked on the next one.

This message was from BIKERDAVE76.

She ignored his message and clicked straight onto his profile.

No point even reading what he has to say if I don't like the look of him. Cut out a bit of the legwork.

BIKERDAVE76 had three profile pictures.

In the first one, it was a body shot of him, holding a pint of lager in his England football shirt. Picture two was of a Rottweiler with the heading "Our Kylie" and the third was a close up of a dragon tattoo on a bicep.

Erm...

Out of curiosity she glanced at his hobbies. These read, football, pool, beer, Jackie Chan films and opera.

She re-read it.

Opera? That's a bit left field. I wonder what Our Kylie makes of that.

Next!

JUSTSTEVE19 was up next.

Ooh, he loves himself a bit.

She clicked straight onto his profile.

I am maverick and a free thinker. I am funny and, in case you hadn't noticed, good looking. Any woman who has a problem with her size, face or any other attributes need not contact me.

If I don't reply, it means you're not my type so don't keep messaging me, ok?

Such arrogance for a man who is five feet three inches tall.

Next!

DAFFYDUCK90 was next.

Suffering Suckertash. You're a bit of a looker.

She looked at his profile.

Profession: Yes, I have one.

Hobbies: Walking, films, eating out and socialising, music and Campervans.

Thanks for getting this far. I'm a grounded guy who finds humour in (just about) anything.

I like the usual - cinema, going out for meals etc. and enjoy experiencing new things and I'd like to undertake that journey with a like-minded soul.

I'll not waffle on, but if you'd like a guy who is happy in his own skin and looking for some relaxed fun times, please message me.

Thanks.

That all sounds relatively normal.

Eliza peered at his photos. There were two.

One with him waving at the summit of a snow topped mountain.

Distant shot but shows he can walk up hill.

Was that a subconscious prerequisite?

What a stupid thing to think.

Well, one has to take what one can from such bare bones of a person.

Stop talking to yourself and look at his face, Eli.

She looked at the main profile picture closely.

He had slightly unruly brown hair. He looked like he'd just taken a hat off and he was evidently outside. He was beaming happily and had smatterings of freckles over the bridge of his nose. His eyes were a deep brown and Eliza realised she was staring into them.

Nope. Nothing. I don't feel anything other than, he looks lovely.

Yup, he's not Jude but on paper he looks very nice indeed.

I've been ruined.

Had I seen Daffy Duck before Jude I'd have been jubilant at him contacting me.

That's just rubbish that is.

Let's face it, Jude was an instant infatuation.

Do I want to live the rest of my life hankering after a man I have no chance of being with, nay probably seeing again thanks to Lydia and her nymphomaniacal streak?

Forget about him.

Find a man I can have.

I'm evidently the only person in Pilkington on the Moors who's not having any form of sexual relationship. I need to equip myself with a man to enable such activities. It's been years since I had sex. That can't be healthy for a woman in her thirties.

In fact, it may well be illegal.

It comes to something when Mrs Hestington-Charles has two on the go and I've got no one. She wears twin sets and pearls for goodness' sake.

And she drives a Micra.

Look at his message.

Eliza clicked on his message:

DAFFYDUCK90: Hi, potential owner of legions of felines.

How are you finding things on this site? How do the pigeons feel about the level of calibre you've come into contact with? I would be greatly interested to learn more about your "tat" and discuss such matters whilst hugging a tree and doing crystal healing on each other.

Please write back. I'm allergic to cats so am hopeful I can save you.

H (as in Henry, not the bloke from Steps).

PS. Please note correct use of apostrophes.

Oooh. He sounds great!

He's obviously read my profile.

He also uses the word calibre.

He's allergic to cats though, Norris would have to remain outside when he comes over.

Have a word with yourself. I've not even met the guy and I've already put Norris in the shed.

Why don't I just hum the wedding tune whilst I'm at it? Dum Dum de Dum.

Eliza instinctively picked up a passing Norris and cradled him. He started purring profusely and kneading her jumper.

Eliza: "I'll not put you in the shed, you're ok, Norris. I'll just pretend to H, not from Steps, you're a stray and I haven't the heart to keep kicking you out. Look at him, what d'ya reckon?"

She held Norris up and pointed his face towards the screen.

Norris carried on purring, waving his paws around in the air, trying to find something to knead.

She put Norris down and brushed the fur off her top.

Eliza to a departing Norris: "I'll reply to him then, what do you reckon?"

Norris meowed on his way out of the back door.

Eliza: "The cat, he say yes."

Eliza clicked on the reply tab.

SHAKESPEARESISTER1: Hi, shame you're not H not from Steps.

Thank you for your message. I can confirm the pigeon and I have been dismayed at the calibre of chaps who have made their presence known.

You seem quite the best of a dubious bunch so I replied with haste.

I note you like walking up mountains. I trust you don't have the prerequisite for a woman to assist you to ski down aforementioned mountains, only I have dodgy knees and can't carry off a bobble hat very well. I do, however, know someone who is selling a snowboard if you're interested.

I would happily discuss my "tat" whilst chanting under a full moon. I would like to hear about your work as you don't mention it in your profile. What do you do?

I look forward to hearing from you.

Yours, and the pigeon, in anticipation, E (as in Eliza, not as in the class A drug).

PS If we meet, please leave your ski jacket and rucksack at home.

She pressed send and went out to put the kettle on. She stared out of the window whilst she waited for it to boil.

Right then, I need to sort out this birthday party for Tom.

Star Wars invites. Hmm, need them you will.

When I pick Tom up from nursery later, I'll ask the woman for the names of other children in his group.

I'll hand them out next week when I drop him off.

I'm so efficient, when I put my mind to it.

It's very nice to see. A level of ongoing clarity.

I bet the ether is very relieved.

We never thought it would show its head again, did we?

Anyway, party.

Party bags can be Star Wars themed. I don't fancy I can fit a lightsaber in each one though.

We could play Pin the Cape on Darth Vader and Pass the Jedi.

I'll call Lydia, see if she fancies coming shopping with me.

She hit Lydia's number who picked it up on the second ring.

Eliza: "That was quick, hello."

Lydia, dispiritedly: "Oh, it's you. Hello."

Eliza: "Charming."

Lydia: "Sorry darling, I was hoping it was Jude. He's not returning my calls."

Eliza: "You sound surprised, Lydia."

Lydia: "Well, I do suppose it must have been a bit of a shock for him. Clarke hasn't returned my calls either, the shit. So, from having two, I appear to now have none."

Eliza: "Well you will play with fire."

Lydia: "Yes, I know. I think I'll find myself another one. I've been back on multitudeofmates and had a scout around."

Eliza: "Blimey, you don't waste much time, do you?"

Lydia: "I told you before, I have my needs and I'm not made to be on my own. I'm not self-sufficient like you. I need a man on my arm to validate my whole being. Sad but true."

Eliza: "So, have you found anyone who takes your fancy?"

Lydia: "Well, perhaps. Do you think I could do deep, darling? Ugly face but marvellous personality?"

Eliza: "I shouldn't think so for one minute."

Lydia: "Do I really come across as that shallow? I might try out this one then, just to see if I can. It would be good for my personal development. It might make me a more rounded person. Plus, he's completely bowled over by me. If there's a pedestal spare, it's got my name on it."

Eliza: "Good luck with that. Anyway, the purpose of my call. Are you free later to get some stuff for Tom's birthday party? We could nip into Dave's for a bit of something to eat, afterwards."

Lydia: "I'd love to but, thanks to your new regime, I have to work in the shop. I have some good news, though. Mr Hicks has bought that wardrobe we did up the other month but had trouble shifting."

Eliza: "Lydia!! I can't believe you've blackmailed him! You and I both know he wouldn't be able to get it up the stairs! Plus, he's perfectly happy hanging his clothes off the curtain pole."

Lydia: "Whatevs. The coffers this month are looking remarkably good! We should catch people shagging more often. We'd be able to open a franchise."

Eliza sighed.

Eliza: "It's the village show next Sunday, are you making a cake?"

Lydia: "I'll buy one and take the packaging off it. I can't be bothered with flour and eggs."

Eliza: "Ok, speak to you later. Let me know how it goes with deep man and please don't force poor Mr Hicks to buy anything else."

Lydia: "I've earmarked him the Louis XIV replica chair but after that, I promise I'll stop. Catch you later, darling. Ciao."

Status: *"Greed, for lack of a better word, is good."*

Chapter Thirty-one

Sub Affirmation for the day: *My financial situation is improving day by day.*

Eliza threw on her sweatshirt, picked up her hastily made party list and went into the supermarket in town. Upon her return, she sat down and checked her multitudeofmates.com messages.

DAFFYDUCK90: Hi E, I'm relieved to hear not as in the Class A drug.

I've never been called the best of a dubious bunch before. Thank you, I'm most flattered.

I note on your profile you have children, I do too. I have a six-year-old girl called Sienna. What do you have?

Looking at your profile, I don't think you live too far from me, I live near the new superstore in Billington. Where do you live? The search says you're less than five miles away.

I work in an auction house. I've been to that new furniture shop in Pilkington on the Moors, that's not yours by any chance, is it? I remember it vividly as I was served by a scruffy fellow, naked, save for a vest and boxer shorts. I bought a recycled commode and when I opened the lid I found a granary loaf in the pan, which was unexpected. Nice touch though. Was that your idea?

I'll cease the twenty questions now.

Yours, still not H from Steps.

Eliza replied.

SHAKESPEARESISTER1: Hi, it's a Tragedy you're not H from Steps.

In response to the white light being shone in my eyes, I reply as follows:

I have a little boy who is nearly four and I do live in the village next to you.

Indeed, I am the proprietor of the bread giving commode shop. You don't get that sort of service everywhere you know. It's a rare thing.

Yours, E as in Exceedingly sorry you were served by a man in his pants.

Eliza put the kettle on and unpacked her Star Wars shopping.

By the time she'd returned and hit refresh he'd replied.

DAFFYDUCK90: Hi, E as in Expanding the meaning of bread on your table.

For fear of looking forward, would you like to chat via our mobiles?

For the record, I haven't offered that before. I'm not a random number giver-outer.

I was wondering, your village has a fête or something coming up, doesn't it? Perhaps Sienna and I could meet up with you and your son there. We went last year and they had some chap tossing a hay bale in the air. All quite odd but fun at the same time.

Let me know.

Yours, H as in Having a bit of a nervous moment.

I like him. Meeting him in a relaxed situation would be a good idea.

I won't have to drink and make a complete arse of myself.

I don't have to get in a car with him.

I don't have to eat with him, thus eliminating any danger of food being spat out on me or me swallowing something whole.

I'll be around friends and children, therefore less likely to have a filthy poem handed to me.

I'll agree and ask for his number.

Eliza typed her reply.

SHAKESPEARESISTER1: Hi, H as in Honestly no need to be nervous.

Yes, I'd like to have your number. I don't really like talking on here all the time.

I think meeting up at the village show would be a lovely idea. They've got a "Whack the Beaver" stall this year so make sure you and Sienna attend. It'll leave you more stunned than the hay flinger.

Yours, E as in Extremely glad to make your virtual acquaintance.

Eliza pressed send and looked at his profile pictures again.

Yep, he seems very nice.

Let's see how this one pans out.

Eliza's mobile rang.

Oh, it's Margaret the shop bookkeeper.

Eliza: "Hi Margaret. How are you?"

Margaret: "Hello Eliza, I'm fine thank you. I've a little query and I wonder if you could help me."

Eliza: "Oh ok, fire away."

Margaret: "Well, I've been doing this month's stock and accounts and there seems to be some deficit between the ratio of stock to purchases."

Huh?

Eliza: "What does that mean in English, Margaret?"

Margaret: "You've been buying stuff that you haven't got."

Eliza: "Eh?"

Margaret: "Last month, money was taken from the business account in cash withdrawals, which I presume was for furniture, yet, I cannot find any receipts of purchase. This is quite concerning as it's becoming a regular thing, Eliza. You need to ensure you keep the receipts for your stock purchases."

Eliza: "I always put in the receipts for any purchase or petty cash I take out."

Margaret: "Yes dear, you do."

Lydia.

Eliza: "Oh. I shall speak to Lydia. How much are we talking here?

Margaret: "Since the business was incorporated, one thousand nine hundred and fifty pounds and forty-five pence."

Shit!

Eliza: "Good god! My, that's very precise!"

Margaret: "Thank you, dear. I've been a bookkeeper for thirty-five years. I'm a stickler for such things. I believe that is why you employ me."

Indeed, Margaret. You of the tweed skirt, twin set and perfectly aligned thimbles in little shelves above your lounge mantelpiece.

Eliza: "Definitely. Oh no! There must be some explanation. I'll speak to Lydia. She's probably got all the receipts in a drawer somewhere at home. She's not very business minded."

Margaret: "This I am aware. Hence the reason why I thought it best to alert you."

Eliza: "Thank you, Margaret. I'll deal with it."

Margaret: "Good girl. I'll leave it with you then. Shall I pay myself last month's invoice?"

Eliza: "Yes of course. Thank you."

Margaret: "Lovely. I'll expect to receive the missing paperwork in due course. Enjoy the rest of your day, dear."

With that the line went dead.

Eliza stood there, in a state of shock with a feeling of dread in her stomach.

Nearly two thousand pounds is unaccounted for.

Lydia, please just have forgotten to hand in the receipts.

Eliza put the kettle on.

What do I do?

Do I go down to the shop and ask her?

No, I can't do it face to face. Looks a bit confrontational.

I'll just text her.

A light-hearted exchange.

Eliza picked up her phone and texted Lydia.

Eliza's text: "Hi, it's only me. Do you have any receipts for furniture stashed somewhere? xx"

Send.

Eliza made her tea and her mobile beeped. Lydia had replied.

Lydia's text: "Hi, when I turned up at the shop, Mr Hicks was making cheese straws. Want me to drop some off on my way home? Receipts? No, don't think so. xx"

Eliza stared at the reply and chewed on her thumb nail. She composed a reply.

Eliza's text: "Are you sure? Only Marg says there's a deficit between the ratio of stock to purchases. xx"

Send.

A reply shot back.

Lydia's text: "What does that mean? xx"

Eliza thought to herself.

How do I word this without looking accusing?

She hit reply and started typing.

Eliza's text: "There seems to be some money gone from the account which we haven't supplied any receipts for or have any stock to show for it. xx"

Send.

She downed her tea and waited. Her phone beeped with a text reply.

Lydia's text: "Oh ok, don't worry, darling, I'll see if I can find anything left about the house. I did buy a picture frame the other week which I might have forgotten to bung the receipt in for. I'll have a look. xx"

Eliza put the phone on the work surface and stared out of the window, absentmindedly watching Philip digging up her vegetable patch.

A picture frame doesn't cost two grand.

Maybe if she has done something, the fact it's in the open might make her come up with the receipts or rectify it.

I feel very uncomfortable about all this.

I'll ring Margaret next week and see if anything's turned up.

Status: *"Show me the money."*

Chapter Thirty-two

Affirmation for the day: *I enjoy cooking and sharing food with others.*

It was the Saturday before the village show.

Eliza: "Tom, pass me the sugar, please."

Tom: "I not Tom, I chef. Call me Chef Tom."

Eliza: "Chef Tom, please pass me the sugar."

Tom: "No. I the Chef. I do it."

Eliza sighed.

Tom was stood in the kitchen, on his little stool wearing his chequered chef's trousers, white shirt and hat.

He was taking the cake baking for the show very seriously indeed.

Tom: "How much sugar, mummy? I can't read yet."

Eliza: "It says three hundred grams. What's that in tablespoons? Oh, I don't have any tablespoons. How many dessert spoons make up a tablespoon, chef?"

Tom: "I don't know mummy, I a child."

Eliza: "Is it two? Dunno. Sounds about right. Here you are, let's count eight spoons of sugar in."

Tom: "Can we get scales mummy, like fish have?"

Eliza: "Fish aren't particularly good cooks, Tom. All the ingredients get wet. I do agree, however, I might need to invest in some form of measuring device. It's all a bit hit and miss, isn't it?"

They carried on haphazardly throwing ingredients into the bowl until it was of a consistency Eliza deemed to be that of brownies.

She put them in the oven and Tom went off to do some drawing whilst they cooked.

Eliza's mobile rang.

Oh, it's Lewis. What does he want?

Eliza: "Hello."

Lewis: "Hi Eli, it's me."

He said it in that familiar tone but I feel nothing.

Good.

I am mended.

I shall have cake to celebrate that landmark occasion.

Eliza: "I know. What can I do for you?"

Lewis: "It is Tom's birthday soon, isn't it?"

Eliza: "How kind of you to remember; it is indeed."

Lewis: "What are we doing for it?"

Eliza: "Well, I am having a Star Wars themed birthday party. What are you doing for it?"

Lewis: "Oh. Erm. I see."

Lewis flustered a bit.

What? Not planned anything?

There's a shock.

Eliza: "Stop sweating. Do you want to come?"

Lewis: "Really? Oh, thank you. We'd love that."

We'd???

Eliza: "Who is this we?"

Lewis: "Gerry and me. She's become very cautious of late, Eli. I'm not sure she's handling pregnancy very well. Not like you at all."

I'm a better pregnant woman. Good.

Eliza: "What's the matter with her?"

Lewis: "She won't go anywhere without me. It's all a bit much, Eli."

A pain in the arse, is she? Shame.

Eliza: "That'll be her hormones. Ah well. Has she bulked up as well?"

Please say she's massive.

Lewis: "She is definitely eating for two. Actually, probably more than two and she's having dreadful trouble with puffy ankles."

Oh, you listened karma fairy! Thank you!

Eliza: "Bummer."

Don't gloat too much. I might have another child at some point and turn into a heifer.

Lewis: "So would it be alright if she came too? I appreciate it would be difficult for you but I wouldn't like to miss out on Tom's birthday party. I've also bought a people carrier so I can sort out my old car for you. I could bring it over and sign over the papers. It's just had an MOT."

Oh, what a predicament.

I would so love the two-seater; my jalopy has had it.

To get it, I have to endure 'Gerry' the pregnant husband stealer in my house.

How do I feel about that?

I want the car.

Forget about the car.

How long do I have to put up with them?

Two hours.

That's doable. I'll put them out in the garden.

Surely, I can handle someone physically and emotionally weak for two hours in return for a sports car?

Would it reflect badly on me? Would it be seen as rather materialistic?

No, it's a reward for a kind gesture.

I'm letting my useless ex-husband go to his son's birthday party with his current oedema ridden clingy partner.

In fact, I'll probably earn karmic forgiveness points. I'll shoot right up the good chi scale.

I might even win the lottery because of this.

Lewis: "Eli? Are you still there? Have I lost the signal?"

Eliza: "Sorry, I was thinking. Yeah, why not? Bring her and the car. Two weeks on Saturday. Midday until two. Don't be early."

Lewis: "Oh brilliant! Thank you, Eli! You really are quite a wonderful woman. I feel very sorry sometimes things didn't work out between us."

Whooooah there. Just because she's eating enough to feed a famine doesn't mean you can try your luck with the mother of your first child.

Eliza: "Ah well. You should have thought about that before running off with someone with straight hair and a black bra."

Lewis: "Pardon? Black bra?"

Eliza: "Doesn't matter."

Tom came wandering into the kitchen.

Tom: "Mummy, I smell something funny."

Eliza: "Bugger! The brownies! I must go Lewis. Speak to you soon."

Lewis: "Goodb...."

Eliza flung the phone on the kitchen worktop and slung on her oven gloves.

Eliza: "Stand back, Tom. Flaming hot brownies alert!"

Tom backed out of the kitchen.

He put his arm out to prevent Ellington running into the kitchen.

Tom, very seriously: "Ewwington. Dangerous. Brownies on fire. Do not enter."

Eliza flung open the door and got caught in a plume of heat.

Eliza: "Jeezus! It's like an oven in there!"

She pulled out the brownies and inspected them.

Tom: "What are they like, mummy?"

Eliza: "They look a bit dodgy around the edges. Let's let them cool off and see how they fair."

She tapped on the top of them and they sounded decidedly hard.

Eliza: "Hmmm."

Tom's bottom lip started to tremble.

Tom: "We have to drop them off to Mrs Hestyton-Charles later. What we gonna do?"

Eliza: "I'll knock up some more, just in case."

Tom: "Chef Tom doesn't want to help. He want to watch Wiggles."

Eliza: "Disrobe then Chef and I'll assume baking duties. I hope the Mortar Compensation Fund is duly impressed with our efforts."

She went and turned the television on, found The Wiggles for Tom before returning to the kitchen.

She saw her phone thrown on the side and stared at it.

I've agreed to let Lewis and Geraldine into my house.

That wasn't very well thought out, actually. I have my parents coming and also Lydia.

Hmmm. What could possibly go wrong?

Don't think about it. Just get on with the next batch of brownies.

Eliza lobbed some more ingredients into the mixing bowl and made another batch of brownies.

This time, she set the timer and halfway through the Wiggles she removed them from the oven.

Ooh, these look a bit more the thing. We'll donate these to the front lawn of Mrs Hestington - I'm knocking two men off - Charles.

Later that evening, Eliza and Tom wandered down to drop off the tin of brownies in Mrs Hestington-Charles's front garden.

When they got there, there were myriad other tins scattered all around the borders. Eliza and Tom chose a spot by a hydrangea to deposit their offering.

Blimey!

I have visions of Mrs Hestington-Charles opening her curtains on Sunday morning to find the sun has been obliterated by a huge pyramid of Quality Street tins.

Status: *"I'll continue to climb to try to reach the top, but no one knows where the top is!"*

Chapter Thirty-three

Affirmation for the day: *I take unexpected developments in my stride.*

It was the day of the village show. Eliza was preparing what had, in recent months, become their usual Sunday breakfast feast; scrambled egg on toast with a rasher of streaky bacon for Tom, two sausages for Ellington and the chopped-up bacon rind from Tom's rasher and a potato waffle for Norris. She was having a bacon and dippy egg sandwich. These days, she had got a bit more with the whole 'eating meals' programme. She confessed she felt all the better for eating a diet which consisted of all the major food groups.

She'd realised it was a chicken and egg situation. When she was down, she felt too depressed to eat but when she did eat, she perked right up. It was almost as if food was a requirement for mental and physical well-being. Astonishing.

As was also usual, all three of them were surrounding Eliza in the kitchen waiting for their food.

Eliza: "Get out from under my feet, Norris! I've got a hot pan."

Eliza stepped over a snaking Norris.

Just then the front door banged.

Ellington let out a surprised woof and stared in the direction of the door whilst resolutely remaining in the kitchen.

Tom: "Mummy, who bang bang at brekkie time?"

Eliza: "A very good question, Tom."

Eliza turned off all the hobs and stepped over them all.

Eliza: "None of you touch anything, ok? All sorts of hospital treatment would be required if you as much as move an inch near those pans. Got it?"

Tom: "Ok, Cheddar Chicken and I come wiv you mummy. We not like hoppy tails, they full of sick people."

Tom and a spatula holding Eliza made their way to the front door when it started banging again.

Eliza: "Blimey, alright, alright! It's half nine on a Sunday!"

Eliza opened the door to be presented with a very red-faced and wide-eyed Lydia.

Eliza: "What the?!"

Lydia: "Hello darling! What a wonderful morning it is! Simply joyous in every regard. I'm just here for my Sunday breakfast. You know, the Sunday breakfast I always have on a Sunday at breakfast time. Here... With you."

Lydia looked imploringly at Eliza.

Eliza: "What the?!"

Lydia continued.

Lydia: "I thought I'd bring my friend. He likes food. You don't mind do you, darling? The more the merrier! Hahaha!"

She laughed hysterically.

Eliza: "What the?!"

Lydia stood aside and behind her stood a heavily eye bagged, big pored, bulbous nosed individual. He was wearing a Panama hat over his thinning grey hair and wore dark blue jeans which didn't meet his black brogues, thus displaying a pair of comedy superman socks in all their glory. Upon his top half, he wore a nylon shirt with a fair isle tank top.

Flipping flip-flops! Who the hell is this?

Upon being presented with the unknown person before them, Tom went and hid behind Eliza's legs and held onto her pyjama trousers.

Tom, warily: "Auntie Wydia, have you gone mad?"

Very succinctly put, Tom.

Lydia blustered in an octave higher than usual.

Lydia: "Haha! So funny you are, Tom. This is Reece, he's coming to the village show with us. Isn't that absolutely wonderful and he turned up extra early, which is simply brilliant!"

Eliza: "Reece?"

Reece moved awkwardly forward and held out his hand and grasped hers in a limp, sweaty grip.

Reece: "Good morning, Shakespeare's Sister One. I am Reece Winksworth, My multitude of mates dot com moniker is Grand Amour Sixty-Nine. I recognise you. I was going to write to you but I don't like blondes."

Be blessed for small mercies.

Lydia: "Oh, Eli dyes her hair, it's not natural."

Eliza looked bemused at Lydia.

Is there really any need?

Reece looked at Lydia and scrunched up his bulbous nose.

Reece: "She should leave it natural then."

What is this interaction I'm witnessing?

Who is this oddball?

What on earth is Lydia and Rancid Reece doing standing on my front step at nine thirty on a Sunday morning?

Lydia has never turned up for breakfast. Ever.

Eliza: "I'm going platinum next week. So sorry."

Shove that up your tank top.

Lydia stood rooted to the spot and widened her eyes further, imploring Eliza to let them in.

Eliza: "I suppose you'd better come in then, seeing as it's the Sunday ritual, eh Lydia?"

Lydia exhaled, audibly, and her shoulders visibly relaxed.

Lydia: "Oh, thank you, darling. Come on you, Reece person, in you go."

Lydia waved Reece through the door and he led the way past a pyjamaed and spatula wielding Eliza and peeping, behind her legs, Tom.

Lydia followed and, standing in the doorway, whispered to Eliza.

Lydia: "Don't ever let me lumber myself with a bloke all day on the first date ever again. I could simply die, darling!"

Eliza: "Who the hell is he?"

Lydia: "He's deep man."

Eliza: "Lydia! That's not deep! That's subterranean! Go much deeper and you'll dredge up the bloody Titanic!

What are you thinking of? Now I'm stuck with him an' all!"

Reece came back into the lounge and clapped his hands.

Rancid Reece: "Chop chop! Some of us are hungry."

Eliza, Lydia and Tom all stared at him.

Eliza found her voice first.

Eliza: "Oh, I do beg your pardon. I wasn't aware I was running a café."

Eliza huffed and continued.

Eliza: "Actually, that's a better idea. Give me ten minutes and after I've fed the animals theirs, we'll go to the Merrythought."

Rancid Reece stalked back into the kitchen.

Lydia, ungraciously: "Do we have to? We'll see other people."

Eliza: "Well, Lydia my dear, the whole village has the joy of meeting Reece later. Isn't that marvellous?"

Lydia: "Oh."

Indeed, oh.

Lydia looked crestfallen and held onto Eliza's arm.

Lydia: "Please don't let people know I'm with him. I've got standards. Can we pretend he's yours if anyone asks?"

Oh, that's just lovely.

Eliza: "No, we most certainly cannot! Anyway, I'm meeting Henry there."

So, nerr.

Lydia: "Oh? Who's Henry?"

Eliza: "I've been speaking to him this week; he seems very nice. He's bringing his daughter too. Have you heard from Jude?"

Jude... Jude... ah, the fleeting thunderbolt that was Jude.

I had to bring him up even when mentioning my potential new suitor.

Lydia shook her head.

Lydia: "No, I haven't. He's not returned my calls or messages. I am quite annoyed about it all really. He was ideal and had the hugest willy I've... oh, you're back."

Reece had returned to the lounge.

Rancid Reece, matter of factly: "Your cat has his head in the frying pan and your dog is on its hind legs trying to reach a potato waffle."

Eliza, sarcastically: "Brilliant."

She sighed.

Eliza: "I'll go and get myself and Tom changed and we'll go to Dave's."

Eliza picked Tom up and left them to it in the lounge before Lydia could protest any further and went upstairs to get them both dressed.

Twenty minutes later, the five of them all climbed into Eliza's car and set off for the Merrythought Café. Lydia was in the passenger seat next to Eliza and Reece had sat next to Tom in the back.

From the back seat.

Tom: "Mummy?"

Eliza: "Yes, darling?"

Tom: "Man wiv hat, don't half pong."

Eliza: "He's called Reece and correctly you should say, Reece really smells, not, don't half pong."

Rancid Reece: "Excuse me, I am sitting here, you know."

Lydia: "All our senses are well aware of that. You're alright Tom, I'll open the windows."

Reece: "I do not smell."

Tom waved his hand in front of his face.

Tom: "Pwoarr, you do! You proper honk!"

Eliza: "Really honk, Tom, not proper."

Rancid Reece: "You child, are mistaken."

Lydia: "If you say so. Are you sure you want to come to the show with us, Reece? I'm not sure it'll be your kind of thing."

Rancid Reece: "I have cancelled work to meet with you Lydia. I am coming to the show."

Lydia really scraped the barrel with this one.

Eliza: "Isn't that just fantastic? Eh, Lydia?"

Lydia, dryly: "Oh yeah. Fantastic."

Lydia shot a look at Eliza, who shrugged in faked nonchalance.

They drove in silence with the windows wide open to the Merrythought. Tom held Cheddar Chicken across his face for the rest of the journey.

They walked in and Dave shot out like a spider from a web to greet them.

Dave: "Oh, oh, Eliza! How wonderful to see you! How are you? Better than last time, I see. Lovely to see you with a bit of colour on your pretty cheeks. Hello Tom."

Tom: "Hello Dave. I sit next to a pongy man in car. We had to drive wiv windows open and I put Cheddar Chicken's feet up my nose so I couldn't niff 'im."

Dave: "Oh? Erm..."

I'd better introduce said pongy man to Dave.

Eliza: "Dave meet Reece. Reece, Dave."

Dave looked Reece up and down and looked at Eliza in dismay.

Dave, incredulously: "He's not yours, is he?"

Eliza: "No Dave. He's Lydia's"

Dave opened his mouth in shock and laughed.

Dave: "Oh, how excellent! Where is Lydia?"

They all looked around and she was nowhere in sight.

Eliza: "She was here a minute ago! Reece, did you see where she went?"

Rancid Reece: "No I did not. I have to say, she's not as entertaining as I was led to believe from the limited correspondence we had. I am prepared to pursue the day, however. I owe it to her, to give her a chance."

Eliza: "Oh, you don't need to do that, Reece. I'm sure she'll cope."

Just then, Eliza's mobile beeped.

She scrabbled around in her handbag to retrieve her mobile. It was a text message from Lydia.

Lydia's text: "Darling, I'm in the bogs. I cannot be seen with this man. My street credibility will nosedive. I think it may even affect sales in the shop. Please, I beg you, get rid of him!! Text me when he's gone xxx"

Marvellous. Just bloody marvellous.

Eliza looked up to find an expectant Dave, Reece and Tom all staring at her.

Eliza: "Oh! Erm. That was Lydia. She's, erm, just been terribly poorly in the toilet."

Dave paled significantly and put his hands over his eyes in horror.

Dave: "Oh no!! My poor toilets! Not after last time! I'll be shut down!"

Eliza removed his hands from his face and patted them with hers.

Eliza: "It's ok Dave, we'll sort it. You go and do your thing in the kitchen and I promise you by the time you come back out, it'll all be sorted."

Dave: "But, but..."

Eliza squeezed his hands gently. Dave flushed scarlet and shifted his legs awkwardly.

Eliza looked him in the eye.

Eliza: "Trust me, Dave, it'll be sorted."

Dave, stammering: "Ohh, ok, ok. I'll go."

Eliza ungripped his hands and he held them up to his lips for a moment. He then adjusted his crotch and went back to the kitchen.

Eliza blanched slightly before returning her attention to Rancid Reece.

Eliza: "Reece, she is as sick as a dog. Hence the non-entertaining nature of her today. Perhaps, it would be better if you rescheduled your date for some other time when she's not throwing up?"

Rancid Reece: "I find vomit most unappealing. She did look rather haggard under all that make up. You're probably right. To be perfectly honest, I'm not sure she's what I'm looking for. I might call up work and see if they need me, instead."

Eliza: "Yes, that's probably for the best."

Rancid Reece: "Eliza, would you stop dying your hair and go out with me?"

When hell freezes over.

Eliza: "I'm addicted to bleach, I'm afraid. The more chlorine the better."

Rancid Reece: "That's a shame."

Eliza: "Yes, isn't it just? Right, I must attend to Lydia. Are you ok getting home from here?"

Rancid Reece: "I shall go on the bus. I believe the number forty-eight passes by here on the hour."

Eliza: "You'd best go now, the next one is in a few minutes."

Rancid Reece: "Ok. I'll send you a message on multitude of mates dot com."

I won't reply.

Eliza: "Fair enough. Goodbye Reece."

Rancid Reece: "Bye for now."

Reece made off for the café door and Tom hollered after him.

Tom: "Bye bye pongy chops!"

Eliza: "Naughty Tom! You mustn't tell strangers they smell! One of us might end up getting punched."

Tom: "It true though, mummy!"

Eliza: "Regrettably, it most certainly is. As you get older, you'll realise when it's pertinent to keep your mouth shut or bare face lie. Come on Tom, let's go and rescue Lydia."

They went off to the ladies and Eliza pushed open the door

Eliza: "Oi! Yellow Back! He's gone so get out here and buy me breakfast!"

Lydia appeared from a cubicle.

Lydia: "Oh thank god! Thank you, darling. I owe you massively! I'll buy you a seven-piece fry-up and Tom, you can have Dave's special bangers."

Tom: "Yay! Special nangers!"

They made their way to a table and Dave came out of the kitchen.

Dave: "Is everything ok in the toilets, Lydia? Only I have a J-cloth if you care to wipe up after yourself."

Lydia: "I beg your pardon?!"

Eliza: "It's ok, Lydia, I made out you were poorly in order to get rid of Rancid Reece."

Lydia: "Oh ok. No, it's fine Dave. No J-cloth needed, thank you."

Eliza looked at Dave.

Eliza: "She wasn't really ill. We needed to get rid of the guy she was with."

Dave: "I'm not surprised. He was a shocking specimen of a man. I would have thought you'd be well suited Lydia. He looked quite your type."

Lydia: "Shut up Dave. Get Eliza a seven-piece fry-up, Tom will have a couple of your dubious bangers and I'll have two crumpets."

Tom: "Please Dave. Manners, Wydia."

Tom was shaking his head at Lydia and using his stern face.

Lydia: "Tut. Please Dave."

Tom nodded with approval.

Dave: "Certainly. I'll bring you a pot of tea too, Eliza. I know it's your favourite beverage, and Tom you can have some milk, yes?"

Tom: "In a big boy's cup?"

Dave: "Yes alright. I'll bring the kitchen roll with it."

Eliza: "Thanks Dave."

Dave scuttled off to the kitchen to prepare their breakfast.

Eliza sighed.

Eliza: "He was so far below your bar, he was limboing."

Lydia: "He was simply diabolical, wasn't he? He didn't look as bad as that in his photo. I should sue, you know. I knew he wasn't the best-looking chap but he shouldn't leave the house, quite frankly. If I looked and dressed like him, I'd become a hermit."

Tom: "You hagrid, Wydia."

Lydia: "Pardon Tom? I'm nothing like Hagrid. He is a bearded giant from Harry Potter. Oh god, Eli! I haven't forgotten to bleach my moustache, have I?!"

Lydia smacked her hand across her mouth in horror.

Eliza: "No, you're fine. He means, you're haggard."

Lydia: "I'm what?!"

Eliza: "Tom's repeating what Rancid Reece said about you, that's all."

Lydia: "Rude, horrible little turd! How dare he?! He's lucky I even gave him an airing."

Tom: "Mummy, what's a turd?"

Great.

Eliza: "It's a lump of poo."

Tom: "Ahh, that's why he ponged then."

Eliza: "Very probably. Oh, look breakfast's up. Eat up guys, we've Pilkington on the Moors Country Show to attend this afternoon."

Dave had approached the table and was dishing out their food and drinks. He put down everything and left half a kitchen roll near Tom for when he inevitably spilt his milk in his big boy's cup.

Dave: "Ooh, you're going? I might come along too. I'll say hello if I see you. What time are you going, Eliza?"

Eliza: "Oh. Erm. About two."

Dave: "I will look out for you."

Lydia: "I bet you will. You can play Whack the Beaver with her, Dave."

Eliza shot Lydia a look.

Dave, flustered: "Oh oh, look a customer! I'll go and attend. See you later, Eliza."

Dave scurried off to another table.

Eliza stared at Lydia and shook her head.

Lydia, innocently: "What?!"

Eliza: "Eat your crumpets and don't say another word."

Lydia: "Yes dear."

Status: *"Say "Hello" to my little friend."*

Chapter Thirty-four

Sub Affirmation for the day: *I am thankful for my friends.*

After breakfast at the Merrythought, they were in the car heading off back home.

Lydia: "Darling, drop me off at mine. I'll meet you at the show later. Roy and Charmaine are taking Freya so I need to put my make-up on."

Eliza: "You already have a face full."

Lydia: "I need a double layer, darling, I need slap armour for this. Please help me through it. I've not seen them out and about as a threesome. I'm not quite sure how I'll react. I'm hoping with serenity."

Eliza: "I don't think that's an emotion you possess."

Lydia: "I'm not sure it's in my repertoire either. I don't want to create a scene so let's have a code word in case my mouth runs away with me."

Eliza: "Ok, how about "cease!" That's effective."

Lydia: "Too obvious. Think of another."

Tom, from the confines of his car seat in the back: "Aubergine!"

Lydia and Eliza looked at each other with surprise.

Eliza: "Crikey Tom, that's a big random word. Well done!"

Lydia: "Perfect Tom. That'll stop me in my tracks. Aubergine is the code word."

Eliza: "Aubergine it is."

They pulled up at Lydia's and she blew a kiss as she got out of the car.

Lydia: "See you later when I'm fully armed for the Battle of Pilkington Show! Who needs a mortar when you have Max Factor! I'll meet you by the cake stall at two. Mwah!"

Back home, Eliza and Tom surveyed the state they'd left the kitchen in when they'd been rudely interrupted by their early morning visitors.

Eliza: "Do you want to help me tidy up this mess, Tom?"

Tom: "Nope. I artist. I draw. I don't do mess."

And he promptly wandered off and got his felt tips out and some paper.

Eliza set about scraping the uneaten food into the animal bowls and started washing up.

Ooh, I'm meeting Henry with an H today.

I hope he's nice.

I could do with a nice boyfriend.

Nice? Is that enough?

I want spectacular, actually.

He might be spectacular.

I might get the same kerpow moment I had with Jude

Yes, because that happens twice in a lifetime. Not.

Let alone twice in a flippin' month.

If it does happen again, I'll put it down to lack of sex and my hormones.

Her mobile rang and Eliza looked at the display. It was Margaret, the bookkeeper, again.

Oh no, what now?

Eliza: "Morning Margaret, how are you today?"

Margaret: "Blessed be the morn on the day of rest, dear."

Eliza: "Indeed, I said just the same to Tom."

Ahem.

Eliza: "Is all well in the world of accounts?"

Margaret: "Perhaps not, dear. Hence my call on a non-workday. Another transaction has occurred and I want to check if it is legitimate."

Eliza hung her head in dismay.

Eliza: "Oh no, what now?"

Margaret: "I have taken the liberty of monitoring transactions on a daily basis; via the online banking facility we have. Two hundred pounds was taken from a cash point on Friday. I would have called you yesterday but Geoffrey and I went to a caravan show in Billericay. The registered location of removal was the cash point at the new supermarket in Billington. I presume this wasn't you?"

Eliza shook her head.

Eliza: "No Margaret, this wasn't me."

Margaret: "If I may put this delicately, dear. Has a new item of stock of this value materialised, or indeed others to corroborate the expenditure we previously discussed?"

Eliza: "No Margaret, I have yet to clap eyes on two thousand pounds worth of furniture or receive receipts to back up any such spending. The only one I must give you is nine pounds forty-eight for a picture frame."

Eliza buried her head in her hands and continued.

Eliza: "What am I going to do, Margaret? This is awful."

Margaret: "Would you wish for the police to be involved?"

Eliza: "No!"

Margaret: "I thought as much. I feel it only correct to advise you to change the pin number on the company debit cards. If I may be so bold as to suggest, knowledge of this remains limited to you."

Eliza: "Ok, I'll nip out in a bit before the show and change it."

She sighed heavily.

Margaret: "I'm sorry to be the bearer of bad news, my dear girl, especially on a weekend. I thought I ought to keep you informed, that's all. You have a fledgling business and it will not succeed at this rate. If it were my venture, I would consider the long-term viability in light of the recent incidents. From an accounting perspective, it is either very shoddy inventory keeping, which quite frankly I will not allow, or there is something more devious afoot. Either way, we must nip it in the bud, Eliza."

Eliza: "We must. Thank you, Margaret, and I'm so sorry you had to interrupt your weekend to keep an eye on my business."

Margaret: "It's no trouble, my dear, I like you and I would not like to see your business suffer due to no fault of your own. I would warn you, however, decisions may need to be made of a personal and professional nature if our doubts prove fruitful."

She's voiced my fears.

Lydia.

Eliza: "You think she's nicking it, don't you?"

Margaret: "I would not put my thoughts into such phrasing. I would only say, my concern regarding matters lie with you, and you alone, my dear."

Take that as a yes, then.

Margaret continued.

Margaret: "I must go, Geoffrey is waving that it looks like rain so I must get the washing in. I will speak to you in a couple of days, Eliza. Try not to worry, I have caught this early. We can address matters as we are made aware of the facts. Good day to you dear."

With that the line went dead.

Eliza expelled a massive sigh.

Brilliant. Just flip-flopping brilliant.

Status: *"It takes a great deal of bravery to stand up to your enemies, but a great deal more to stand up to your friends."*

Chapter Thirty-five

Sub Sub Affirmation for the day: *I am comfortable in a crowd.*

After an impromptu trip to the local cash point, Eliza and Tom held hands as they wandered down the garden path on their way to the show.

Tom: "You awight, mummy? You look sad."

Eliza: "I'm ok Tom, I've got something on my mind, that's all."

Tom looked above Eliza's head.

Tom: "I don't see anything on your mind."

Eliza tapped her temple.

Eliza: "Inside Tom. In my brain. Thoughts."

Tom: "Ohhh, I have them. I tell Cheddar Chicken about them. You can too if you want."

Eliza: "I might take you up on that, Tom."

Tom: "I let you chat to him later."

Cheddar Chicken. Therapist.

Eliza: "Good lad. By the way, we're going to meet a friend of mine at the show. He has a daughter called Sienna who is a similar age as you."

Just then a car horn beeped at them.

It was Brian and Clive. Brian stuck his head out of the window and hollered at them.

Brian: "Yoo Hoo!! We'll park by your house and walk down with you. Wait there, poppet!"

Eliza and Tom waved.

Tom: "I didn't know Bwian was coming. Yay!"

Eliza: "That makes two of us, Tom. How lovely."

They waited a couple of minutes and were joined by Brian and Clive.

Brian and Clive greeted her and Tom with hugs.

Clive: "Hello Tatty Head. How's things?"

Eliza: "Ok. It's a wonderful surprise to see you."

Clive: "Lydia told us about it, so we thought we'd join you. Just ok?"

Eliza: "Ah, it's alright, it'll sort out, I'm sure."

Brian: "'Ere, we heard she was bringing another fella. What happened with Jude?"

Eliza: "She didn't tell you?"

Brian: "Well, she said she'd dumped him and had gone for someone more intellectual. She said she was going for deep now rather than looks."

I bet she did.

Eliza: "Something like that. Yes, Tom and I had the delight of meeting aforementioned man this morning. I'm afraid you won't be witnessing the pleasure of his attendance. He was a bit too deep."

Tom: "We met a man this morning and he was a lump of poo."

Clive: "Really Tom? Well, we did think it a bit of an unlikely pairing. Lydia likes her lookers."

They all headed down towards the village park.

Brian nudged Eliza and whispered in her ear.

Brian: "If Jude's not with Lydia anymore, that means you can pursue him."

Eliza: "I'm not sure if it's quite that simple, Brian. Things were left a bit, er, restricted."

That's an understatement.

Brian: "Ah well, what's meant to be, will be, poppet."

Eliza: "I'm meeting a guy here today, actually. He's called Henry. Works in an auction house and has a little girl. He bought a commode from the shop. He seems quite nice."

He patted her hand.

Brian: "Good, good. We'll vet the antique bog buyer for you, won't we Clive? See if he's up to scratch."

Clive: "Naturally. That last one was a right dead loss. Licking his plate. Honestly."

Eliza shook her head.

Eliza: "Sorry about that."

Clive: "Don't you apologise, Tatty Head, it's not your fault. The path of true love and all that."

The four of them walked along chatting companionably and paid their entrance fee.

Eliza: "I need to meet Lydia by the cake stall."

Brian stopped by a stall near the entrance.

Brian: "We'll meet up with you in a minute, I've just seen chutney."

Brian and Clive wandered off to a stall laden with homemade chutneys, jams and other such gingham lidded wonders.

Lydia was waiting by the cake stall in what can only be described as "a racy little number".

Blimey!

Eliza: "Hi, are you going clubbing after flinging the hay bale?"

Lydia: "Hello darling, a bit OTT?"

Eliza: "Just a bit."

Lydia: "Excellent! I want to remind Roy what he's missing."

Eliza: "Oh, he'll get a full view of what he's missing, alright."

Eliza's attention was diverted towards the cake stall.

Eliza: "Good heavens! Look at all those cakes! Pilkington on the Moors must have created a power surge when they put on their ovens to cook all that lot!"

Lydia: "I know, I added mine to the pile earlier. No power surge created by me, though."

She winked and tapped her nose.

Brian and Clive joined them and greeted Lydia with a hug. Brian held her back at arm's length and looked her up and down.

Brian: "Is there a "Hook a Fuck" stall or are we on the pull?"

Eliza shot him a stern look and pointed at Tom.

Brian: "Sorry, poppet, I forgot my language. It was shock brought about by Lydia's get up."

Eliza: "She's on a "look what you once had" mission as Roy and Charmaine are coming today."

Lydia: "How do I look?"

She did a little twirl.

Clive: "A bit like a sex worker. But in a good way."

Lydia: "Brilliant. I've gone for military meets slut."

Brian: "You're there, poppet."

Lydia clapped her hands and did a little jump with glee.

Just then, there was a tap on Eliza's shoulder and she whipped her head around.

Eliza: "What the..? Oooh hello! Henry?"

Perhaps Henry: "Hi Eliza, I thought it was you. Sorry, I didn't mean to make you jump. You look exactly how I thought you would!"

Crikey, you're very good looking.

Very good looking, indeed.

Your photos don't do you justice, which on that site is a first.

Eliza: "Goodness, you're lovely! I mean, how lovely to meet you! Is this Sienna? Hello."

She turned round and took in the little girl with soft brown ringlets wearing a beautiful lace trimmed dress. She was carrying a basket with a little pot of jam in it.

Sienna: "I've got jam. I like strawberries."

Eliza: "I do too. Meet my son Tom, he also likes strawberries."

Henry: "Hello, young man."

Tom: "Hello mister. I like your handbag."

Henry laughed.

Henry: "That, my young sir, is what they call a 'man bag'. It's for knickknacks and folding cheeky little boys into!"

Tom: "Ooooh!"

Sienna interjected.

Sienna: "I said, I've got jam. Look!"

Tom went and roughly pulled at Sienna's basket to have a closer inspection.

Sienna: "Oi! You not eat mine. Gerroff!"

Sienna pulled her basket away. Tom's bottom lip shot out and started to quiver.

Henry: "Sienna! Don't be so mean. Say hello and be nice!"

Sienna, sulkily: "Will not."

She crossed her arms defiantly and glared at them.

Henry looked dismayed.

Okay, perhaps I should introduce them to the others.

She turned her attention back round to her friends. She was faced with large fixed grins on Brian and Clive's faces and a stupefied Lydia. She was stood there shoulders slumped, staring at him, stunned.

Eliza: "Henry meet Brian and Clive and this is Lydia. You lot, this is Henry."

Brian and Clive greeted Henry, warmly.

Lydia, meanwhile, remained gawping at him.

Eliza: "Lydia... Lydia?!"

What's the matter with you woman?!

Eliza, continued: "Do you need food? You've gone a bit pale."

Lydia visibly shook herself and extended her hand.

Lydia found her voice, about an octave higher and in a very fluttery tone.

Lydia: "Henry! How marvellous to meet you. You and your delightful, well mannered, little girl. She's absolutely wonderful!"

Brian, Clive and Eliza all looked at each other, bemused.

Henry, laughing: "Haha, not the best mannered, I'm afraid but thank you, she does have her delightful moments. Nice to meet you, Lydia. I'm sure I recognise you from somewhere."

Lydia shook her head, feverishly.

Lydia: "Oh, most definitely not. I've never been seen before in my life. You must be mista..."

Lydia stopped mid-sentence and looked straight past all of them towards the entrance of the show.

Lydia, hissing: "They're here..."

Everyone, including the children, followed Lydia's gaze.

Coming towards them was Roy, Charmaine and Freya.

Freya was between them both and holding a hand of each of them. She was laughing, joyously, as they swung her by the arms.

Eliza looked at Brian and pulled a "what do we do now" face.

Brian: "Well, let's go and be frightfully British and say hello."

Lydia clung onto Eliza's arm.

Lydia: "Remember the code word, darling. I have no idea what might spill forth."

Well judging from your performance just then with Henry, we're in for a right old treat.

Eliza: "No worries, just stick close to me. We will just say hello and then leave them to it."

Henry looked on slightly bewildered.

Eliza: "It's Lydia's ex-husband and girlfriend. They're here with Lydia's daughter. Anything could happen."

Henry: "Ohhhh, right you are. One of those sort of situations, is it?"

They walked over towards the entrance and Freya caught site of Lydia and ran over to greet her.

Freya: "Mummy! You look like a dancer!"

Roy and Charmaine stopped in front of them.

Roy, derisively: "Yeah, a lap dancer. Casual as ever, Lydia."

Lydia looked at Charmaine with her greasy hair pulled back into a tight ponytail. She was wearing tight black leggings with a black vest top. On show were the straps of a once white bra but which was now decidedly grey. She had a tattoo on each of her biceps. On the left was "Roy" in script and on the right arm, in a matching script was "Freya".

Lydia's eyes bored into Charmaine's right arm.

Lydia: "Better than looking like one of the Hairy Bikers, like someone I could mention."

Here we go.

Eliza scratched her head, looked down and muttered.

Eliza: "Ohhh, aubergine."

Roy: "What? Oh, hi Eliza, you look pretty. Though, saying that, you always did."

Lydia: "I thought you only found corpulence to your taste now, Roy."

Eliza: "Ohhh, more aubergines. Look over there! A stall full of 'em!"

Brian: "Really?! Oh, Clive we should go and see. Carlos would love some, I'm sure."

Brian hurriedly grabbed Clive's arm and steered him away from the group.

Clive: "Huh? Where am I looking?"

Brian: "I don't care, come on. Eli's seen them so let's just go and investigate."

Brian guided Clive behind Roy and Charmaine, pulled an Edvard Munch "Scream" face behind their heads and ran off quickly.

Coward!! Now I'm left to deal with it.

Lydia was still staring at Charmaine's upper arm.

Lydia, full of hostility: "You have my daughter's name on your arm."

Charmaine, proudly turning it to the group: "Yeah, I had it done last week. Great innit? Freya's idea weren't it, Freya?"

Freya looked up at her adoringly and nodded proudly.

Lydia, almost spitting: "Very classy. Also, completely unnecessary seeing as she's nothing to do with you. Who the fu...?"

Eliza interjected, wildly.

Eliza, hollering: "AUBERGINE!"

Henry stepped forward to rescue the situation.

Henry, calmly: "Hello, please allow me to introduce myself. I'm Henry. You must be Roy and Charmaine. Hello Freya, you look about the same age as Sienna. Why don't you say hello, girls?"

Sienna and Freya, shyly: "Hello."

Freya: "What have you got in your basket?"

Sienna: "Jam. Do you like strawberries?"

Freya: "I love them."

Sienna: "Me too, you can have some of my jam if you want."

Freya: "Yay! Yes please."

Tom harrumphed next to Eliza and she ruffled his hair, affectionately.

Charmaine: "Hi Henry, you're a bit fit, incha?"

Henry laughed.

Fit Henry: "Ha! Thank you, Charmaine. Very kind of you to lie so admirably!"

Lydia: "Oh she's not lying, you're gorgeous."

Ahem!!

Eliza, coughing: "Lydia. A big prize-winning aubergine."

Lydia, apologetically: "Soz."

Henry sized up the situation.

Henry: "Well, an absolute delight to meet you. I'm sure we'll see you around the show. We're off for a look around, aren't we ladies?"

Lydia and Eliza in unison and relief: "Yes."

Roy: "Yeah mate, catch you later. Are you staying with us, Freya, or going with your mum for a bit?"

Freya: "I'll stay with you and Charmaine please, daddy."

Lydia, over brightly: "Fine! That's just fine!"

Ooh, that's got to hurt. Poor Lydia.

As they walked away, Eliza put her arm round Lydia and gave her a squeeze.

Brian and Clive materialised from behind a bouncy castle.

Brian: "Everyone still standing?"

Eliza: "You blinkin' cowards! I think it went quite well considering. She didn't punch anyone which is a bonus."

Lydia shook her head.

Lydia: "I'm not happy about the tattoo. Not happy at all. I think that inking might be illegal. It's like stealing, isn't it? Branding someone else's daughter on your body."

Eliza: "I do agree it's perhaps stepping over boundaries but I don't think she meant any harm. Tattoos are just the latest accessory these days. People don't appear to give them a great deal of thought."

Lydia: "She's probably riddled with them. I bet she has 'cake' tattooed on her arse."

Brian: "She seems nice enough though, Lydia. Try and be pleasant for Freya's sake, eh?"

Lydia: "Meh."

Clive: "It's Roy you should be venting any residual anger at, not her."

Lydia, crossing her arms: "Don't you all start on me. I think I did very well under the circumstances."

Eliza: "Can we have a code word in future that doesn't make me sound like a lunatic?"

Lydia: "Certainly, darling. Going forward, we'll use the word "penis". How about that? Oooh penis, a big prize-winning penis!"

Tom: "What's a penis?"

Eliza gave Lydia a look and she poked her tongue out at her.

Eliza: "Maybe "quiet!" would be more prudent. Thank you, Henry, for rescuing the situation."

Henry: "No problem at all."

He smiled at Eliza and pulled her briefly towards him by wrapping an arm around her shoulders.

Lydia switched her attention back to him.

Lydia: "Yes thank you, Henry. I was in mortal danger from an avalanche of aubergines."

Brian: "Our Eli says you work in an auction house Henry, is it the one in town?"

Henry: "Yes, I live near the new supermarket in Billington, so very handy in that respect."

Lydia: "Ooh, I've not been there. Is it good?"

You've not been to the new supermarket in Billington?

Are you sure? Not when you used the cash point the other day? Hmmm?

Henry: "It's the future, Lydia. It's a big shop that sells lots of products all in one place. You should visit."

Lydia laughed.

Lydia: "Eli and I go to the other one. The one near the Merrythought."

Eliza: "We do indeed. Are you sure you've never been to it, Lydia?"

Eliza watched her carefully.

Lydia: "No darling, shall we go next week. Check it out?"

Tom tugged Eliza's leg.

Tom: "Mummy, I bored with talking. Can I go on bouncy castle?"

Eliza: "Yes, of course."

Tom: "Oooh fank you mummy! I loves bouncing!"

Henry: "Everyone loves a good bounce, Tom. Sienna, are you going on?"

She nodded and stalked off promptly to join the queue.

Henry was looking at Lydia intently and she smiled at him, coquettishly.

A realisation dawned on his face and he then pointed at her.

Henry: "I've got it! I know where I recognise you from!"

Lydia's face fell and her eyes widened. She shook her head, pleadingly.

Hello. What is this exchange I'm witnessing?

Henry remained oblivious to her unspoken begging of silence.

Henry: "You're on that dating site too, aren't you?"

Lydia, cautiously: "Er, yes. You must have seen my photo or something."

Henry, incredulously: "You wrote to me! I remember now! You're the one who wrote me a smutty poem!!"

I beg your pardon!

Eliza: "Lydia?! I thought only Jesus did that!"

Lydia, hurriedly: "No, no Henry! You must be confusing me with someone else. I don't have any rhyming ability, whatsoever. Anyway, we can't stand here tittle tattling, there's children to bounce and lots of absolutely marvellous stalls full of tat to peruse. Come on!"

Lydia turned her back on them all and rushed off towards the Whack the Beaver stall.

Brian shot a knowing look at Eliza who rolled her eyes.

Henry: "Whoops! Sorry Eli. I didn't mean to upset your friend."

He whispered, conspiratorially.

Henry: "It was exceedingly graphic. I was quite shocked when I received it. I nearly dropped my Hobnob. For the record, I didn't reply. I am a bit old fashioned and like to pursue a girl rather than the other way round. Anyway, you caught my eye and I like you. You seem very normal."

Eliza smiled.

So deluded.

Eliza: "Thank you."

Brian: "You chose well, Henry. Our Eli is very normal. Be sure to ask her about the dead body in her back garden."

Thank you, Brian.

There was a screech from the bouncy castle.

They all looked to the castle to find Sienna had cornered a child by the turrets and was grabbing on to her hair.

Henry: "SIENNA! Let go of that girl, immediately!!"

Sienna, still retaining her hair grip: "She started it!!"

Henry: "You have a count to five! One...! Two...!"

Sienna let go and the other girl jumped off the castle and ran to her mother.

Henry to child's mother: "I'm so sorry. She's a bit highly strung."

The mother glared at him and walked off with her daughter.

Eliza got Tom off the castle and caught up with Lydia. The others followed behind.

Eliza: "Did you really write him a filthy poem?"

Lydia: "Not that filthy. Uh oh. Stalker at ten o'clock."

Eliza looked to the left and lumbering towards them was Dave from the Merrythought Café.

I've never seen him in daywear.

I've only ever seen him in his café get up.

He looks as if he doesn't belong.

He should only ever be seen with a J-cloth in his belt hook, carrying a notepad.

Dave: "Hello Eli, you look lovely. Would you like to hit the beaver with me?"

Eliza: "Certainly Dave. How could I refuse?"

The others caught them up.

Eliza: "Dave, meet Henry and Sienna. I think you've met Brian and Clive in the past."

Dave: "I have. Hello all. Oh, a man. Is he with you?"

Eliza: "He is Dave. Sorry."

Dave sighed, heavily.

Dave: "It's to be expected, one as beautiful and bountiful such as you. You must have them queuing up."

Beautiful and bountiful.

We're on the B words of flattery today.

It's like Sesame Street.

Eliza: "I'm not sure about that, Dave, but thank you. Let's hit the poor old mammal, shall we?"

Dave: "We shall."

They all had a go at the stall. Brian was jubilant when he was the only one to whack the much-beaten beaver.

Status: *"I solemnly swear I am up to no good."*

Chapter Thirty-six

Sub Sub Sub Affirmation for the day: *I am serene at all times.*

There was a tap on the microphone and then a massive screech of feedback over a tannoy.

Tannoy: "Turn it down for Christ's sake, Eunice!"

The tannoy tapped again.

Tannoy: "Testing? One, two, three."

There was a moment's silence, a man's cough, and then it piped up again.

Tannoy: "Good afternoon, ladies and gentlemen. Thank you so much for joining in the festivities of this year's Pilkington on the Moors annual country show. We hope you're all having a wonderful afternoon. I'd like to take this opportunity, ahead of the re-enactment and mortar display, to announce the winner of this year's fabulous cake baking competition. The winner of which will win a coveted place on Mr Culpepper's willow weaving course. A marvellous prize, I'm sure you'll agree. Thank you all for your contributions."

There was a pause as the microphone was put down.

Tannoy, in the distance but definitely audible: "Eunice! Pass me that bit of paper. I'm not a bleedin' octopus for Christ's sake!"

In the background, there was a rustling of paper.

There was another cough and the microphone was picked back up.

Tannoy, back with composure: "After much deliberation, the winner of the cake competition is... drum roll... Lydia Perkins! A very worthy winner with her absolutely sumptuous Black Forest Gateau. A true culinary masterpiece."

There was a round of applause around the park.

Lydia: "Oh shit."

Eliza, muttering: "Marks and Spencer's will be thrilled."

A woman ran over from behind the White Elephant stall up to Lydia.

White Elephant woman: "Oh Lydia! I had no idea you were such a wonderful cook! I was involved with the judging and yours was the best by far. I've got the Rotary club annual luncheon coming up, would you mind giving me the recipe? It'd go down a treat."

Get out of that one Lydia, dear.

Lydia: "Oh, er, I'd absolutely love to divulge the ingredients used but it's an old family concoction from the 1980's. It's against our tradition to pass it on to anyone other than the next generation so you're definitely out of the running. Sorry. Come on guys, let's get in place for the mortar display."

She literally dragged Eliza by the arm. The others trailed after her.

Brian: "Good heavens, poppet! I didn't know you could cook either. Did you, Clive? Would you make us one? We like a bit of cake, don't we, Clive?"

Clive: "We do indeed."

Lydia: "No worries, I'll nip into town and get one, I mean, the stuff. Ahem."

She plonked herself down on the grass ready to watch the re-enactment.

Henry was keeping a safe distance from Lydia and had stuck close to Eliza's side throughout their time at the show and sat beside her with Sienna to his other side. Tom plumped himself on Eliza's lap. Dave sat to her right next to Brian and Clive and Lydia was on the end.

The tannoy crackled back into life.

Tannoy: "Hello again ladies and gentlemen, boys and girls and, as Eunice has reminded me, apropos of her Zoom inclusivity course, I also extend a huge welcome to all the pronouns who roam our green and pleasant land. You are now in for a treat. I am delighted to present the Pilkington Re-enactment And Theatrical Society who will perform a pike skirmish, to commemorate the 370th anniversary of the Battle of Pilkington on the Moors. Due to the trauma sustained by Mrs Campbell last year, we have taken advice and all shafts will now be sheathed. So, with without further ado, in the words of Alan Partridge 'Let Battle Commence!'"

There was another screech of feedback and the tannoy stopped speaking.

From behind the pavilion ran out a load of people carrying pikestaffs.

The whole group in unison: "What the…?!"

Brian: "Well, I'll be buggered!"

Lydia: "I wouldn't recommend it with one of those, darling!"

A group of flamboyant, overweight, middle aged men with colanders strapped to their heads started prancing around. They were clad in various tea trays and plastic toboggans as makeshift breastplates, carrying pikes with an array of fruit and vegetables pierced on the end.

Henry: "Oooh, they've really pushed the boat out, haven't they?!"

Dave, grumbling: "I do not believe at any time the English Civil War was fought by a man wearing a tray bearing the words "Keep Calm and Make Tea" on it."

There were more taps from the tannoy and the disembodied voice started speaking again.

Tannoy: "As you can see ladies and gents, boys and girls and adverbs, in the spirit of "make do and mend" we have taken the liberty of utilising the fruit and veg from the "Wonders from the Allotment" stall and the actors have made their own costumes. A true testament to their abilities."

Brian: "Indeed. RADA must be so proud."

The re-enactment carried on and then Mr Regis proudly wheeled out his mortar and prepared it to fire.

People hurriedly cleared out of the firing line.

Henry looked sideways along the line and his eyes settled on Eliza and he nudged her and smiled.

Henry: "Would you like to see me again, Eli?"

Just then, a massive bang erupted across the park as the mortar went off and a plume of smoke billowed out of it.

The whole park sat stunned for a moment as the smoke cleared, before a wave of expletives murmured throughout the onlookers. Then children started shrieking, dogs across the whole of Pilkington on the Moors started barking and babies started crying.

Tom: "Whaaaahhh!!! Mummy! My skin nearly jumped off!"

Eliza hugged Tom close to her and kissed him all over his face.

Eliza: "Dear Lord, Tom! Are you ok? Jeezus! I think I've gone deaf in one ear!"

Their little group all checked on each other to make sure they were all in one piece.

Eliza: "Are you ok, Henry? Sorry, did you say something before we all nearly got blown up?"

Henry, a bit less confidently: "Yes, I wondered if you'd like to see…"

Just then a boy and his father walked straight through the middle of them, chatting.

Son to father: "That was awesome, dad!!"

Father to son, wistfully: "I'd love a mortar."

Son to father: "Shall we ask mum?"

The father sighed heavily.

Father to son: "P'raps not, Luke. She wouldn't even let me have a shed."

They carried on past.

Eliza: "Sorry? What did you say? I got a big distracted by the man wanting a mortar."

Henry, exasperatedly: "I just wanted to know if you'd like to see me again. That's all!"

All right, all right! Keep your hair on!

Dave: "Yes Eli, I want to know that too."

Huh?

Oh, I forgot about you.

Eliza: "Well seeing as you asked so nicely. Yes Henry, I would."

Henry looked visibly relieved.

Dave looked visibly crestfallen.

Brian clapped his hands.

Brian: "Come on you lot, let's celebrate not being blown up by a mortar with a slice of cake. We'll see if there's any of Lydia's 'culinary masterpiece' left."

Dave: "I'm very surprised, Lydia. I thought all of your expertise lie outside of the kitchen."

Lydia: "Shut up, Dave."

Henry winked at Dave.

Henry, laughing: "Me too mate, though there was a mention of whipped cream in the sonnet I received."

Lydia, honestly.

Lydia, flustered: "You can shut your face, an' all."

She strode off towards the cake stall and left the others in her wake.

Status: *"You're only supposed to blow the bloody doors off!"*

Chapter Thirty-seven

Affirmation for the day: *I am gracious and forgiving.*

It was the day of Tom's birthday party and Lydia and Eliza were in the throes of decorating the house.

Eliza's mother had come over and taken Tom down to the park for the morning. Her father had made his excuses as he had a big project on at work so at least that was one less person in the queue to punch Lewis.

Lydia: "I can't believe you're letting both of them come, Eli. Had you been sniffing varnish?"

Eliza: "It's just this once. I think it will be good for us all to move on."

Lydia: "It does help that she's a mess at the moment."

Eliza: "There is that benefit, yes."

Lydia: "And you get the car."

Eliza: "That too..."

They were each perched on a chair either end of the lounge pegging up some bunting.

Eliza: "Plus, I should earn some karmic points for allowing them across my threshold."

Lydia: "Bollocks to karmic points. I warn you now, there is absolutely no guarantee I will be nice to either of them."

They got down from their respective chairs and looked up at the bunting and nodded with approval at each other.

They started blowing up balloons. Lydia nonchalantly enquired between puffs.

Lydia: "How's it going with that Henry then?"

Eliza: "It's ok. He seems very nice."

He's not Jude.

I hope Jude's alright.

Not with anyone or anything.

But I do hope he's happy.

Do I? No, actually I hope he's thinking about me.

Yeah, and the likelihood of that?

Lydia: "He's more than 'nice' Eli. He's a stunner!"

Eliza: "Who? Jude?"

Aargh!! Shut up! Think before engaging mouth!

Lydia: "Eh? Jude who? How'd he get into the conversation? No, I meant Henry."

Jude who?? How can you be so dismissive?!

Lydia continued.

Lydia: "Have you invited him today?"

Eliza: "No, I didn't fancy having him meeting Lewis and Geraldine. I've got enough on my plate keeping the peace with them here."

There was a knock on the door and Ellington woofed his obligatory solitary bark.

Lydia: "I'll get it."

She answered the door to a tray-carrying Brian.

Lydia peered behind him.

Lydia: "What've you done with Clive?"

Brian: "He's had to go to the Cash and Carry. Carlos has used up three quarters of our last shop concocting some pork belly effort. He's turning into a bleedin' money pit. There are more trays of food in the car."

Lydia went out to fetch them whilst he offloaded his one into the kitchen.

Eliza: "Ahh, thank you Brian."

Eliza pulled him into a hug.

Brian: "No problem, poppet. Glad to be of service. Carlos has made the most marvellous cake."

He went to help Lydia with the rest of the food.

They spent the next hour sorting the food out and finishing off the house in preparation for the visitors.

Just before midday, Eliza's mother came back with a very excited Tom.

Tom: "Mummy, mummy! I get changed, quick!! Need to be Stormtrooper!"

Tom and Eliza ran upstairs and he put on his outfit.

When they came down, some of his friends from nursery had turned up in various Star Wars themed outfits and were thwacking each other in the garden with lightsabers.

The door banged again and Eliza went and opened it.

There, stood on the doorstep was a very awkward looking Lewis and hanging onto his arm, an extremely puffy, red-faced Geraldine. She had on an olive-green maxi dress which skimmed over her very prominent bump.

Bloody hell! You look shocking!

How absolutely marvellous!

You've literally ballooned.

Lydia came up behind Eliza.

Lydia with very clear hostility: "Lewis."

She nodded curtly.

Lewis: "Lydia."

He nodded back, curtly.

Lydia: "And you must be his current bint."

With that she whisked back off into the kitchen.

The three of them stood there for a moment.

Eliza gathered herself.

Eliza: "Right, ok. Well, I'd better let you in then."

She opened the door wider and led them through to where some of the other guests were.

Eliza's mother, acidly: "Hello Lewis. A long time no see."

Lewis: "Indeed, Mrs Turner. I'm very grateful to Eli for letting us join you today."

Eliza's mother: "Well that's because she's a wonderful young lady with a thoughtful disposition. I do believe that was one of the qualities you loved about her when you married her."

She looked pointedly at Geraldine.

Lewis: "Er, yes. Most definitely."

Geraldine tugged on Lewis's arm.

Geraldine, grouchily: "Lewy, introduce me to everyone."

Lewy?

Lydia: "Yeah, Lewy. Introduce her."

Lewis waved vaguely in Geraldine's direction.

Lewis: "Everyone, this is Geraldine. Geraldine, this is everyone else."

Geraldine: "Where's your son? I'd like to meet him."

Eliza's mother, pointedly: "Oh, of course you've not had the chance to meet my grandson as you've only been with his father for eighteen months."

Lewis looked suitably shamefaced.

Lewis: "I mean to amend the error of my ways, Mrs Turner."

Lydia: "How do you propose doing that then? Are you getting rid of her?"

Lydia pointed at Geraldine.

Suddenly, Brian rushed in from the garden holding a lightsaber.

Brian, grabbing his crotch: "Those kids mean business! I've just been whacked in the nuts by Jar Jar Binks!"

He stopped in front of Lewis and Geraldine.

Brian: "I see you both came, then. How frightfully brazen of you. Hello again, Lewis."

He extended his hand to Lewis who shook it, warmly.

Lewis: "Hello Brian. I've missed you. How's Clive and the restaurant going?"

Brian, politely: "All splendiferous, thank you."

Geraldine tugged on Lewis's arm again.

Geraldine, whining: "Lewy, I need a wee. Ask her where the toilet is."

Lewis opened his mouth to speak.

Eliza: "It's ok, Geraldine, I do understand English so translation isn't required. It's upstairs on the left."

Geraldine released her limpet grip on Lewis and made off upstairs.

Lewis shouted after her.

Lewis: "Remember, three points of contact at all times, Gerry! Safety first!"

The others all exchanged looks.

Rule boy. Get a life.

Eliza: "Yes, it's very hazardous walking upstairs. I'm seriously considering a bungalow."

Lewis: "The door to safety swings on the hinges of common sense, Eliza, I've always maintained that."

Eliza: "Indeed, you have. It's one of the things I don't miss about you."

Yay! Go me.

Brian guffawed and clapped his hands.

Brian: "What do you reckon to some party games?"

They all agreed and went off to the garden to play with the children, whilst Lewis remained at the bottom of the stairs waiting for Geraldine to return.

Brian whispered to Eliza.

Brian: "Do you know, I do believe he did you a favour running off with that old barge. I'd forgotten that he was as boring as fuck."

Eliza laughed.

Shortly after, they were joined by Lewis and Geraldine who puffed her way across the garden to a seat under a tree. She plonked herself down heavily and sat with her legs splayed apart. Lewis joined her and perched on the edge of the seat, awkwardly.

Over the ridiculous boundary fence from next door, stepped Philip.

Philip: "Hello Eliza! How absolutely wonderful! A party! May I be so bold as to enquire if I may join your celebrations?"

Eliza: "Of course, Philip, let me to introduce you to the people you haven't met. You know Lydia and Brian."

Lydia and Brian waved and wandered over.

Philip: "I do indeed, I'm dismayed, dear Lydia, to see you in more conservative apparel today. You look most engaging in your catsuit. I've drawn upon that memory on many an occasion."

Oh dear.

Lydia grimaced.

Lydia: "I don't wish to know, thank you."

Brian: "Found any more treasure for our Eli, old boy?"

Eliza: "He's well on the way to a kitchen's worth of utensils, aren't you Philip?"

Philip: "I am dear girl. Ooh, who's the big old bird in green?"

His attention was aimed at Geraldine who was fanning herself with a Darth Vader mask under the tree.

Lydia: "That's the old bird Eli's ex-husband left her for."

Philip, visibly shocked: "Is the man blind?! She's a hideous specimen of womanhood. I'd never get it up if I were faced with that."

Too much information!

Eliza: "To be fair Philip, she is very pregnant and, by all accounts, it's taking its toll."

Lydia: "You were a lovely pregnant woman. You bloomed. You never wore a tarpaulin by way of a dress."

Eliza: "Ahh, thank you, Lydia. Shall we go and join the others with the party games?"

Eliza and Lydia sat within earshot of Geraldine and Lewis whilst her mother fussed about in the kitchen with Brian sorting drinks and nibbles for the children.

Geraldine snuggled up to Lewis.

Geraldine: "I was talking to Eleanor the other day. You know the one I told you about?"

Lewis looked at her blankly. Geraldine tutted.

Geraldine: "The one with the husband who has the jaw?"

Lewis, nonplussed: "The jaw?"

Geraldine: "Yes. The jaw. Anyway, she told me they'd been saving up and they'd just bought a new car. How exciting is that?"

Unless it's a Lamborghini Gallardo, I fear I'm eavesdropping on a very dull conversation.

Lewis: "Oh right. What did they get?"

Geraldine: "A Vauxhall. How great is that?"

Lewis: "Oh, that is great. What colour?"

Geraldine: "Blue metallic. I never had them down as metallic people, did you?"

They talk the language of Dullard.

Where all expression has been removed and must be spoken in a monotone and all exclamation marks are redundant.

Surely, he wasn't this boring when we were together?

Maybe I was just too exciting for him.

I do get quite animated about things.

She's no better than me, she's just more suited to him.

She's as boring as him.

Everyone has a match and maybe a dull, boring old limpet is his.

I wonder who my match is.

Jude? Henry?

Jude.

Eliza's mother came out and informed everyone that the birthday cake was ready.

All the children assembled around the dining room table and Eliza shut the curtains and turned the lights off.

Eliza's mother lit the four candles and came into the dining room with the cake and placed it in front of Tom.

Tom blew out his candles and they all cheered and sang happy birthday.

Eliza flicked on the light and they all saw the cake for the first time.

Tom exclaimed with delight.

Tom: "It's Gewaldine!!"

Oh!! I love my child!!

Brian clamped his hand over his mouth and Lydia shrieked with joy and spat out her drink.

Eliza, matter-of-factly: "No Tom, it is Jabba the Hutt."

Geraldine looked down at her dress and at Lewis and pulled his arm.

Geraldine, very very sulkily: "Come on Lewy, We've done our bit. I want to leave now."

Lewis shrugged her off.

Lewis: "I want to stay for the cake cutting and I've got to give Eli the car papers and stuff."

Geraldine stared at him, willing him to obey her. When it became evident he wasn't going to, she huffed, sourly.

Geraldine: "Fine. I'll wait in the car."

Lewis: "Yes, good idea. Off you go. Here's the keys."

He lobbed the car keys at her from his pocket.

Geraldine: "Ten minutes max, Lewy. Got it?"

Lewis, sighing: "Yes, yes. Ok."

Geraldine flounced off without saying goodbye to anyone.

Eliza's mother, shaking her head: "Her aura is in a shocking state."

Lewis: "I think it's her hormones, Mrs Turner. She's changed considerably since she's been pregnant. I'm struggling to cope with her mood swings, to be honest."

Eliza's mother: "Ah well, you've made your bed so you'll have to lie in it. She could definitely do with some chakra therapy, though. I'd recommend it ahead of the baby otherwise you'll not get a wink of sleep."

Lewis: "I'll suggest that to her. Thank you, Mrs Turner."

Lydia: "You might want to recommend retail therapy to her whilst you're at it; sort her dress sense out."

Philip: "Whilst you're in town, you should check yourself into the Opticians dear boy. You must be barmy."

Okay everyone. Time to change the subject.

Geraldine has enough to contend what with the rubbish boyfriend, water retention and impending birth.

Eliza: "Who wants Jabba's bottom?"

Lydia: "Lewis!"

Lewis took the slice of cake and handed over the car documents and keys to Eliza.

Lewis, despondently: "I'd better go, Gerry will be getting fretful. I could do without a scene. Thank you, Eli. I hope to see you all again soon. I've missed you. Even you Lydia."

Lydia: "Christ, things must be bad."

Tom shouted to him as he went towards the front door.

Tom: "Are you Auntie Wydia's friend?"

Lewis turned back sadly to Tom and shook his head, forlornly.

Lewis: "I am your father."

Tom: "Oh."

With that Lewis walked out of the front door and back to a waiting Geraldine.

Eliza's mother to the remaining group: "Well, I think that all went rather well don't you, dears? Now, who wants a cup of tea?"

Status: *"Help me Obi-Wan Kenobi. You're my only hope."*

Chapter Thirty-Eight

Affirmation for the day: *I am superior to negative thoughts and actions.*

The Monday afternoon after Tom's party, Eliza's mobile rang. It was Margaret. Eliza put down her paint brush.

Oh no. Please not more bad news.

Eliza: "Hello Margaret. How are you?"

Margaret: "Hello Eliza. I am well thank you. Much better now Geoffrey's finally finished weeding the borders - after much coercion, I might add. I have some news with regard to the funds that have been unaccounted for."

Eliza: "Oh, please don't tell me more has been taken out."

Margaret: "No dear, you changing the pin number appears to put paid to that foul play, hence the purpose of my call. One of the company debit cards is being held by the bank due to the incorrect pin being entered three times."

Eliza: "Really? When did this happen?"

Margaret: "Saturday, at one fifteen."

Eliza: "This Saturday just gone? Are you sure?"

Margaret: "Quite sure. They telephoned me this morning and I enquired as to the time and circumstances."

It can't have been Lydia then! Oh, thank goodness.

Eliza: "Lydia was with me then, Margaret, at Tom's birthday party!"

Margaret: "Ahh, really? That must be a source of comfort to you, Eliza."

Margaret cleared her throat.

Margaret: "My dear, you need to find out who the perpetrator is before it goes any further. Do you still wish to keep the police out of this?"

Eliza: "Yes please Margaret, for the moment. I'll see if I can get to the bottom of it. I need to find out where Lydia kept her company card and who could have had access to it."

Margaret: "As you wish, Eliza. I shall request the bank sends you the card back, directly. Keep me informed."

Eliza: "I will. Thank you, Margaret, and thank you for keeping this between you and me for the moment."

Margaret: "It is not a problem, my dear. I must go, Geoffrey is wanting a cup of tea. I shall speak to you again soon."

Eliza put down her mobile and shook her head.

You bad, bad person Eliza.

How could you have ever doubted your best friend?

The karma fairy will have something massive in store for you.

You will never have sex again and will definitely be a mad cat lady.

I can't have that.

I'll book myself in for a complete ethereal overhaul.

I'll email mum see if she can Reiki me and get my kundalini back on the right track.

Eliza put her hands on her hips and stared out of the window.

But if Lydia didn't do it.

Who did??

I need to find out where she keeps her company debit card.

She hit Lydia's number.

Lydia: "Hello! Hang on, I'm being a domestic goddess. My Marigolds have been on and off more times than a whore's drawers."

Eliza heard Lydia removing her plastic gloves and pick up her phone again.

Lydia: "What can I do for you?"

Eliza: "Hi. Aren't you in the shop?"

Lydia groaned.

Lydia: "Now don't start. I'm going in later. I have chores, darling. Mr Hicks is watching it until twelve then I'm taking the reins."

Don't beat about the bush.

Ask outright. Get to the bottom of this.

Eliza: "Where do you keep your company debit card?"

Lydia: "Huh?"

Eliza: "Where do you keep it?"

Lydia: "What is this? What's got into you?"

Eliza, shouting: "Just tell me where you keep it!"

Lydia, mardily: "Fine. I keep it in the drawer by the till in the shop."

Eliza: "Where do you keep the pin number? In your head?"

Lydia: "Have you been drinking? What on earth is the matter with you?"

Eliza: "Just answer the question!"

Lydia sighed, heavily.

Lydia: "Now promise you won't tell me off?"

Eliza: "I promise. Sort of. Depends. Just tell me."

Lydia: "Ok. I keep the pin number on the back of a bit of paper in the till. I can't be doing with memorising numbers."

Eliza: "Excellent!"

Lydia, surprised: "Is it? I was expecting a proper bollocking then."

Eliza: "When was the last time you saw the card?"

Lydia: "Erm. Lemme think."

There was a pause.

Lydia: "Friday. I was ordering that special paint online. You know the snooty place that won't let us have an account so we have to pay upfront? Retrogloss or whatever the stuck-up wholesaler is. Are you going to tell me what's going on, seeing as I've capitulated to the cross-questioning?"

Eliza: "Someone has been taking money out of our business account and they've had access via our debit card."

Lydia, incredulously: "My one?!"

Eliza: "Yes."

Lydia: "The effing lowlife!"

There was another pause.

Lydia: "Who do you think it is?"

There was another pause.

Eliza and Lydia in unison: "MR HICKS!"

Lydia, shrieking: "The cheating bloody bastard! After us letting him stay there and make cheese straws an' all. What shall we do? Shall we go down there and smack him in his bread-making face?"

Eliza: "We don't have any proof. We need to catch him red handed then we can confront him."

Lydia: "Good idea."

There was another pause.

Lydia: "How do we do that then?"

Eliza: "I don't know. Leave it with me, I'll think of a plan."

Lydia: "Ok. Shall I come over to yours when I've put some make-up on?"

Eliza: "We don't have that long. I'll pick you up in half an hour. I should have thought of something by then."

Lydia: "Okidokes. I'll be ready. Ciao, darling."

Status: *"Of course you realise, this means war!"*

Chapter Thirty-nine

Sub Affirmation for the day: *I accept others and their frailties.*

Half an hour later, Eliza parped her horn outside Lydia's and she came running out dressed in a raincoat and sunglasses.

Lydia slipped beside her into the passenger seat.

Eliza: "Bloody Nora! Who are you? Inspector Gadget?"

Lydia: "We're being sleuths, aren't we? I'm wearing the correct bib and tucker. I've been wanting to wear this get up for ages. It's very Audrey Hepburn in Breakfast at Tiffany's, don't you think?"

Eliza looked at Lydia, baffled.

Eliza: "And you say I'm deranged."

Eliza started the car and drove one hundred yards down the road and parked up.

Lydia: "Why are you stopping here? We're nowhere near the shop."

Eliza: "Exactly. We don't want him to know we're there. We need to be stealthy and somehow creep into the shop without him noticing. Set a trap and then wait to see if he takes the bait."

Lydia: "Stealthy? Should I wear a more Ninja type outfit then? I can change. Drop me back."

Eliza: "Shut up! This is serious Lydia. He's been nicking money from us. We need to confront him and put a stop to it."

Lydia: "I was being serious, actually."

Lydia paused and scratched her head.

Lydia: "How do we creep into the shop without him noticing? What trap shall we set? Where do we wait for him to take the bait?"

Eliza, shaking her head: "I don't know."

Lydia, dispiritedly: "Oh. I thought you were going to have a plan."

Eliza: "That is a plan! I just haven't thought out the finer details, that's all! I think I did very well coming up with that in such a short time."

Lydia: "Let's think."

Lydia tapped her forehead, deep in thought.

Lydia: "I've got it! We need to create a diversion so we can get into the shop. Let's call his phone upstairs. While he's up there we can run in and hide."

Eliza: "Ooh, I like it. We need to put some bait down."

Lydia: "Hmm. Have you got your company debit card?"

Eliza: "Yes."

Lydia: "Great. Let me scribble a made-up number on a bit of paper and leave it in full view with the card on the side. When he picks it up and keeps it, we'll have him!"

Eliza: "Inspired! I love it. What could possibly go wrong?"

Lydia: "Exactly. You see. Dress the part, feel the part and you become the part. Method acting, darling."

They, nonchalantly, walked down the main village street to their shop and hid around the side.

Lydia peaked in through the corner of the shop window.

Lydia: "I can see him. He's scratching his balls by the bureau."

Eliza rolled her eyes.

Eliza: "That's nice. Are there any customers in there?"

Lydia: "Nope. Probably why he's taking full advantage of the opportunity to scratch his testicles."

Eliza: "Ring him. Let's get in there."

Lydia punched in Mr Hicks's home number and they heard it vaguely ringing out upstairs.

Lydia watched as Mr Hicks cocked an ear to the air, released his crotch and scooted off upstairs.

Lydia: "GO. GO. GO!!"

Eliza and Lydia charged in.

Lydia: "Shit! Where do we hide?!"

Eliza pointed to an art deco wardrobe.

Eliza: "Get in!"

Lydia: "I need to hang up before he answers!"

Lydia hit end on the call and they huddled in the wardrobe.

Lydia, whispering: "Can you see anything?"

Eliza: "Not really. I'll hold the door open a bit so we can see out the middle."

Lydia: "Cool. I can see the till."

Eliza: "Shit! We forgot to put the card out with the number!"

Lydia: "Bollocking bollocks!"

They heard him thundering down the stairs.

Eliza: "Call him again! I'll run out and put it on the side."

Lydia: "I need to take these sunglasses off! I can't see a bleedin' thing!"

Lydia hit redial and the phone starting ringing again upstairs just as Mr Hicks got to the bottom.

They heard Mr Hicks swear under his breath and charge back upstairs.

Eliza shot out of the wardrobe and threw the debit card and number on the side and ran back to their vantage point in the wardrobe.

Lydia hit end call on her phone.

Eliza, whispering: "Now we wait."

Lydia, also whispering: "We'll catch the thieving bastard! No retired baker gets one over us!"

Eliza: "What if he does one four seven one?"

Lydia: "Don't worry. I hide my number so Roy doesn't know it's me stalking him."

Eliza: "Oh."

Note to self: Have a conversation with Lydia about her last statement when this is over.

A couple of minutes later, a puffing Mr Hicks came lumbering back into the shop, muttering.

Mr Hicks: "Who would call and hang up like that? Not once, but twice? Maybe it's Patricia. Maybe the weather is too balmy for her. She never could handle the heat. Maybe she wants to come home. Back to her Honey

Monster. Oh, please let it be Patricia. Ohh Patricia... I miss you so much."

He looked forlornly at his shoes and wiped a tear from his cheek.

Lydia and Eliza looked at each other in the wardrobe and Eliza put her bottom lip out and mouthed "Aww" to Lydia.

Just then, a customer came in and Mr Hicks gathered himself.

Mr Hicks: "Good morning, Gerald. What can I do for you today?"

Apparently Gerald: "A good morning to you too, sir. I'm looking for a little side shelving unit. One suitable for the missus to bung her pots of beauty stuff on. She's sent me down as she's trying to make a Black Forest gateau for the Rotary Club. She's on her fourth attempt. She's desperate to make it as good as whatsername who owns this."

Lydia beamed at Eliza.

Mr Hicks: "Eliza? She's a wonderful woman."

Eliza beamed at Lydia.

Apparently Gerald: "No not her, the other one. The old floozy."

Lydia's face turned to thunder. Eliza patted her gently with her spare hand.

Mr Hicks: "Really? Lydia? I had no idea she even ate, let alone knew how to utilise a cooker."

Apparently Gerald: "Yes, she won this year's show with it."

Mr Hicks: "Ah, well done Lydia. She's a lovely girl underneath it all. You mustn't be rude about her. Both she and Eliza have been most kind to me. I won't hear a bad word said about either of them."

Eliza and Lydia smiled at each other.

Good old Mr Hicks.

Hang on. Thief Mr Hicks.

Of course, he thinks we're wonderful, he's been pilfering money off us.

Mr Hicks continued.

Mr Hicks: "Now then Gerald, let's see if we can find your wife this shelf, shall we? Oh, hang on. What's this?"

Mr Hicks looked down to the counter and picked up the debit card and looked around him.

Mr Hicks: "That's very odd. I'm sure that wasn't there earlier. A piece of paper too? What's that? One, two, three, four? No idea."

He shook his head and scrunched up the piece of paper and threw it in the bin. He hit the button to open the till and placed the debit card in it and turned his attention back to Gerald.

Mr Hicks: "How about that one over there?"

Mr Hicks proceeded to show Gerald around all the units in the shop trying to make a sale.

Lydia and Eliza looked at each other, perplexed.

Gerald settled on a duck egg blue, hand painted pine unit and went on his way.

As Gerald was leaving the shop, they heard him greeting Mrs Hestington-Charles, who was on her way in.

Apparently Gerald: "Morning Bunty! How's Seb? Still working all the hours, eh?"

Bunty Hestington-Charles: "Hello Gerald. I'm afraid so. We are but ships that pass in the night these days."

She let out a tinkly, little laugh.

Definitely Gerald: "What are you in here for? I've just bought Joyce this."

He held up the shelving unit.

Bunty Hestington-Charles: "Ah, that's divine! I'm here for my weekly fix of indulgence."

Oh no.

Not again!

Lydia and Eliza exchanged disapproving looks.

Definitely Gerald: "You're right, Bunty, there are some lovely novelties in there. Right, must be off. Send my regards to Seb. We'll have to meet up for golf soon."

Mrs Hestington-Charles went over to Mr Hicks.

Mrs Hestington-Charles, lasciviously: "Hello my Big Bear. How are you today?"

Mr Hicks: "All the better for seeing you my little Goldilocks. Grrrr."

Lydia and Eliza groaned in unison from within the wardrobe.

Goldilocks Hestington-Charles: "How about my Big Bear going to get little Goldilocks her favourite treat? Hmmm?"

Big Bear Hicks: "Big Bear would like that. Give me two minutes."

Mr Hicks pranced off to the kitchen.

Eliza and Lydia watched as Mrs Hestington-Charles ensured he'd gone into the kitchen then went round to the back of the till and furtively looked around.

Eliza and Lydia both stopped breathing.

Mrs Hestington-Charles then quickly tapped open the till and took out a mass of notes and the debit card and stuffed them all into her back pocket.

Eliza and Lydia both gasped in shock and Lydia hurled herself out of the wardrobe.

Lydia hollering: "You bloody bollocking stealing witch of a whore!"

Mrs Hestington-Charles: "What the?!"

Lydia threw herself at her behind the counter and Mrs Hestington-Charles fell backwards onto the floor. Lydia straddled her and pinned her arms down.

Eliza fell out of the open wardrobe doors, picked herself up and stood in the middle of the shop in stunned silence.

Just then Mr Hicks came out of the kitchen stark naked except for a macaroon on the end of his cock.

Mr Hicks: "Yoo hoo! Goldilocks! Big Bear has your elevenses! What the...?!"

Oh, dear Lord.

I'll never look a macaroon in the eye again.

Mr Hicks took in the situation of Eliza standing in the main shop gawping and Mrs Hestington-Charles flat on her back with a rain coated Lydia straddling her.

Mr Hicks: "Bunty?! What's going on? Lydia get off her this instant!"

Lydia, struggling against Bunty: "She's been stealing from us, Mr Hicks! We've just caught her red-handed!"

Mr Hicks looked at Eliza with confusion as the macaroon rolled across the shop floor.

Eliza found her voice.

Eliza: "I'm sorry, Mr Hicks. It's true. We've just caught Mrs Hestington-Charles taking a load of money out of the till."

Mrs Hestington-Charles, shrieking from the floor: "You can't prove it! It could be my money!"

Lydia: "Stand up!"

Lydia yanked up Mrs Hestington-Charles.

Lydia: "Empty your pockets! Specifically, the back ones."

Mrs Hestington-Charles: "You cannot make me! I have rights!"

Lydia roughly shoved her hands into Mrs Hestington-Charles' beige chinos.

She pulled out a few notes and also the debit card.

Mr Hicks gasped in horror.

Mr Hicks, shouting: "BUNTY! NO!!"

He buried his head in his hands.

Just then, a customer started to come in. Eliza shot over to the door and shooed them away and put the closed sign round.

Mr Hicks, crying: "Bunty! Was it all a ruse? Us?!"

Mrs Hestington-Charles slumped forward and rested her arms on the counter.

Mrs Hestington-Charles, dejectedly: "No, Big Bear. I'm so sorry. It was a moment of weakness."

Eliza: "Two thousand pounds worth of weakness, I think you'll find, Mrs Hestington-Charles."

Lydia, screeching: "You what?! Two buggering thousand pounds?! Ohhhh, you're going to have to pay for this Bunty. Big time."

Mrs Hestington-Charles, remorsefully: "Things have been very difficult since Sebastian's buyout failed. We haven't been able to pay the mortgage. I am so sorry ladies. How can I repay you?"

She started crying.

Eliza sighed.

Eliza: "Have you got the money to pay it back?"

Mrs Hestington-Charles shook her head.

Mrs Hestington-Charles, snivelling: "No. We're in danger of losing the house at any moment."

She started sobbing, uncontrollably.

Eliza: "Mr Hicks, would you mind terribly putting some clothes on?"

Mr Hicks: "Oh. Certainly. Sorry Eliza."

He ran back into the kitchen to get changed.

Lydia: "I say we call the police and let them deal with it."

Lydia stared at Mrs Hestington-Charles with her lip curled.

Mrs Hestington-Charles, stammering: "Please! I beg you! Don't! Sebastian would leave me! The shame it would bring on the family. Think of Hermione. You're mothers, please!"

Think Eliza. They live in a massive Edwardian house in the most expensive part of the village.

Eliza: "Do you have anything of any worth?"

Mrs Hestington-Charles: "What do you mean?"

Lydia: "Yeah, what do you mean, Eli? Can't we just ring the law? I'd much prefer that."

Mrs Hestington-Charles and Lydia glared at each other with mutual dislike.

Mr Hicks came back from the kitchens, ashen-faced and fully clothed. He stared hard at Mrs Hestington-Charles.

Mrs Hestington-Charles: "I'm not sure if I have anything."

Mr Hicks maintained his stare.

Mr Hicks: "You have that French antique armoire."

Mrs Hestington-Charles: "But that's from my great aunt!"

Mr Hicks: "It's worth a fair penny. I would suggest you offer them that as part payment for the money you have misappropriated."

Mrs Hestington-Charles: "Big Bear?"

Mr Hicks, matter of factly: "Also, by my recollection, you have a Spanish marquetry table. I would estimate that would reach over a thousand pounds in auction."

Mrs Hestington-Charles: "But that was from Sebastian's grandfather!"

He turned to Eliza.

Mr Hicks: "It is nineteenth century. Sold to the right market you will make up everything she has stolen and be compensated for the damage she has caused."

Mrs Hestington-Charles, her voice quivering: "Big Bear?"

Mr Hicks switched his attention back to her.

Eliza and Lydia just stood there motionless, watching the exchange.

Mr Hicks: "I wish to be addressed as Mr Hicks in all further dialogue if you would be so kind, Mrs Hestington-Charles. I propose you agree to my suggestions or I shall call the police myself."

Mrs Hestington-Charles, wailing: "Ohh, Big Bear. My beautiful Big Bear. Don't do this to me!"

Mr Hicks kept his stance. Resolute.

Mr Hicks: "Do we have an agreement, Mrs Hestington-Charles?"

There was a long pause.

Mrs Hestington-Charles, nodding sadly: "Yes. If that is what you want, Mr Hicks."

Mr Hicks nodded, curtly.

Mr Hicks: "That's settled then."

He turned his attention back to Eliza.

Mr Hicks: "Do you know any places that could value and auction the furniture off?"

Eliza thought for a moment.

Eliza: "Actually, yes I do. I know a guy, Henry, who works at the auction house in town. Maybe I could get him, or one of his colleagues, to come over."

Eliza turned to Mrs Hestington-Charles and continued.

Eliza: "That way, it'll be kept discreet."

Lydia, muttering: "Bollocks to discreet."

Mrs Hestington-Charles, ignoring Lydia: "Thank you Eliza. I'm most grateful for your consideration."

Eliza: "Ok, well we should make a day and time when it's convenient to come over and go from there."

Mrs Hestington-Charles: "Wednesday afternoon, at two. Sebastian and Hermione won't be there. I'll think up some reason why the pieces have gone."

Eliza: "Fine. I'll call my friend and see if he can bring a van and also to value them."

Mr Hicks interjected.

Mr Hicks: "If they aren't worth as much as I anticipate, Mrs Hestington-Charles will have no problem donating other items to reach the value you desire. Will you, Mrs Hestington-Charles?"

Mrs Hestington-Charles, forlornly: "No, Mr Hicks."

Mr Hicks: "Good, then that is a deal."

Mrs Hestington-Charles: "Yes. You have my word."

Lydia: "A right load of old shit that's worth, innit?"

Eliza looked at Lydia, then turned her attention back to Mrs Hestington-Charles.

Eliza: "Thank you, Mrs Hestington-Charles. If you give me your mobile number, I'll call you to confirm."

Mrs Hestington-Charles picked out the scrunched-up piece of paper with the fake pin number from the bin and scribbled her mobile number on it and handed it to Eliza.

Mr Hicks: "I might go out if that's alright with you Eliza, Lydia? I wish to clear my head."

Lydia: "Of course, Mr Hicks. I'll take over now."

Lydia looked disdainfully at Mrs Hestington-Charles.

Lydia: "And you can clear off an' all."

Mr Hicks left and so did Mrs Hestington-Charles. Both going in opposite directions once they left the shop.

Eliza flopped down on a carver chair.

Eliza: "Blimey Lydia, I didn't expect that!"

Lydia: "Eli?"

Eliza: "Yes?"

Lydia: "What's an armoire?"

Eliza shook her head.

Eliza: "Go and put the kettle on."

Status: *"Round up the usual suspects."*

Chapter Forty

Affirmation for the day: *My life is just beginning.*

It was the day of the auction.

Eliza was sat on an uncomfortable plastic chair waiting for her lots to come up. Henry had valued Mrs Hestington-Charles' donations and assured her they would far exceed the two thousand pounds she was hoping for.

She'd looked through the catalogue at some of the other items on sale that day and a Victorian Ottoman had caught her eye. Henry had tipped her the wink that the guide price was way lower than he thought it should be. She reckoned she'd be able to get the upholstery tidied up and sell it on for a good profit.

As she sat there, with the quiet hum of chattering in between people bidding at the auction, she thought about how much she'd changed over the past year.

She realised that one day she'd just given up conforming. She didn't quite know when that was, but it just happened.

The resulting effect was the most profound feeling of liberation. An acceptance of self.

Those hippy books had, perhaps, worked after all.

She realised she lacked the sophistication gene and she was fine with that.

She realised Geraldine wasn't any better than her.

She realised men didn't find her hideous and whilst she might not appeal to all men, she appealed to some and that was good enough for her.

She realised she could live on dry cornflakes for weeks on end without getting scurvy.

She realised she enjoyed having Tom and being a mother.

She realised she wasn't actually an incompetent mother.

She realised she didn't need to write a blog about her life. Instead, she realised she was happy just to live it.

She realised joy could be found every day in the little things.

She realised she could cope.

She realised she actually liked herself.

She realised she didn't want Lewis.

She realised she'd made it out the other side.

She smiled and nodded her head in silent acknowledgment that Lewis had done her a favour.

Eh?

Auctioneer: "Eighty-five, ninety... Do I hear ninety-five?"

Eliza: "Oh, flipping flip-flops! My Ottoman's up!"

Eliza shot her hand up in the air.

Auctioneer: "I have ninety-five. Do I have one hundred? I thank you, sir. One hundred."

Who is this sir? Piss off!

It's my Ottoman!

Eliza looked around the room to where a rotund man sat, squatting on a plastic seat. He smiled at her.

Is it you?

Eliza put her hand up again and stared hard at him.

Auctioneer: "One hundred and five…"

The smiling, rotund man raised his catalogue.

Auctioneer: "One hundred and ten!"

It is you! Go away, it's mine!

What do you want a storage box for?

Eliza bid again and narrowed her eyes at him with steely determination.

Karma fairy! Make him stop!

I did a good thing not calling the police with old Bunty. Surely that counts for something, eh?

I appreciate I mentally blamed my best friend and then my poor beaten down stand in employee of stealing, but let's gloss over that bit, please.

Auctioneer: "Thank you madam. One hundred and fifteen, I have. Do I have one twenty?"

The rotund man shook his head.

Yay! Thank you, karma fairy.

See, mentally accusing doesn't count. I'll remember that.

Auctioneer: "Are you sure sir? Anyone else in the room? Am I hearing one hundred and twenty? It's a lovely little piece."

He paused momentarily.

Oh, it's mine! It's mine!

Auctioneer: "Thank you. I have one twenty. You madam. One twenty-five?"

Huh? Who now?

Karma fairy! Nobble whoever it is!!

Eliza nodded. She looked around to try and see who it was but couldn't see anyone.

What's my limit? I need to make sure I don't go mental.

One fifty. That's my lot. Not a penny more.

She carried on bidding against her new opponent.

Auctioneer: "…One hundred and sixty-five, madam?"

This must be my last bid. I'm getting carried away.

Eliza nodded.

She was quickly counterbid.

Aargh!!

Eliza looked desperately around the room to see who was bidding against her but couldn't see anyone who was actively showing any interest in the lot.

She sighed heavily.

Ok. One seventy-five is my highest bid. That's my lot. Not a penny more.

Eliza bid again.

Karma fairy! Listen to me!

Auctioneer: "I have one eighty. Madam, do I have one eighty-five."

Eliza huffed.

Have some restraint. I must stop.

I'm not very happy with you karma fairy. We'll be having a chat later.

Eliza shook her head.

Auctioneer: "Sold for one hundred and eighty pounds. May I have your number, sir?"

Who's bought my Ottoman then?

Show yourself.

Eliza spun around on her chair to scan the whole room.

A woman at the back of the room stepped aside and there she saw him.

Jude.

He held up his card and turned to face Eliza with surprise.

Eliza and Jude, in unison: "Oh!!"

They stared at each other, both motionless.

Auctioneer: "Thank you sir, I've taken a note of your number. You can put your card down now."

Jude gathered himself and put his card down.

Jude made his way across the auction house towards her.

Oh, karma fairy!

You work in such mysterious ways but you do listen!

Thank you, thank you!

Jude pulled up a spare plastic chair and sat next to her.

Jude, cautiously: "Hello Eli. Do you mind if I join you?"

Eliza, stammering: "He... hello Jude. No, no, feel free."

Has it suddenly got very warm in here?

Jude's brow furrowed.

Jude: "Was I bidding against you?"

Eliza: "Erm, yes, actually."

Jude tutted.

Jude: "I'm so sorry, I had no idea. If I'd known, I'd never have bid. I only want it for my towels."

Eliza: "It's ok, I didn't really want it."

Ahem.

Jude looked at her, nervously, and ran his hand through his hair.

Jude: "How have you been?"

Eliza: "I'm fine. It's all very peaceful in my life."

If we forget your ex-girlfriend with the bondage fetish, the blow jobbing money stealer, garden looting neighbour, pregnant ex-husband and my sudden aversion to macaroons.

Jude.

He's here, right next to me and he's got my Ottoman.

Please don't let him be with anyone. Ask subtly.

Eliza: "So, have you met anyone else?"

Perfect. Just perfect.

Idiot.

Jude looked at her, cautiously.

Jude: "Perhaps."

Oh crap.

Jude continued.

Jude: "How are things going with you and the guy in red?"

Who?

Ohhh! Neville!

Eliza: "It was meant to be green, but anyway, no, no. That's all done with. I couldn't ski plus I didn't fancy learning all the words to Edelweiss."

Jude looked at her, perplexed.

Jude: "Oh, ok."

Shut up, fool.

Be demure and sophisticated.

I can't.

I've already ascertained I don't possess that gene.

They both sat there awkwardly for a minute.

Say something!! Anything!

Eliza and Jude both started talking at the same time. Then both stopped.

Eliza: "You go on. Sorry."

Jude: "No, no. I'm sorry. You go ahead."

Eliza, firmly: "No, I insist!"

Calm down.

There was a pause.

Jude ran his hand through his hair again.

Jude: "Would you like to have a cup of tea with me after the auction?"

Did I just hear that correctly?

Say pardon just to hear him ask again and to make sure I didn't imagine that.

Eliza: "Sorry?"

Jude: "Oh, erm, I just wondered if you'd like to have a drink with me after the auction but if you don't want to then that's fine."

Yay! I did hear correctly and he is definitely asking me out.

My chakras must be fully aligned after all!

Eliza: "Yes please. Let's go now!"

That's it. Play it cool.

Oh, hang on, I'm flogging Bunty's bits.

Eliza: "Oh, wait a minute, I have two lots up for sale but will be free after that."

Jude exhaled, audibly.

Jude: "Brilliant! I mean, yeah that's cool. I'll go and pay for my box and will come back and wait with you."

He got up from his plastic chair and smiled at her as he left.

Oh, that smile! Thank you, karma fairy.

As she sat there waiting for her lots to be sold, she realised it was time for the credits to roll on her past.

She realised she was ready for her future.

She realised she had the chance to be with the man of her dreams.

Status: *"Alright, Mr. DeMille, I'm ready for my close-up."*

Bibliography of status film quotes:

Prologue:	Mermaids	1990
Chapter 1:	The Wizard of Oz	1939
Chapter 2:	Gone With the Wind	1939
Chapter 3:	The Wizard of Oz	1939
Chapter 4:	Psycho	1960
Chapter 5:	The Godfather	1972
Chapter 6:	Willy Wonka & the Chocolate Factory	1971
Chapter 7:	Dead Poets Society	1989
Chapter 8:	Maverick	1994
Chapter 9:	Silence of the Lambs	1991
Chapter 10:	When Harry Met Sally	1989
Chapter 11:	Calendar Girls	2003
Chapter 12:	Hicksshank Redemption	1994
Chapter 13:	Toy Story	1995
Chapter 14:	A Few Good Men	1992
Chapter 15:	Life of Brian	1979
Chapter 16:	Ice Age 3	2009
Chapter 17:	Cool Hand Luke	1967
Chapter 18:	The Terminator	1984
Chapter 19:	All About Eve	1950
Chapter 20:	Another Fine Mess	1939

Chapter 21:	Arsenic and Old Lace	1944
Chapter 22:	The Wizard of Oz	1939
Chapter 23:	Bridget Jones's Diary	2001
Chapter 24:	Dirty Dancing	1987
Chapter 25:	Top Gun	1986
Chapter 26:	Good Will Hunting	1997
Chapter 27:	Alice in Wonderland	1951
Chapter 28:	Apocalypse Now	1979
Chapter 29:	Pirates of the Caribbean	2003
Chapter 30:	Wall Street	1987
Chapter 31:	Jerry Maguire	1996
Chapter 32:	Jiro Dreams of Sushi	2013
Chapter 33:	Scarface	1986
Chapter 34:	Harry Potter and the Sorcerer's Stone	2001
Chapter 35:	Harry Potter and the Prisoner of Azkaban	2004
Chapter 36:	The Italian Job	1969
Chapter 37:	Star Wars IV – New Hope	1977
Chapter 38:	Duck Soup	1933
Chapter 39:	Casablanca	1942
Chapter 40	Sunset Boulevard	1950